RHYTHM OF LOVE

A SWEET SECOND CHANCE ROMANCE

TINA NEWCOMB

Rhythm of Love

❀ Created with Vellum

DEDICATION

Thank you, Bruce, Jane, and Joe, for introducing me to the Tennessee River.

PROLOGUE

*K*enzie Rivers stared at her father. The energetic, horseback-riding, hay-hauling, always-smiling man who raised her was too quiet.

His hair, habitually windblown, was slicked down too neatly, his cheeks too smooth-shaven, his expression too rigid, and his lips too . . . pink. Although his brown suit was the right choice, the decision between the traditional tie or the sterling silver galloping horse with the inlaid turquoise bolo had been harder. She'd finally decided on the bolo, which was also the right choice.

The part that was all wrong—the casket. The interior fabric washed out his usually tanned complexion making her perfect father's skin look sallow and waxen.

A hand touched her waist. She knew without turning that it was Kyle. Her brother resembled their father so much, with his dark hair and chestnut eyes, she was almost afraid to look at the living version.

"Hey, baby girl, people will start arriving in about fifteen minutes."

She swallowed a fresh wave of tears. "Dad would hate to

have all his friends file past, looking down at him. He would hate this."

Waylon Rivers would rather everyone celebrate his life at the ranch, with a backyard barbecue, lots of music, and dancing.

"People want to pay their respects. Are you going to be okay?"

Kenzie nodded.

"I asked Mr. Stewart if someone could wipe off that gaudy pink lipstick. The makeup lady is on her way." Kyle squeezed her waist. "Are you sure you're okay?"

Frustration, anger, and pain leaked through her tiny *I'm fine* fissure. "I've never had someone close to me die before, so I'm not exactly sure how I should feel or act. Am I doing it wrong?"

"It's okay to cry, Kenz," he said, ignoring her harsh tone.

She glanced up at her brother's handsome face, now etched with sympathy. And concern. "Have you?"

"At the hospital."

"You were with me the whole time."

"No. While you were in the hospital chapel, I sat in my truck and bawled like a baby."

In all of her twenty-four years, she'd only seen Kyle shed tears once, and that was on the day their mother drove away.

Rubber-soled shoes squeaked down the carpeted aisle, growing louder with each step. Kenzie cringed until the sound halted next to her.

"Mr. Stewart says you're unhappy with your daddy's makeup." The gray-haired lady, her curls as tight as corkscrews, peered into the casket. "What's the problem?"

"If you could just wipe off the pink lip color," Kyle said.

"He needs some color on his cheeks too," Kenzie added. "He looks yellow. My father worked outside every day of his life. He even had a tan during the winter months."

The lady squeaked closer and set a makeup case on their father's chest, then pulled out a white towel and tucked it inside his loose collar. "We don't want to get your daddy's white shirt smudged."

She pulled another tissue out of a box, dipped the tip in a small pot of something that looked glossy, and wiped at the lipstick.

Kenzie wanted him to grin, leap out of the casket, and shout, "Gotcha!"

He didn't.

Dizzy, she backed into a chair. She couldn't bear to watch the lady swiping and brushing at her dad like he was dead. Waylon had been a force of nature all their lives. He was resilient and kind and funny, and the backbone of Rivers Equestrian Ranch. He'd taught her to be strong and said the ranch and her brother needed her unique womanly power. Funny thing, she didn't feel powerful. At the moment she was a quivering mess.

She ran a hand over her burgundy skirt, her dad's choice for her funeral attire. "Do not wear black," he'd instructed. "I want you to wear that pretty, flowery blouse with the skirt you bought for Easter Sunday. And tell Kyle to wear his blue suit and that bright tie you gave him for his birthday last year. That's how I want you both dressed for the occasion."

Not *my funeral*, but *the occasion*.

The woman stepped back from the casket. "How does that look?"

Kenzie stood and moved next to her brother.

"He looks better." His lips were a more natural color now and bronze tinted his face. "He looks better," she repeated before glancing at Kyle.

He nodded.

The lady pulled the towel away and tucked everything back in her case. "You kids have a nice night."

Kyle and Kenzie stared at the lady as she squeaked her way back down the aisle, leaving behind a parting comment that was ludicrous enough to be laughable.

Tall, lanky Jeremy Knight passed the woman on his way down the aisle. He'd cut his shoulder-length, sandy-colored hair shorter than she'd ever seen, and his brown eyes, usually twinkling with mischief, conveyed as much sorrow as she felt.

"How are you guys? You okay?" He ran a finger under his collar, his Adam's apple bobbing when he swallowed. "Sorry. Stupid question. Man, I hate the quiet in this room." His eyes darted to Waylon, then back to them. "So does your dad. I can tell by the look on his face."

The comment made Kenzie smile. Jeremy and Kyle had been friends since they were toddlers, and he and his parents were like extended family.

Minutes later, Kenzie stood between her brother and Jeremy while people filed through the room, expressing their condolences, hugging, kissing, shaking hands.

Dove Hill, Tennessee was a small town, population eight thousand, and most people within fifty miles knew Waylon Rivers. Either Jeremy or Kyle had their arm around her, supporting her through the endless evening while they talked with friends and neighbors, people they'd known all their lives, and people who did business with the ranch.

*T*he next day was a blur for Kenzie. She scanned the gathering at the church, hoping to see the one face who could shore her up through this. His mom and dad were there, but she didn't see him. After the moving funeral service, during which many friends got up to share memories of her father, and the equally emotional graveside service, there was still no sign of Nick Marshall.

Everyone converged at the Rivers' ranch following the service. Jeremy had tables and chairs delivered from an event rental party place in Nashville, so people had plenty of places to sit and visit under the shade of huge trees.

A Nashville catering company delivered barbecued brisket, pulled pork, and fried chicken. Fresh buns and sides of potato salad, baked beans, and coleslaw filled the tables, along with veggie trays and separate bags of chips. Neighbors contributed platters of cookies and brownies, cakes, and pies.

The ranch house and surrounding yard overflowed with people consoling and reminiscing, story after story told and retold.

After two hours, Kenzie escaped down a path, past Kyle's small house, through the pecan grove, to a big shed almost hidden behind a wall of dogwoods that had already dropped their spring blossoms.

The day smelled fresh, like new growth and sunshine. The sky was too beautiful, the temperature too perfect for a funeral. Her mood called for black clouds and booming thunder, followed by a torrential downpour.

Bypassing the big sliding doors, she walked around to the side door and stepped inside. Kyle, Jeremy, and Nick, along with all three of their fathers, had turned this old building into a practice space for the band Kyle and Jeremy had started in junior high school. Nick joined a year later, and the other three members joined a few months after that. And they still practiced here every Tuesday, Thursday, and Saturday.

Knight Rivers band—named after Jeremy Knight and Kyle Rivers—had only lost one member over the years, when Nick left just three months earlier to pursue bigger dreams.

Wandering around the inside of the building brought back so many memories. Over the years they insulated the walls, added windows, heating, and air for comfort. Her dad even built a small kitchen in the back that he kept stocked so the boys had food when they were too busy practicing to eat.

She grew up loving music as much as the boys did, and she'd spent hours and hours in here. Kyle taught her to play the guitar, Jeremy taught her to play the drums, and she taught herself to play the piano.

She started writing songs at fourteen. Total fluke, a pop singer heard one of her demos and bought the song and sang it all the way to number one on the charts. That was the beginning for Kenzie. Since then she'd written jingles and sold songs to music artists who specifically asked for her work. A couple of songs even found their way onto movie soundtracks.

All that changed six months ago, when her dad suffered a severe stroke and his health deteriorated quickly. She still wrote for top artists, but rarely left the house while taking care of the man who had taken care of her most of her life. Until two weeks ago, when Waylon came down with pneumonia and, in his weakened condition, couldn't fight it.

She sat at one of three keyboards and plunked out a tune she'd been working on. The haunting melody seemed appropriate for the occasion.

The door swung inward on squeaky hinges, and she looked up to see Jeremy standing in the opening, backlit by the setting sun, which cast him in a golden glow, like an angel swooping in to rescue her from the path of darkness she was headed toward.

"What are you doing out here alone, sweet pea?"

"Escaping, same as you. Or are you here to check on me?"

He sat down at the drums, picking up a pair of sticks and twirling them through his fingers. The beaters, as he called them, were as much a part of Jeremy as his hands. "Kyle's worried about you."

She knew her brother. No matter how often she told him she was okay, he'd continue to check. He'd looked after her since the day their mother left with *the nice insurance man*. Kenzie was four and Kyle eight when he became her surrogate guardian. *I'll take care of you, baby girl. Daddy will take care of the horses, and I'll take care of you.*

Kenzie plunked another few keys. "You can tell him I'm fine, Jer."

"You've been through a lot the past six months. Your father's stroke and then Nick leaving."

Nick.

Even though the band he was playing with was in nearby Nashville, he hadn't come yesterday or today. The worst days of her life, and Nick, who was less than an hour away, hadn't been here for her. That he missed her dad's funeral hurt more than him leaving in the first place—which wasn't fair of her. The opportunity he'd been offered was too big to pass up.

Kenzie got up and walked to a window. From here she could see the pristine horse stables—painted right before her dad had his stroke—and the pastures beyond. After several days of rain last week, the grass was such a vivid green it looked unreal—like someone had painted it a shade richer for her father's last days.

She sensed Jeremy's approach. He put his hands on her shoulders, squeezing lightly, letting her know she had a support system at the ready.

"I'm sorry about Waylon. We're all going to miss him."

She reached up and linked their fingers. "I know."

He turned her around so she faced him. "I'm sorry about Nick, too. He shouldn't have left like he did. And he should have been here today."

She wanted to defend Nick, say she understood, but if the

tables were turned, she would have moved heaven and earth to be here for him.

His leaving cut deep. That he asked her to come, even though he knew she couldn't, had deepened the wound. She would never leave her dad when he was so sick. After all the years Kyle had taken care of her, she'd never leave him with the responsibility for the ranch and the care of their father, too.

Nick knew her hands were tied. He also knew she'd never ask him to stay because playing bass guitar with a rising country star's band was his dream come true.

The tears that refused to come since Nick's departure and her father's death flooded her eyes. Jeremy drew her close and held tight. She hated crying in front of people, but the sobs came without warning, shaking her.

"Go ahead and cry, sweet pea. Let it out. You've been holding it in for too long." Gently rubbing her back, Jeremy stood unwavering and let her soak his shirt. Once she settled into shuddering breaths, he tipped her face up and dried her cheeks with the pads of his thumbs. "You think you're done?"

Kenzie could count on Jeremy as much as she could count on Kyle. He'd always be there for her, just like she'd been there for him when he buried his wife and their unborn daughter after a drunk driver ran a red light and hit her as she crossed a street.

Her smile wobbled at the corners. "You can now report to Kyle that I cried. He'll be so ecstatic."

He chuckled and kissed her forehead. "Do you feel better?"

"No, but *he* will."

"Anytime you need an ear"—he lifted his wet tie—"or tissue, just give me a call. I'll be here in minutes."

She tried to swallow around the tears that spilled over a second time.

"Oops, you're not done yet," he said with another chuckle. He kissed her cheek.

She swiped under her burning eyes just as he aimed for her other cheek, but their lips met instead. And neither of them pulled away. It started as a gentle brush of lips and an inkling of wonder that turned deeper in a split second.

This is wrong, ran through her mind as she got up on tiptoe and wrapped her arms around his neck. He pulled her tight against his chest. She could feel his heart pounding against hers, and she lost herself in a moment of comfort, of not feeling so alone.

The hinges on the door squeaked, and they wrenched apart to face Nick.

CHAPTER 1

THREE YEARS LATER

*K*enzie took a deep breath to calm the nervous jitters. She'd performed with the Knight Rivers Band on many occasions over the past few years, but not to a crowd this size. A hundred thousand people were expected in Belle Haven, Kentucky, over the Memorial Day weekend.

When the van they rented entered the security gate, she looked out over the sea of people clapping and dancing to the band currently performing onstage, which was set on a barge anchored to the shoreline of the Cumberland River. Blankets and chairs covered the grass from the water to the forest behind.

As the band members piled out of the van, Kenzie glanced at the blue, blue sky. The weather was perfect for an outdoor concert. Warm with a nice breeze coming off the water. As nervous as she was, she'd be able to relax a couple of hours from now, once they were on their way to Jeremy's property for their own holiday celebration.

Jeremy draped an arm over her shoulder. "You okay, sweet pea?"

"Nervous enough that I wish I'd skipped lunch." She looked up into his brown eyes. "I've never performed in front of a crowd this size."

"Sure you have. You won two awards, the show televised to millions."

"Millions might be pushing it. And I couldn't see the people in television land, only the crowd in the theater."

Nick had been at the award show with his pregnant wife, the first time she'd seen him since he walked in on her and Jeremy's one and only kiss.

"You'll be fine. We've been practicing for this all month. You know the songs. You sound like you've been singing with us all along." He pulled her tight against his side. "You got your beaters?"

Kenzie held up her drumsticks, "And my guitar."

"You ready?" Kyle asked as he approached them.

"No," she replied with a hand to her heart. The cheering behind her was so loud she had to shout. The band onstage had the crowd in a frenzy.

Kyle smiled down at her. "Want to know who's in the audience?"

"Not if knowing will make me more nervous."

"Why are you so nervous? You've been with us all month."

Though she'd talked to him about this before, Kyle still didn't understand—or chose to ignore—her love/hate relationship with the final few minutes before performing. She loved the nervous anticipation and hated it. Excited. Scared. Intense. A lot of the same emotions involved with falling in love. Once on the stage, she was fine. Looking into the audience and watching people sing along was exhilarating. But the before terrified her.

"Just remember, you come on after our second number."

"I will."

She, Kyle, and Jeremy had written new material for this

festival. After the band's female vocalist, Bonnie, was confined to bed rest for the remainder of her pregnancy, Kyle begged Kenzie to fill her spot over the summer. She knew the songs, knew the lineup, and was as ready as she'd ever be.

A home-grown, much-loved comedian hit the stage to entertain the crowd, and while a stage crew shifted the previous band's instruments off one side of the barge, another crew moved the Knight Rivers gear into place. When everything was set, the comedian introduced Knight Rivers to wild shouts and applause. Kyle and Jeremy had built a loyal fan base over the years, dating back to high school.

The band members ran onstage, waving and saluting the crowd.

"Welcome to the Cumberland River Music Fest!" Kyle shouted. "We're proud to be back for another year of fun in the sun, and we have a few surprises for die-hard Knight Rivers fans."

After the first two songs were met with grand applause and cheering, Kyle took the microphone in hand. "We know you've missed Jeremy and his wild antics up front. Well, grab your fiddle, Jeremy, because Kenzie Rivers is back!"

Kenzie ran onto the stage waving her drumsticks. While she took Jeremy's place at the drums, he grabbed his fiddle and held it high to a standing ovation. Yes, it felt good to be back up here. Bodhi Hyde waved his rhythm guitar in the air. Tripp Cross plucked a few strings on his banjo in welcome. From the keyboard, Tripp's brother Ryder winked. Jeff Davidson performed a short riff on the bass guitar. Just weeks ago, he became the band's third bass player since Nick left.

"And now for another surprise. We've written a new song for crazy Jeremy, and you're going to be the first to hear it!"

More thunderous applause.

The tune was upbeat and fun and matched Jeremy's personality perfectly. Kenzie stayed on the drums for the next song, then Jeremy moved back to take her place. She grabbed her guitar and moved to the front of the stage. A loud whistle caught her attention.

Becky Marshall.

Nick's family was front and center in the audience. Only Nick was missing. She blew a kiss their way.

Of course, they were here to see Nick. He now played with Aaron Vance's Band, scheduled to take the stage later this afternoon.

Since her dad's funeral followed by her breakup with Nick, she'd only seen the Marshalls in passing at the grocery store or in the post office. She didn't ask about Nick, and they didn't offer any information, which was fine. She didn't want to know details.

Becky had asked Kenzie to be a bridesmaid at her wedding scheduled for the end of June. And Nick was one of the groomsmen. Then Knight Rivers was scheduled to sing at the wedding reception.

So yippee, I have that to look forward to.

That was a mean thought. She was very excited that her friend had found love and that she'd been asked to help celebrate a happy occasion.

Cara, Jeremy's wife of one year, along with Kenzie's new sister-in-law, Jessi, were next to the Marshall family. The other band members had family or girlfriends scattered through the audience, but *her* only family was onstage.

She looked out over the crowd. She'd been to this festival many times with her father, and even though he'd been gone for three years, she still missed him every day. Kyle had hired a fabulous ranch manager, and life went on as before, but a sad undercurrent still pulled at her most days.

Jeremy gave them a count, bringing her back to the

present, and they began to play another new song with a foot-stomping tempo and tongue-twisting lyrics. Once the crowd caught on to the chorus, Kyle unhooked the mic, held it out toward the audience, and they joined in. She'd imagined just this scenario when she wrote the happy song about smiles and sunshine and summertime.

Being back onstage was exhilarating, and the crowd was jamming. Kyle and Jeremy had a way of getting the crowd revved up and begging for more.

The next song planned was a duet with Kyle, and then she'd ease the crowd down with a solo. After that, she'd return to the drums so Jeremy could get them pumped up again with his fiddle and crazy behavior.

When Kyle struck the chords for something other than what they planned, Kenzie turned to him with open mouth. She told him last night she didn't feel comfortable singing this song. The harmony was tricky, and they'd only practiced it a couple of times.

Turning her back to the crowd, she glared at Jeremy, hoping he'd take pity and change his tempo, forcing Kyle into the song they planned.

Jeremy flashed a grin while ignoring her silent plea.

She pressed fingers to one ear and hummed the harmony to herself. She was going to strangle Kyle as soon as they got off the stage.

When she turned toward the mic, she spotted Nick. Though his eyes were hidden behind reflective sunglasses, she knew he was watching her. She flexed her fingers, then fisted her hands, digging her nails into her palms.

Three years ago this weekend—a month after her dad's funeral—she found out Nick had married a concert groupie who was two months pregnant. She distanced herself from everyone that summer, spending all her time on the ranch, writing songs, and mourning the loss of two men who'd filled her life with joy.

Since the Aaron Vance Band wasn't due onstage for several hours, she hadn't thought she'd see him. Hoped was a better word. She had hoped Knight Rivers would be long gone before Nick arrived.

She missed her cue but recovered quickly. This was a song she and Kyle had written years ago, but never performed, and based on the crowd's reaction, they loved it. During a keyboard solo, she moved over to share a mic with her brother. After the song ended, she turned her back to the audience. "I can't sing the next song. Nick's here. I don't want him to think I wrote it about him."

Kyle signaled Jeremy, who went into a drum solo. The guys caught on quickly and started playing with him.

"Where is he?"

"Over my left shoulder."

"Sing your new one," Kyle said without looking.

Perfect.

Kenzie turned and smiled. "I wrote the next song for my father, who passed away a little over three years ago. He loved music and taught us to love it too. He was a rock, a pillar of strength, and a teddy bear at the same time. We miss him every day." She looked skyward. "This one's for you, Daddy."

~

*N*ick Marshall gritted his teeth and turned his back on the stage. Didn't matter. Kenzie's voice surrounded him, tickling over his skin, seeping into his soul. He closed his eyes, but his imagination was as clear as his sight. He knew her, knew the way she moved, the way her skin felt and smelled.

Her song touched a spot deep inside his heart. Waylon Rivers was like a second dad to him, and he'd missed the man's funeral because Juliette had hidden his keys. She didn't want to be left behind, and he couldn't take her. Missing Waylon's funeral was just one of many regrets he'd never outlive.

He'd read the lineup of today's bands and knew Knight Rivers would be here, but he didn't expect Kenzie to be singing with them again. Since arriving, he'd been searching the crowd for her, figuring she'd be here to watch Jeremy. Instead, she was on stage, singing a song so full of heart his chest tightened uncomfortably.

He knew the second she spotted him, felt the same cord of energy pass between them. He also knew she wouldn't look his way again.

Feeling judgmental eyes boring into him, he glanced in the direction of his parents. Both were looking at him. His dad had texted him to say they'd come early enough to get right up front.

He tipped his head down and made eye contact over the rim of his sunglasses. They'd voiced their disapproval often enough that he knew what they were thinking. They were still disappointed because of the stupid mistakes he made when he started playing bass for Aaron Vance.

He was now paying for those mistakes. Juliette had packed her bags and left two months after she gave birth, leaving him to raise their beautiful daughter, London, alone. So he could spend more time at home, he'd gone from being Aaron Vance's bass guitarist to managing his band.

When Kenzie's song was over, he turned back to the stage. The crowd gave her a standing ovation before she returned to the drums. Jeremy picked up his fiddle and the crowd went wild. Kyle, Jeremy, and Kenzie had always been expert entertainers.

Nick moved farther into the crowd so he could see her better. She looked happy to be back onstage, and if the crowd's reaction was any indication, they were just as happy to have her back.

His phone vibrated and he glanced at the message.

Where are you?

Nick scanned the crowd, spotting Aaron and a couple of his bodyguards moving in the opposite direction.

Behind you, just south of center stage.

Aaron turned and shaded his eyes with a hand. He was wearing a baseball hat and dark glasses to hide his identity. Otherwise, the up-and-coming country star would be swamped with adoring fans. Two of his songs climbed to number five on the charts over the past six months, and he was aiming for that number one spot, but couldn't quite make it up those last few rungs.

"That girl can sing," Aaron said when he reached Nick's side. "The whole band is great. You used to sing with them, right?"

Nick nodded.

"Why haven't I heard of them?"

Aaron didn't understand what it took to make a name for yourself. His uncle was a music producer in Nashville, so he'd been given an easy in. The guy was talented, but he wouldn't be where he was without his uncle, and he'd never get where he wanted to be if he didn't rein in his partying ways.

"The lead singer's dad had a massive stroke a few years ago, which kept Kyle and Kenzie at home. They're just getting back up and running."

"You still talk to them?"

"Once in a while." Not exactly true. He hadn't talked to Kyle since the awards ceremony where Kenzie won for not only the best song of the year but the best songwriter award.

He'd walked over to where Kyle and Kenzie were sitting before the show started. Kenzie had quickly excused herself and didn't return until he was back in his seat next to his very pregnant wife, Juliette.

"I'd like to meet her." Aaron flashed a grin. "Them. I'd like to meet them."

"Why?"

Aaron patted him on the shoulder. "Make it happen before I go on."

You're wasting your time, buddy. Kenzie's already taken.

Kenzie was back at the mic, rolling her shoulders in her sexy way, and Jeremy was eating it up for the whole crowd to see. The thought of Kenzie with Jeremy had festered for three long years.

There was a bro-code. Buddies didn't date your girl, even if she was an ex, but once he started touring with Aaron, Jeremy hadn't wasted any time moving in on Kenzie.

Worse, he couldn't get any information about their relationship from his parents or Becky. They were tight-lipped and protective when it came to Kenzie.

"The band usually goes camping on Memorial Day weekend. They'll probably head out as soon as their set is finished."

"Work your charm, Nick. That's what I hired you for."

Nick blew out a breath, reaching for patience. Privileged from birth, Aaron was used to getting what he wanted. "Where's the RV?"

One of the bodyguards pointed toward a dirt road that ran parallel to the river. Nick could see the top from here. He pulled out his phone to see the time. One-fifty. Aaron didn't go on until four. Plenty of time if Knight Rivers didn't have plans.

A meeting would put him closer to Jeremy and Kenzie than he wanted, but Aaron didn't accept no gracefully. "They should be wrapping up in the next ten minutes. Head to the RV before the crowd recognizes you, and I'll see what I can do."

After Aaron and his burly bodyguards walked away, Nick headed toward the barge.

~

*K*enzie strummed the last cords of the song, lifted her guitar strap over her head, and took a bow with the rest of the band. She straightened and waved to the audience before leading the guys off the stage. When she reached the gangplank, she stopped short. Nick stood at the other end.

Kenzie felt an arm go around her shoulders, and she was propelled toward the man who'd ripped out her heart.

"Be strong for just a few more minutes," Kyle said close to her ear.

She nodded.

When they reached the bottom, Kyle extended his hand. "Nick. It's been a long time."

"Good to see you guys again. The band sounded great."

She hated her reaction to seeing Nick, to hearing his voice. Her heart should be racing because of their thrilling performance. She should be relishing that high for a while, but Nick thoroughly crushed it.

"I came to ask if y'all have a few minutes before heading to the river. Aaron Vance would like to meet you. His RV is parked down the road," he said pointing to his left.

Kyle glanced around at the other band members. "Everyone up for meeting Aaron Vance?"

"Why does he want to meet us?" Bodhi asked.

"He enjoyed your music and asked if I could set up a meeting."

Kenzie wanted to escape, but the other band members were nodding.

Cara and Jessi rounded the gate separating the band from the audience. After congratulatory kisses were exchanged with their husbands, the women were introduced to Nick.

Cara smiled and held out her hand. "Hi, Nick. I've heard so much about your days with the band."

Nick glanced at Kenzie with raised brows, then shook Cara's hand. "It's nice to meet you, Cara." He glanced at Jeremy. "I didn't know you got married. Congratulations."

Jeremy nodded in reply.

"Jessi and I will wait by the van," Cara said.

"I'll wait here too," Kenzie was quick to add. "I can make sure our gear gets loaded."

"No, Kenz. Cara and I will take care of that. Go with the group," Jessi said, shooing her away.

Kenzie tried to give Jessi a pleading look, but her sister-in-law had already turned toward the stage to oversee the gear.

Tripp gestured to Nick. "Lead the way, buddy."

Aaron's RV was parked under a stand of trees along with several other country stars' RVs and buses. Two muscled men sat in lawn chairs just outside the door.

"Come on in," Aaron called with a smile, swinging the door wide. "Glad you agreed to meet."

"Aaron, this is Kyle Rivers and his sister Kenzie. Jeremy Knight, Bodhi Hyde, Tripp Cross, and his brother Ryder." Nick stopped at Jeff. "Sorry, we haven't met."

"This is Jeff Davidson," Jeremy told Nick. "He took your place on the bass."

Aaron shook hands all around while Nick opened the well-stocked fridge and offered everyone drinks.

"I really enjoyed your music, so did the crowd," Aaron said. "How long have you been playing together?"

Kyle chuckled. "A long time."

"How long?"

"Jeremy and I started the band in middle school. Nick came aboard shortly after, and everyone else joined three months after that. Jeff has only been playing with us for a few months."

"And you only play locally?"

"Pretty much," Jeremy said. "We do a couple of county fairs and a few music festivals every year."

"And we have a standing slot at a local bar on Friday nights," Tripp added.

"I've rented out a party venue and would love for y'all to join me tonight after the concert. There will be plenty of food and music. And plenty of big names."

Kyle shook his head. "We appreciate the invite, but we have a long-standing tradition of meeting at the Tennessee River on Memorial Day weekend. People are already there waiting for us to provide some music."

"You and your band are welcome to join us," Jeremy said. "Nick can give you directions. He knows the way. It's nothing fancy. We camp out, cook our meals over fires, boat and swim during the day, and sing every night."

Kenzie wanted to clap a hand over friendly Jeremy's mouth. The Marshalls would be there, but Nick hadn't attended since he got married. If he showed up, this would be an awkward weekend—at least for her.

"You've told me about your weekends there, haven't you, Nick? Said you missed going the past few years."

Nick nodded.

Aaron smiled at Kenzie. "You wouldn't mind if we crashed?"

She minded. She didn't want to be anywhere near Nick. "It's Jeremy's property."

"We'll be there until Tuesday morning," Kyle said.

"How many people?"

Kyle and Jeremy glanced at each other. "Thirty to forty," Kyle said.

Jeremy nodded. "People come and go. Not everyone can stay the whole weekend. Some come in late, some leave early."

"Nick, order enough barbecue to feed everyone tomorrow night," Aaron said.

Surprised, Kenzie glanced at Nick. Didn't Aaron have a manager who ordered food? Why would he ask his bass player?

"That's not necessary," Jeremy said. "We always have plenty of food."

"It's the least I can do. Nick can set everything up to arrive at—what?" Aaron looked from Jeremy to her. "Six okay?"

"The property is in a remote area," Nick said. "There isn't a lot of takeout nearby. And it's a holiday weekend."

"If you pay someone enough money, they'll deliver," Aaron said to Nick like he was addressing an inferior. He turned back to Jeremy. "Plan on barbecue tomorrow night."

Kenzie didn't want to make things easy for Nick, but Jeremy's property was *way* off the beaten path. "Dad used to meet a friend at a place called Ramey's. It's about thirty minutes away from camp. You could try there."

"Thanks. I'll give them a call." Nick pulled out his cell phone with a look of relief. "I'm sorry to rush you guys out, but Aaron needs some time to get ready."

"Hey, it was great to meet you." Aaron shook their hands as they left his RV, holding onto Kenzie's a beat longer than was comfortable. "I'll see you tomorrow."

Oh, yay, her inner sarcasm cheered, while she smiled on the outside.

As the band members headed for their van, Jeremy slung his arm around Kenzie's neck with a laugh.

She glanced up at him. "Glad someone enjoyed that encounter."

"Did you notice the surprise on Nick's face when I introduced him to Cara?"

Kenzie nodded. "Yeah, what was that about?"

"He thought we—*you and me*—were together, sweet pea."

"Oh." That made sense, since the last time Nick saw them, they were kissing. After Nick stormed out, both she and Jeremy had tried to get in touch with him, to explain their kiss meant nothing. It had just been two sad people caught in a moment of grief. He never returned their calls or texts.

His sister, Becky, delivered a double kick to the gut a month later. Nick had run off to Vegas to marry a woman who was eight weeks pregnant. Which meant Nick had been with Juliette before her Dad's funeral.

"You need to be careful around Aaron this weekend, Kenz," Tripp said. "He stared at you the whole time we were in his bus."

Bodhi nodded. "I noticed that too."

Tightening his arm around her neck, Jeremy snorted. "He'll have to go through the six of us to get to her."

Kenzie could always count on the guys she'd known forever to protect her. She just wished they could have protected her heart from Nick Marshall.

CHAPTER 2

enzie turned off the highway and onto a county road that turned to dirt after three miles. She wove through dense trees where the sun barely filtered through, to sudden clearings lined with green corn stalks. Passing single wide trailers and cottages, cabins, and elaborate homes, she topped hills and dipped into vales. At one point, she emerged from the trees with a clear view of the Tennessee River in the distance. A sharp left and she was back in the thick ponderosa pines. A mile farther, she turned left and passed under a cypress arch with Knight carved across the top.

Dirt dusted her car as she drove around a bend in the road and saw the sweet log cabin Jeremy had built for Cara tucked back in the trees. The thirty-foot Pioneer trailer he'd sold to Kenzie when he upgraded sat on the raised deck he built to keep it dry if the river rose with floodwaters. He'd placed it so the front windows faced the creek and the rising sun, the bedroom in the back, shaded by the huge trees surrounding the property.

She parked next to the deck, climbed out, and took a deep

breath of warm earth and musky river, setting loose the memories that always fluttered through her mind every time she came here.

Jeremy's parents gifted him this three-acre parcel of land for his high school graduation. The property ran along a creek that joined the Tennessee a hundred yards downstream with cypress trees lining the shore on both sides of the boat launch.

A T-shaped dock extended from the muddy shore out into the creek where two pontoons were tied. One belonged to the Marshall family, the other to Jeremy's parents. Five boats bobbed in the slips off an arm of the dock that ran parallel to the shore.

RVs and trailers were lined up on the other side of the road leading to the boat launch. The Marshalls' huge RV sat between Kyle's and Becky's trailers. She was so glad Jeremy had set his old trailer away from the others, giving her a little more privacy—which she'd need if Nick and his wife showed up.

Chairs and benches circled a large firepit Jeremy built in a clearing since last she'd been here. Picnic tables and camp chairs dotted shady spots under surrounding trees.

Jeremy's parents were coming down the trail from their cabin just beyond Jeremy's. They'd built as far away as they could from the noise generated once the after-dark music and dancing got started.

They both stopped long enough to give her a warm hug.

Her dad, Jeremy's parents, and the Marshalls had made meeting here with family and friends a summer holiday tradition.

Tripp and his girlfriend pulled in, towing another trailer, followed by Ryder with a camper on the back of his truck. Bodhi and Nick's brother, Griffin, were setting up a volley-ball net in another clearing. She looked over to where her dad used to park his trailer. The spot still sat empty. Kyle tried to get her to use their dad's trailer after he passed, but she never could, so Kyle finally sold it last summer.

Tomorrow most of the gang would pile into boats and head two miles downriver to an island with a great beach. They'd spend the day waterskiing, wakeboarding, and enjoying the heat of the sun and the cool of the water.

She grabbed three grocery bags out of the back seat and climbed the steps to her cute little weekend home. She'd fixed it up a little since Jeremy sold it to her. Stripping the ugly wallpaper, she'd painted the walls barely yellow and the ugly brown cabinets white, brightening up the former bachelor pad.

She'd also re-covered the benches, added colorful curtains, replaced the threadbare carpet with tile, and updated the appliances. Jeremy complained that she made it too girly, but she loved every square inch of her now-bachelorette haven.

A light glowed from the kitchen window, letting her know Cara had been here in case she arrived after dark. She went inside and set the groceries on the table.

When she went back outside, she found Jeremy already unloading her bag and guitar from the trunk.

"What took you so long?"

She went down the steps. "I had a conference call."

"Country or pop artist?"

"Ned Gray."

"Ah." Jeremy gave her a sidelong look. "Moving into the big leagues, talking to producers. You thinking of going solo?"

She rolled her eyes. Jeremy knew better than anyone how she felt about performing. "Has everyone already eaten?"

"Yeah. Cara put a plate in your microwave."

"She's such a sweetheart." She glanced around the camp.

People were coming out of their trailers, setting up chairs, ready to enjoy the evening that was settling over the Tennessee, a river that was wide and deep enough that twenty-five to thirty thousand barges transported goods over its waters every year.

"Nick's in the Marshalls' RV putting his daughter to bed."

The words were like ripping a bandage off a raw wound. So, Nick was already here, and she'd have to endure seeing him with his wife for a whole weekend. Unless she got in her car and drove home right now.

"Don't even think about it," Jeremy warned.

"What?"

"I know exactly what's going through that pretty little head of yours. You can't let Nick run you off, Kenz."

The music scene was a close-knit community, but she'd been careful to stay away from the gossips and news. She didn't want to read that Nick and his wife were expecting another child or see pictures of their Nashville home. She didn't want to hear that Nick and his family were jetting off to some exotic location.

A door closed, and both she and Jeremy turned to find Nick standing on the bottom step of the Marshalls' RV staring at them.

Kenzie looked away first. She went to the back door of her car and stacked the three cover dishes she'd premade for their potluck dinners, then followed Jeremy up the deck stairs and set everything on the table until she could make room in the small fridge while Jeremy carried her bag into the bedroom.

"What's his wife like?" she asked, ripping off another bandage.

"I don't think she's here yet. At least I haven't seen her." He leaned a hip against the counter. "By the end of this weekend, seeing him won't be so hard anymore."

Kenzie turned away so she wouldn't see Jeremy's expression. "I think I'll always have a hard time being around Nick."

"Not if you meet someone. Cara has a single friend—"

"No. No blind dates."

"Cara and I can go with you. Dinner and bowling or a movie. We won't leave you alone."

Her laugh held no humor. "Right, because the only thing more awkward than a blind date, is having your friends there to witness the catastrophe."

"At least think about it." He walked to the door. "Eat, then grab your guitar, so we can get this party started, baby girl."

Kenzie followed Jeremy out onto the deck. Because, why not? Get another look at Nick. Pick at the raw edges around the scab. Rip out her heart one more time.

Nick had joined his family. Just the sight of him sent her into near panic. "I don't know if I can do this, Jer. I've loved this place since I was tiny, but I don't want to be here right now."

Leaving right after getting here would cause a scene, but she could sneak away once everyone went to bed.

Jeremy pointed a finger at her nose. "Don't you dare let him chase you away, Kenz. If I wake up and you're gone, I'll drag you back. Do you hear me? This place wouldn't be the same without you. It's time to get over the schmuck."

She nodded, unable to speak for fear her voice would crack. Folding her arms, she looked over the gathering group. "I thought I was over him enough to not care, but I'm not."

"How can you be over him when you won't let yourself move on? How many dates have you been on? Two? Three?"

"I've been out four times."

He hooted out a laugh. "Nope. You can't count the fair with Dwayne Ellis. He made you pay your way. And his."

"Poor Dwayne," she said, with a laugh. "I should never have told you about him forgetting his wallet."

He snorted. "You're the only one who actually believes he forgot his wallet."

Kyle, Nick, and Doug Marshall started playing "Sweet Home Alabama."

"Nick isn't playing bass anymore," Jeremy said almost as an afterthought.

"What?"

"His dad says he's managing Aaron's band instead."

Ordering barbecue wasn't a band manager's job, but Aaron telling Nick to do so made more sense now. "Nick loves playing music. Why would he do that?"

"According to Doug, he took the job so he could spend more time with his daughter. I'm sure we'll learn more over the weekend."

She didn't want to learn more. She just wanted Nick, his wife, and his daughter to go somewhere far away.

They both turned at the sound of motors. Two big tour buses stopped at the gate.

"Looks like the celebrity has arrived," Kenzie said.

"I didn't figure they'd get here until tomorrow." Jeremy turned to her. "Didn't he say he was having a big party tonight?"

"I guess his plans changed. Where are you putting them?"

"In that clearing on the other side of my house. I warned my parents this might be a noisy weekend," he said with a chuckle. At the bottom of the stairs, he looked back at her. "Remember to be careful around Aaron while he's here, sweet pea."

"I will."

"Go make some music while I show the celebrity where to park."

After Jeremy jogged toward the gate, Kenzie went back

inside to finish putting the last of the groceries away and microwave the plate of dinner Cara set aside for her. She spent ten minutes picking at the chicken breast and green beans, not really hungry, just delaying joining the group for as long as possible. But she knew if she didn't go down soon, Kyle would be up here checking on her.

She unpacked, then changed into jeans and a T-shirt, but pulled a hoodie off a hanger and tucked it under her arm. Though the night was hot and the air heavy, the breeze coming off the river could get cool, especially this early in the season.

The last thing she grabbed was her guitar case. Leaving the light on over the sink, she closed the door and headed down the slight hill toward the group. When she finally gathered enough courage to glance up, relief that Nick wasn't there washed over her. If he was managing Aaron's band, he'd probably walked up to check on where they were parking.

Bodhi and Kyle saved her a place between them. After hellos and a few hugs, she pulled out her guitar and got down to business.

They rarely played their own music for these occasions. Instead, they played songs from George Strait, John Denver, Brad Paisley, Tim McGraw, Alabama—songs people were familiar with. They always threw in a little Charlie Daniels so Jeremy could show off his fiddling skills. Kenzie and Becky added something from The Judds, Loretta Lynn, or Taylor Swift for the women.

The moon was nearly full, lighting the treetops and glittering off the creek. She held her guitar close, like a shield, while she glanced around at the group—friends she'd known forever.

People didn't need to have the same blood running through their veins to be family.

Like her sister-in-law. She and Jessi were as close as two blood relatives could be. Her brother's wife spoiled Kyle, which he deserved after taking care of a little sister his whole life. He treated Jessi like a queen in return.

Kenzie was only sorry their dad died before he got to meet her. He would have been so proud of Kyle and the sweet wife he picked. He would have been equally as proud of the way Kyle handled the ranch while still playing the music he loved.

Kenzie didn't see Nick join the group while she was singing Bebe Rexha's "Meant to Be" with Kyle and Bodhi, but felt his presence as physical as a touch on her shoulder.

Tripp turned up the tempo with Zac Brown's "Chicken Fried," and Ryder jumped up and pulled her to her feet. She didn't want to be the first on the dance floor Jeremy built under a stand of trees, but it wasn't in Ryder's DNA to sit idle when he could be dancing.

Jeremy took the next song by grabbing his fiddle and segueing into "The Git Up," which had the group laughing while she and Ryder hammed it up. She'd been dancing with Ryder for years, and he cued her into their next moves with a simple touch or nod.

Kyle and Tripp shifted into a slow, sexy tune.

When Ryder pulled her close, she closed her eyes and felt the night settle in around her. She didn't want to see Nick singing along, and she didn't want to see him dancing with his wife. She didn't want to see him at all.

Crickets and tree frogs competed with the music, and the engine of a passing barge blended with the atmosphere and river noise. When the song ended, Aaron Vance was waiting for the next dance. She'd rather sit safely between Jeremy and Kyle, but both were dancing now. Nick's dad and his brother, Griffin, were playing guitars, and Ryder had pulled out his harmonica.

"I'm glad you're here. I wanted to tell you how much I enjoyed your music today," Aaron said as he led her around in a lively two-step. "You were impressive, moving so easily between the drums and guitar. Do you play any other instruments?"

"The piano." When Aaron twisted her around, Nick came into view. He was standing with his back to a tree, watching them.

"Are you with that guy?"

"Who?" she asked, immediately assuming Aaron meant Nick.

"The guy you were dancing with."

"Oh, Ryder? No."

"Good," he said with a grin.

"How did you get started in music?" she asked, looking for an exit from this particular conversation.

"My uncle bought me my first guitar when I was seven. He's been in the music business for years. He used to sing, but he's a producer now."

"Really? What's his—Oh! Marc Vance is your uncle."

"You know him?"

"I've worked with him a couple of times. He's very talented."

"I can't wait to ask him about you."

Kenzie chose to ignore his remark, grateful when Doug Marshall appeared for the next dance. She hadn't danced with Nick's father since Nick's parents' anniversary party five years ago. Twirling her around the floor made her wish her dad was here, dancing and singing along with the group. He used to love their holiday weekends on the river.

"It was great but unexpected, to see you up onstage today," Doug said.

"I'm just filling in for Bonnie. It was great seeing you in the audience. I was sure you were there to watch Nick."

"Ah, I thought you knew he isn't singing with Aaron's band anymore."

"Jeremy just told me. I'm sure he misses it."

"I'm not sure he does. How's the writing going?" Doug asked, not very smooth in his attempt to change the subject.

"Good."

"Working on another award-winner?"

"I wish. I'm pretty sure that was a fluke. The artist put so much—"

Doug lifted her chin, making her look him in the eye. Nick inherited his intense blue eyes from his dad. "Take some credit, Kenzie. You wrote a good song."

She smiled. "I wrote a good song. The artist made it better."

Doug shook his head. "You wrote it. Own it."

"Actually, I was going to ask if I could come over sometime next week and have you play one of my songs with me. Maybe Griffin could join us, and Becky, if she's still in town. I need to hear the music the way I wrote it."

"Kyle won't play it with you?"

She glanced at Kyle. He was grinning at something Jessi was whispering in his ear. "You know my brother. He'd try to add a country twist to my pop."

He chuckled. "I don't work on Thursdays or Fridays. You can come over anytime on those days, baby girl."

Hearing him use her dad's nickname for her warmed her heart and hurt at the same time.

"Email the music to me so the kids and I can run through it a couple of times first. Becky's here until next Saturday, and Griffin will be in town all summer. We'd love to play with you."

"Thanks, Doug. I'll send an email when I get home, and I'll plan on coming over at eleven on Thursday."

~

*W*atching Kenzie dance with Ryder had always shot a streak of jealousy through Nick. Three years away hadn't changed that. The two of them moved together as if they were one. People who watched them dance often mistook them for a couple.

Before making his move, Nick noticed Aaron watching Kenzie like a hawk eyeing his next meal. After their one dance, Nick's dad put a nix on any progress by asking Kenzie to dance. But that wouldn't deter Aaron. He was like a bloodhound when his interest was piqued. And Kenzie filled that interest for the weekend. Lucky for Kenz, Aaron's attention could be turned elsewhere at the drop of a hat.

In a surprise move, his little brother, Griffin moved in for the next dance. Grif was nursing a broken heart after his girlfriend of nine months left him to backpack through Europe with a trust fund baby.

After their dance, she and Griffin grabbed their guitars, moved over to a picnic table, and started picking out a tune. Just the two of them. Griffin played music, but he'd never been serious enough to join a band.

Nick pushed away from the tree and wandered down to the dock. The water in the creek was still as glass, and he gazed into the darkness until a rustling in the bushes farther down the bank turned his attention. Possibly a family of raccoons hoping to rummage through the remnants of the camp's garbage once everyone was in bed.

When Kenzie was dancing with Aaron, she glanced at him once, but she looked away and never glanced his way again. He couldn't blame her. He'd hurt her. Abandoned her when she needed him most. Something he wouldn't forget soon, even if his family stopped throwing out little reminders as often as possible.

To tell the truth, when a buddy mentioned Aaron was holding auditions for a bass player, there was nothing more important than trying out. He had to go or forever wonder. And where had that gotten him? Married with a baby he was raising on his own.

Kenzie finally stood, hugged his brother, tucked her guitar into the case, and moved through the group, offering hugs and good nights before heading toward Jeremy's old trailer.

Before she got very far, Aaron made his second move. Nick couldn't tell what he said, but Kenzie shook her head. He was probably asking her to his RV for a drink because that's what Aaron did. Very rarely did he retire alone. Unless Kenzie had changed in three years, Aaron would be going to bed alone.

After what Nick had done, while traveling with Aaron's first tour, he had no right to judge anyone.

Aaron followed Kenzie up the stairs to the deck, but she stopped him at the door of her trailer. He knew Aaron as well as he knew Kenzie. The guy had hoped for an invite inside, even though she already turned him down once.

Good girl, Kenz.

Several Knight Rivers band members, as well as his dad, were watching. She had an army of protectors.

After Kenzie shut her door, Aaron walked down the stairs tugging his phone out of his pocket. Nick's cell rang a second later. He connected the call. "Yeah."

"Where are you?"

"On the dock."

"I have a fantastic idea."

Those words always scared Nick. While playing in Aaron's band, he'd learned *I have a fantastic idea* was usually the beginning of something he wasn't going to like. "Sure. Let me check on London, then I'll meet you at your RV."

CHAPTER 3

*W*hile Kenzie peeled an orange for breakfast, she watched Kyle, Jeremy, and Nick approach her trailer through the window. Unlocking the door, she pushed it open just as Kyle raised his fist to knock. Leaning against the frame, she popped an orange section into her mouth. The sun was bright and the temperature already hot.

Bodhi opened the door of his trailer and pulled a T-shirt over his head, then crossed the dirt road toward them.

"Good. You're awake," Kyle said.

Jeremy had followed Kyle up the stairs, but Nick stayed at the bottom. He again wore reflective sunglasses that hid his eyes. She'd give anything for a pair so she could do the same.

Jeremy frowned. "Would you stop stealing my underwear? Cara keeps blaming me for losing them, and all the while it's still you pilfering through my stuff. I should buy stock in guys' underwear companies."

Kenzie looked down at the SpongeBob boxers she was wearing. "If you do buy stock, go with Jockey. I prefer the way they fit."

Bodhi, who'd stopped next to Nick, chuckled. "Kenz looks much better in them than you do."

"She should since I don't have any left. Why do you think I'm wearing swim trunks?" He turned back to Kenzie. "And that's my Titans T-shirt. When did you sneak in and nab that?"

She peeled another section off her orange, popped it in her mouth, and looked out over the camp. Most everyone had gathered around tables for the pancake breakfast Nick and Jeremy's moms were cooking.

"I know you're not here to talk about what I'm wearing."

"Get dressed." Kyle thumbed over his shoulder. "We need to talk."

"Bring all my underwear with you," Jeremy grumbled before he hopped off the deck.

Kenzie walked out minutes later, wearing a swimsuit top and cutoffs, to find Becky sitting in a lawn chair under her trailer's awning, a darling little girl on her lap. The second she saw the vibrant blue eyes she knew the child was Nick's daughter. All this time she worried she'd have to play nice around Nick's wife, and never gave a second thought to how she'd react when faced with his daughter.

Her hair was as dark and curly as Nick's and she'd inherited her daddy's right-cheek dimple, which was apparent the second she grinned.

"Sorry, Kenz. I thought it might be easier for you to meet London alone rather than in front of the whole crowd," Becky said.

Kenzie felt every reaction she might have expected. Hurt. Anger. Soul-sucking sorrow. Like a blender, her heart mixed the emotions together and served them up with a punch of envy that had her swallowing tears. "She's beautiful."

Becky pushed to her feet and patted the little girl's bare leg. "London, this is my friend, Kenzie. Can you say Kenzie?"

The little girl pointed at Kenzie. "Mama."

Kenzie's heart squeezed to the point of pain.

A grimace contorted Becky's expression. "No, London. This is Kenzie."

The little girl looked at her aunt in confusion, then grinned at Kenzie. "Kamma."

Kenzie couldn't help but smile at her two-year-old's attempt at a hard name. "Close enough." She took London's soft little hand in hers. "Hello, London. You sure are pretty."

London held out her foot.

"She's showing you her new shoes."

"I love your pink sandals."

"Pink," London repeated in her adorable little voice.

Kenzie felt her smile wobble even before Nick's mom and dad joined them on the deck.

"Congratulations on your sweet granddaughter."

"Thank you." Vicki Marshall took London from Becky when she reached out for Kenzie. "She's fun to have around."

"Mom and Dad are in for a treat with Miss London's terrible twos. They're keeping her while Nick's touring with Aaron Vance for four months."

"Where's her mother?" Kenzie blurted out before she could stop herself.

Doug raised his eyebrows. "You haven't heard? Nick's wife divorced him and gave up all rights to London," he said, his tone hushed like the two-year-old would understand. And maybe she would. Kenzie didn't know much about children.

"I'm sorry."

"Don't be sorry. We aren't. Juliette was nothing but a—"

"Becky." Vicki gave her daughter a stern mom glare. Something else Kenzie didn't know much about.

Becky folded her arms and stuck out a hip. "Well, it's the truth."

40 | TINA NEWCOMB

"I'm sure Kenzie doesn't want to hear any of this."

Vicki was right. She didn't want to hear about Nick or Juliette—or even darling little London. She'd rather drive back to the ranch and spend the weekend alone, where her heart didn't have to hurt every time she heard his name or saw his face.

She shoved her hands in her cutoffs' back pockets and nodded toward a picnic table where the band members had gathered. "The guys want to talk about something, so I better head over."

"You didn't get any pancakes," Vicki said.

"I ate something here."

Nick was with the band, watching this uncomfortable moment along with everyone else in camp, so Becky's plan hadn't worked out after all.

"I'll see you all later," Kenzie said.

She walked down the stairs and across the camp to where Bodhi patted a space between him and Ryder. Still processing the Nick's-wife-left-him information, she stepped over the picnic table bench while watching the newest member of the band cross through the middle of camp on his way to their picnic table.

She didn't know much about Jeff Davidson. Though he'd been with the band for three months, something seemed off about him, and she couldn't quite figure out what. Apparently, Kyle felt it too. Though they hadn't discussed Jeff, she'd seen Kyle watching him more than once.

"Sorry to get you up a little earlier than you would have liked, especially after our late night, but Nick came to me this morning with—" Kyle stopped and glanced at Nick, who stood just outside their gathering, looking uncomfortable. "Nick, why don't you explain?"

Since they were in the shade, Nick had removed his

sunglasses. He looked around the group before he stopped at her. "Aaron was really impressed with your performance yesterday. *And* last night. I've been with him for three years, and he's never invited an artist, let alone a whole band, to his trailer."

He stopped and rubbed his thumb across his bottom lip, a telltale sign that he was uneasy. Was he uncomfortable because of what he had to say, or because she was sitting there watching him? She hoped it was the latter. He should feel way more uncomfortable than she did.

"He thinks Knight Rivers could become headliners if offered a break, so that's what he wants to do. Aaron starts a four-month tour the first of July and would like Knight Rivers to be his opening act. The schedule is intense. He's playing at ninety-six venues in one hundred and eight days. That's twelve days off in four months. And we'll be in a different city almost every night. Twice we have two concerts in one day. He's booked at concert venues, as well as state fairs and a handful of music festivals."

"Why us?" Tripp asked.

"Pretty sure I already explained why. Aaron was impressed with your performance and the number of loyal fans following Knight Rivers."

Nick looked at her again, like what he said should mean something to her specifically. Becky said her parents were taking care of their granddaughter while Nick was on tour with Aaron, so he'd be there the whole four months. And Bonnie would be out on bedrest and then taking care of a new baby until at least November.

"Aaron just bought a new tour bus. He offered to let you use his previous bus, no charge. It has six bunks and a king-sized bed in the back."

"I get the king!" she called, raising her hand.

Bodhi hooked his elbow around her neck "Bull crap you do."

"I'll get you a schedule of the cities and venues where we'll play," Nick continued. "You may want to hire a manager to take care of hotel reservations when we don't have to drive through the night, and to schedule catered meals, plus you'll need a bus driver. I can give you some names or,"—he toed the dirt beneath one of his flip-flops—"I can take care of the details for you if you want. I'll include my fees, which will give you an idea of cost, plus some other manager's names with the schedules. If you decide to do this, we have a lot to go over in a short amount of time."

"How long do we have to decide?" Kyle asked.

"I need your decision before Aaron leaves tomorrow. I know you've already agreed to sing at my sister's wedding at the end of July. I have another band that can fill in for three days to give you some time off over that weekend." He took a step back, and then another as if impatient to escape. "Any questions before I leave so you can talk?"

"Let us talk first." Kyle clapped Nick on the shoulder. "I'm sure we'll have plenty of questions afterward."

Kenzie turned when she felt a hand on her back. London stood behind her with arms outstretched. "Mama."

The shock on Nick's face would have been comical if she'd been in the mood to laugh.

"Awkward," Ryder sang under his breath, but loud enough for all of them to hear.

Kenzie picked up the little girl. "Kamma," she pronounced slowly, hoping the name stuck rather than Mama.

London grinned, flashing her darling dimple. "Kamma."

Nick held out his arms. "Come on, London."

London twined her arms around Kenzie's neck. "Mama."

Every eye in the camp was on them. "I'll watch her," she said, without looking up at Nick.

"You don't have to do this, Kenz," Nick said.

"She's fine."

The moment hung for eternity, the tension thicker than fog. Finally, Nick relented and walked away. London took a moment to look at everyone sitting near, then ducked her head under Kenzie's chin.

"Let's get this over with quickly," Kyle said. "We all know this opportunity could be a game-changer. Both good and bad. If our music takes off, our lives won't be the same."

"I say let's do it," Bodhi said, drumming the table with his palms.

Tripp nodded. "I agree. This is a once-in-a-lifetime chance. We'll never get this kind of an offer again."

"We need to discuss money before we make a decision," Jeremy said. "Most of us have day jobs that we'll need to give up if we're gone for four months."

Kyle pulled a slip of paper out of his jeans pocket and handed it to Jeremy.

"This is what Aaron offered?" Jeremy asked, surprise evident in his tone. He passed the paper to Bodhi, who grinned before passing it to her.

Kenzie was also surprised at the amount. Concerts, after expenses, didn't always pay well. The merchandise sold at the venues was what made most of the money. "Will we be able to sell merchandise as well?"

Kyle pointed at her. "I also thought of that. Aaron's attorney is drafting a contract promising that amount if we agree. I'll have him add that we get to keep the proceeds from *our* merchandise."

"What merchandise?" Ryder asked after Kenzie passed the piece of paper to him.

Kyle leaned forward, planting his hands on the picnic table. "Ryder, you're going to finally put that college degree from UT to use. If we do this, we'll need a logo. Then you can design T-shirts, hats, posters, drink koozies, keychains, and anything else we can think to sell, but you'll have to do it in a hurry." He pointed at the paper Ryder passed to his brother. "That number, divided by seven, won't make us rich—"

"But it'll get our music in front of people," Tripp said.

Kyle nodded. "Exactly."

"It's more than I expected. If we tack on merchandise, it will make four months on the road worth it," Tripp said, holding the paper out for Jeff to see. "I'm in."

"I'm in too," Jeff said after taking a look.

"What do *you* think?" Jeremy asked Kyle.

Kyle grinned. "I don't think I've ever been more excited about music in my life."

Jeremy turned to her. "What about you, sweet pea? You'll be on the road with Nick for four months. Are you okay with that?"

Kenzie looked around at the band members, her family. Singing on a stage wasn't her dream, but it was theirs. Four months wasn't a lifetime. She had songs to write, which could be done on a bus as easily as at home. "I'll go along with whatever you guys decide."

"Jeremy's right." Kyle sat down at the table for the first time since they gathered. "Since Nick's the tour manager, he'll be around most of the time. Bonnie won't be back by the time we leave."

Bodhi barked out a laugh. "Be realistic. If Bonnie had been with us at the Cumberland Festival, we wouldn't be having this conversation. This offer came about because Aaron Vance has his eye on Kenzie."

Kenzie turned to Bodhi. "What happens when he finds out I'm not the tiniest bit interested?"

"Hopefully, he won't until after we sign the contract," Tripp said.

"You might have to sleep with him," Bodhi added, slipping his arm around her shoulder.

Though she knew he was kidding, she shrugged his arm away. "Yeah, that's not happening."

Kyle waved a hand. "We haven't signed up for anything yet. We have to make sure this is going to work for all of us." He pulled his cell phone out of his pocket. "What are some questions you want answered?"

They spent several minutes brainstorming while Kyle typed notes into his phone.

"We have other people to consider. Let's discuss the offer with the people in our lives. Jeremy, can we meet in your cabin right after dinner tonight?" Kyle asked.

"Sure. Your significant others are welcome to join us. Like Kyle said, this decision doesn't only involve four months of our lives, but theirs as well."

"This opportunity could change everything for us, or we may get dumped back here with nothing," Kyle added. "Going on tour with Aaron doesn't guarantee success. This will be a grueling four months where we're locked up together on a tour bus a lot of the time. Think this over seriously. We'll meet at Jeremy's around seven-thirty."

Bodhi, Jeff, Ryder, and Tripp got up from the table. Kyle held Jeremy in place while motioning Kenzie to stay. He looked from the little girl in Kenzie's lap to her. London had been an angel the whole time they talked, content to finger Kenzie's braid.

Jeremy shook his head. "Nick shouldn't have left his daughter for you to look after."

She ran a hand over London's soft curls. "It was my idea to watch her. She hasn't been a bother."

"You're not his babysitter."

"He didn't ask me to watch her, Jer. I said she could stay."

"You need to be really sure about this because there won't

be any going back once we start. A contract will commit us for the entire tour," Jeremy said.

"We can't do this without you, Kenzie," Kyle quickly added. "We're a stronger band with you."

Jeremy turned to Kyle with raised brows. "Nothing like laying on the pressure, bro. Just like the rest of us, she needs to decide what's right for her." He glanced at her. "If you decide you can't do it, we'll either turn down the offer, tell Aaron we accept but without you, or we'll try to find someone who can replace you. I know singing with this band isn't what you want to do."

"I'm willing to tour for four months. For you guys. For the band. After that, you'll have to find someone else," she said, aiming her last comment at her brother. "I'm serious, Kyle. Four months and then I'm done."

Music and being onstage were as important to her brother as his next breath. He'd never been able to understand why her passions ran in a different direction.

"Okay," Kyle said. "What about Nick?"

"I won't have to be around him alone. And I can keep myself occupied with writing while we're on the road. Most of you have jobs you'll have to quit and people you'll have to leave. I don't."

Her comment hit just under her ribs, taking her breath away, making her feel very alone.

～

*N*ick kept an eye on the woman holding his daughter. Kenzie didn't seem uncomfortable with having London in her lap. As she listened to what the other band members had to say, she ran her fingers through London's hair or smoothed a hand down her leg. Her actions seemed to be unconscious while his daughter sat quietly, which was an anomaly in and of itself. London never sat still. She seemed mesmerized by Kenzie's touch.

And "mama?" Where had that come from? Juliette left before London was three months old.

Becky sauntered toward him and wrapped an arm around his waist. "Kenzie looks like a natural, doesn't she?"

Yes.

"You made a huge mistake, Nicky." She glanced up, her dark eyes sad at the corners. "But you know that already, don't you?"

Yes.

"Wouldn't it be great if time machines really did exist? We could go back and change the past."

Juliette had been with a pack of groupies who'd followed Aaron's tour bus from town to town, waiting outside the concert venues with the rest of them for the band to exit. He'd been flattered when the beautiful blond set her sights on him rather than Aaron. The first three nights he'd turned her offers of a good time down. The fourth night he succumbed to her flirty smile and enticing promises.

Becky pinched his side lightly. "It might not be too late."

"It is."

"Have you tried apologizing? A simple 'I'm sorry I acted like a complete moron. I still love you' might soften the blow when she finally doubles up her fist and socks you in the nose. By the way, I want to be there for that moment."

He glared at his sister over the top of his sunglasses. "Why didn't you tell me Jeremy got married? All this time I thought Kenzie was with him."

"What did it matter? You were married to Juliette and she was pregnant."

When he arrived late to the barbecue after completely missing Waylon's funeral, he'd expected Kenzie to be waiting for him since they hadn't seen each other in weeks. When he couldn't find her, his temper flared. Kyle finally pointed him toward their practice shed. To walk in on one of his best friends and the woman he still considered his, locked in a passionate kiss had pushed him over the edge. A month later, he and Juliette jumped on a plane to Vegas.

That night—at least in his feeble mind—Kenzie and Jeremy had given him the justification he needed for his past actions.

"You could have told me."

Becky leaned close. "Did you lose sleep wondering? Were you plagued with thoughts of her and Jeremy together? If so, good. You got what you deserved."

He folded his arms. "Will you go get London? Please?"

"Why don't *you* go get her?"

"Because Kenzie will think I don't trust her."

Becky smiled. "Sure. I'll get London while you figure out how to apologize."

The band members dispersed, but Jeremy and Kyle kept Kenzie at the table. They were asking her if she was sure about being on the road with him for four months. He knew them, knew how protective they were of her. He used to be right there with them, protecting Kenzie until he turned into the one who hurt her.

Kenzie would agree to the tour now she was singing with the band again. She probably didn't want to go, but she wouldn't let the guys down.

His daughter put up a fight when Becky lifted her up off Kenzie's lap. London, who was skittish around most strangers, had attached herself to Kenzie. Why? What had Kenzie done to make London so captivated with her?

He'd been completely enraptured by this tiny human being from the moment she was born. She was beautiful, with her little rosebud lips and head of black hair, so tiny and vulnerable. London had changed every aspect of his life.

Every thought, every decision he made, was with London in mind.

He was awed that Kenzie had so readily picked up his daughter. In a reverse situation, he wasn't sure he could do the same.

CHAPTER 4

*a*fter grabbing a granola bar, Kenzie jumped onto Kyle's boat along with a group of people. The trip to the island two miles downriver wouldn't take long once Kyle motored beyond the creek's no-wake zone.

She settled onto the bench seat in the forward bow. While Kyle backed the boat away from the dock, she glanced toward camp. Everyone was hauling grills and coolers and stacks of towels toward the boats still at the dock.

She'd been able to steer clear of Aaron this morning, but now he and his band members were climbing aboard the Marshalls' pontoon.

He'd asked her to come to his tour bus last night for a nightcap. When she said no, he followed her to her own trailer, obviously hoping for an invite in, and she almost wished she was marginally attracted. Her attention on someone other than Nick for the weekend would be wonderful. Aaron was nice-looking and friendly, but he was also a player. Even without reading gossip magazines, she could tell if it wasn't her, he'd find someone else quickly enough.

As soon as the creek flowed into the river, Kyle opened up the engine, lifting the nose of the boat in the air, and Kenzie pulled the bill of her baseball cap lower to keep it from flying away. When they neared a barge putting out a sizable wake, Kyle slowed so the water wouldn't swamp his boat. The pilot waved from his loft high above.

Once they were past, Kyle hit the gas again, and the boat glided over the glassy surface of the river. Minutes later, he slowed and rounded the west side of the island, where their group would avoid the worst of the wakes kicked up from boats passing through the main channel.

They were early enough to unload a grill, a couple of coolers, and set up a large canopy for shade-seekers.

Jeremy pulled in next to Kyle with a boat full of friends, and they set up another canopy and staked a couple of huge umbrellas.

When the Marshalls' pontoon came into view, Kenzie grabbed a towel and her beach bag and headed to the far side of the gathering. Spreading her towel over the sand, she slathered on sunscreen, popped in her earbuds, and turned up the music, hoping to drown out the world until lunch.

But alas, London's adorable little laugh broke through the country crooner singing in her ear. She opened her eyes, fortunately, hidden by sunglasses, and looked in the direction of the laughter. The little girl was up to her knees in the river, trying to splash her daddy. He would splash her back, just enough to make her squeal with delight.

Earbuds aren't cutting it. I need major league noise-canceling headphones and pulse-pounding rock music.

Someone initiated a raucous volleyball game in a small clearing behind her, so she rolled onto her stomach to watch the fun, smiling when Jeremy spiked the ball and Cara jumped up and down cheering.

Jeremy said he'd never love again after losing his first

wife, but he'd been wrong. Cara was perfect for him, and they made a great couple. Kenzie wondered how Cara and Jessi would react to their husbands being on the road for four months. When Nick went on tour with Aaron the first time around, he was gone for eight weeks, and she'd been torn between missing him and feeling abandoned and completely helpless while caring for her dad.

If Aaron's tour wound through southern states, at least Cara and Jessi could travel to a few of the concert venues. And they would be home for Becky's wedding at the end of July.

The tune she and Griffin played around with last night whispered through her mind. She wished she was sitting at the piano in her little house at the ranch so she could refine the melody. This song was coming backward for her. Usually, she wrote the lyrics and then fit the music to the words.

She woke up a week ago with this tune running through her mind. It was haunting and sad, which was unusual for her. She liked upbeat and fun, so she was stymied by this tune, wondering how it would play out.

Someone plopped down next to her and she turned.

Aaron.

"What are you doing over here so far from the group?"

Kenzie popped out an earbud and smiled, glad he wouldn't see it didn't reach her eyes. "Writing a song."

"I'm pretty good at songwriting. Maybe we could combine our musical talents and come up with a winner."

"Maybe."

"I wrote two of the songs I'll be singing on tour. I'm going into the studio to record them next week."

"Great."

A slight frown wrinkled his brow. She must not have

responded the way he expected, so she tried again. "You'll have to let me know which ones."

His grin told her she'd done better the second time around. "Your brother said we could take his boat out. You up for a ride?"

The boat's motor would drown out London's laugh and Nick's voice, and carry her away from people's sympathetic, yet curious, glances. The boat would be an escape. She jumped to her feet, slipped into her cutoffs, and grabbed her bag. "Let's go."

Kyle didn't look as anxious as she felt. He tossed a Frisbee to Tripp and joined her and Aaron near the bow. "Going for a ride?"

She sent him a reassuring smile. "We'll stop at the marina for gas."

Kyle's attention bounced from her to Aaron. "Want me to go with you?"

"No need. We won't be long."

"I was just going to fire up the grills for lunch."

"We'll be back before the coals are ready," she assured him.

"Be careful," Kyle said close to her ear after Aaron climbed aboard.

"This is survival one-oh-one."

Kyle turned to look behind him where the Marshall family sat. "Don't cut off your nose to spite your face."

"I'm here for the whole weekend, Kyle, and I'm going on tour for four months."

He put his hands on his waist and blew out a breath. "No one is forcing—"

Kenzie held up her hand to stop him. "I'm not playing a martyr here. I told you I'd go, so let's not rehash it."

"Are you going to hold this over my head for years to come?"

"Absolutely." Though Kyle knew she wouldn't. She made the decision because she loved her brother and she loved Knight Rivers. And it was only four months. Not life-changing. Just sixteen weeks while she wrote on a bus rather than at home—no big deal. And she'd get to see the country.

She patted his arm. "Do you need anything from the marina?"

"Ice. Grab about four bags. I left a cooler in the back of the boat."

"Okey-dokey."

When she turned toward Aaron, he held out a hand to help her up. She'd been scampering on and off boats since she was tiny, but she let him lift her aboard.

Kyle waited until she was at the wheel, then pushed the boat back off the sand. She started the engine and shifted into reverse. Aaron took the passenger seat and leaned his head back.

"Careful. There's a wicked sandbar on the end of the island," Bodhi called from his boat as he maneuvered around to take the spot she just vacated. Shifting forward, she eased around the south end of the island, giving the barely visible sandbar a wide berth.

She'd forgotten her baseball cap, so she pushed her sunglasses to the top of her head to hold the flyaway hair that had escaped her braid, stuck a foot on the seat behind her to hold her balance, and opened up the engine. Flying past trees and cabins on either side of the river, waving to passing boats, she reveled in the moment.

She glanced at Aaron. He had his eyes closed, a smile on his face. Maybe he needed this weekend of freedom too. She hadn't really given much thought to the busy life he led.

As soon as she passed a boat of tubers, the driver flipped the boat around and hit her wake at high speed. The two people on the tube shot into the air with shrieks before hitting the water. Luckily, everyone was wearing a lifejacket.

Crazies.

Aaron shouted something, but she couldn't hear over the wind and the motor. She shook her head.

He stood and put his mouth to her ear. "How often do y'all come here?"

"We try to come every couple of weeks during the summer, and always on holiday weekends," she shouted.

"So not during winter months?"

She shook her head and then pointed at a large sign attached to a tree. "I'm going to pull into that marina."

He nodded and held onto the windshield while she turned the boat into a creek just beyond the sign, slowing when they entered a canopy of trees that blocked all but a few rays of sun. A quartet of turtles was lined up along a log. Just as she pointed them out, they slid off into the water barely making a splash.

Aaron smiled.

After a bend in the creek, they emerged onto a small lake, and she turned the boat toward the long dock at the far end. As she neared, a man who looked like Santa Claus—but wearing a T-shirt with the sleeves ripped off and cutoff jeans that should have been thrown away years ago—pushed off a bench sitting under a large umbrella. He grinned, showing a missing incisor. Kenzie cut the engine and he grabbed the rail on the bow and pulled the boat close to the dock.

"Can you get the back bumper?" she asked Aaron.

Santa tossed her a rope that she looped around a cleat, then she stepped out onto the dock and into his waiting arms.

"Hey, sweet pea. How you been over the long cold winter?"

"Great." She gave the man a tight squeeze. "How're you doing, Eddie?"

"Glad it's finally warm enough to see you in a bikini again."

She kissed him on the cheek. "How many females have you fed that line to so far this weekend?"

He huffed out a belly laugh and held out his hand to welcome her friend before he realized whose hand he was shaking. "Wow, Kenz, you've improved the company you hang around with these days. Aaron Vance is standing on my dock."

"Yep. You get your fill of eye candy with the ladies, so I brought someone for your wife to ogle. Is Betty Sue inside?"

"Yeah, she's behind the register." He turned back to Aaron. "Could we get a picture for our celebrity wall?"

"Sure." Aaron extracted the hand Eddie had been pumping.

"By the way," Eddie hollered as Kenzie headed inside. "Me and the wife saw you onstage at the festival yesterday. The band sounds real good now you're back."

Short term, Eddie. "Thanks. Fill 'er up for me, will you? And I need four bags of ice."

~

"*M*ama!"

Vicki Marshall looked in the direction her granddaughter was pointing. "What does she want, Nick? That's the third time she's said that."

Nick glanced down the beach for the thousandth time since Kenzie and Aaron left on Kyle's boat. She was just pulling back in. "She can't say Kenzie."

Under different circumstances, he would have laughed at the look of shock on his mother's face.

"She's calling Kenzie, mama?" his dad asked.

"Mama," London said, pointing down the beach.

His mom closed her eyes. "Please, tell me Kenzie hasn't heard her."

"She has," Becky said from her towel on the other side of Nick. "At least twice."

"I was worried something like this might happen if you came to the river. Hearing that has to hurt Kenzie to no end," his mom said.

"It was time for Nick to come," his dad said. "What happened changed several lives, but it's been three years. Coming to the river is as much a family tradition for Nick as it is for Kenzie. London should grow up with those same traditions."

"Kenzie's the one who's getting hurt. Not Nick. Not London. Kenzie. She shouldn't have to deal with a little girl" —his mom took a deep breath—"*Juliette and Nick's daughter*, calling her mama."

Nick heard the unspoken words—*Who should have been hers. Who is someone else's child. Who came about because Nick cheated*—in his mom's deep-breathed pause. There was any number of ways to fill the break in her sentence. The constant guilt ratcheted up another notch. He should have given Kenzie more time, enjoyed a weekend at home with London rather than coming to Jeremy's property for the annual Memorial Day get-together. Three years away hadn't erased the memories of his and Kenzie's times here on the river. If anything, his awareness of her was heightened. Was it different for her?

"I'm not trying to be coarse or hurtful, Vicki. You know I love Kenzie." His dad touched his mom's chin. "I don't imagine it will ever be comfortable, but it can be tolerable."

His mom turned to Nick, years of blame emanating from her look. "It won't be better for Kenzie—" she stopped.

"Earlier London ran up to Kenzie and held out her arms to be picked up," Becky said, sitting up and reaching for a bottle of sunscreen.

"Don't do that to Kenzie," his mom said to him.

"In Nick's defense," Becky said before he could protest, "he tried to take London away, but she wrapped her arms around Kenzie's neck, so Kenzie said she'd watch her. Nick tried to protest, but Kenzie said it was okay. By doing so, she avoided a two-year-old's meltdown, which would have turned the *whole* camp's attention on Kenzie rather than just half of them."

"I didn't want Kenzie to think I don't trust her." Nick glanced between his mom and dad. "I also didn't want to force the issue and make a scene in front of Knight Rivers. It was awkward enough without adding to the situation."

His parents looked at each other, then at their grand-daughter. She was piling sand on the edge of a towel.

Kenzie's laughter reached them, and London looked up and pointed. "Mama!"

"That's Kenzie," Becky said.

"Kamma," London said with a grin. She jumped up and started running toward Kenzie.

Nick pushed to his feet, scooped up his daughter before she got very far, and splashed into the river to eliminate the possibility of a meltdown. His beautiful daughter loved water. Slipping his hands under her belly, he held her horizontal with her little round tummy just under the surface. "Kick your legs, baby girl."

He hated that he and his family got into the habit of calling London by the same nickname Waylon Rivers had called Kenzie since her birth. He tried to catch himself before the words came out, but was never quite fast enough.

London pointed. Nick turned in time to see Aaron grasp Kenzie around the waist and lead her to the volleyball game.

Another vicious jolt of jealousy shot through him, physical enough to leave a bitter taste in his mouth.

"Boad," London said, a threat of tears in her voice.

"Want to go for a ride on Pappy's boat, beautiful?"

"See Mama," she said, pointing down the beach.

"Maybe later, baby girl." He gathered his daughter close. "Can you splash daddy?"

She squealed and did her best to splash water in his face.

"Give daddy a kiss." He smiled when London puckered her little lips and gave him a peck. "I love you."

"Wuv voo," she repeated, hugging his neck.

After lunch, his mom, dad, and Becky took London out on the pontoon for a trip back to camp to pick up Becky's fiancé.

While they were gone, Bodhi offered to take him out on his boat for a little wakeboarding and Nick jumped at the chance. He used to love the sport but was rusty after three years. Once he got his river legs back, though, he let loose, knowing his muscles would be screaming tomorrow.

He'd missed this, the comradery with Knight Rivers. His dad was right in that sense. Nick wanted London to experience family traditions. Coming here had built lifelong memories for him.

But his mom was right too. He didn't want to hurt Kenzie more than he already had.

⁓

*K*enzie sat at the kitchen table in Jeremy and Cara's cabin, unsure why she needed to be at this meeting. She'd made her decision and wouldn't change her mind, despite all the cons Kyle was throwing out—with good reason. He wanted Knight Rivers members to be absolutely sure before they committed.

By choice, Jeff was the only band member sitting outside of the band's circle besides her. He'd been invited to pull his chair closer but chose to remain at a distance.

She'd reminded Kyle after lunch that he also had to take Bonnie's opinion into consideration. Even though she was out on bedrest, she'd be back after the tour was over. If Knight Rivers music took off like the band was hoping, it would mean more time on the road. When Kyle called Bonnie, she was on the fence about leaving home for months at a time, but she was in the minority. Kenzie imagined Kyle would have to replace her by the end of the tour.

She looked over the schedule Nick had provided. They would be traveling from one side of the United States to the other. South as far as Key West, Florida, and north to Seattle, Washington.

"We'll be in cramped quarters, so if one of us has a problem, we can't let it fester. We have to talk things out and be open any time a disagreement arises."

"What about merchandise?" Bodhi asked. "Will we be able to sell our stuff at concerts?"

"Nick said he would get that added into the contract."

Tripp patted his brother's shoulder. "Get to work, Ryder."

"I already have." Ryder picked up a sketchbook and flipped to a page. "This isn't finished, but I want to see what y'all think."

Kenzie got up and looked over Ryder's shoulder. He'd drawn an outline of the state of Tennessee with a guitar running kitty-corner through it and Knight Rivers Band along the neck.

"I love that, Ryder. Good job."

"Is it good enough to keep you singing with the band after the tour?" Tripp asked.

"Nope. I'm here for four months," she said, directing her

remark to Kyle. She walked toward the door. "I'm going to head out. Count me in no matter what you decide."

*O*n her deck minutes later, Kenzie plunked out the tune that was still giving her trouble. She glanced up at the patter of little feet coming up her steps. London ran across the deck, then stopped in front of her and shyly ducked her head.

"She wants to say good night," Nick said from the bottom of the steps.

All through dinner, Kenzie caught herself watching how cute Nick was with his daughter. His attention was one hundred percent on her when she was near, and she was the same with him. She stood on his thighs and cupped his cheeks with her tiny palms when she wanted his attention, and she hugged his neck often. When reading her a story, he used all the animal sounds, punctuated by her cute giggles. They were pretty adorable together.

After the barbecue had been delivered for dinner, Nick cut everything into two-year-old pieces and wiped her tiny fingers. She pouted when he cleaned her mouth and he laughed and teased her with a kiss on the nose. More giggles followed.

Kenzie set her guitar aside and beckoned with a finger. London grinned and closed the distance between them. Kenzie picked her up, and the little girl snuggled against her, the scent of lavender shampoo enveloping them both.

How Nick's wife could leave such a perfect bundle of happiness and love was unfathomable to her.

"Is it bedtime?"

London nodded until her curls bobbed.

"Do you have a dolly you sleep with?"

She tipped her face up, her eyes lighting with happiness. "Bunny!"

"You have a bunny?"

Another vigorous nod followed.

"Maybe you'll dream of twinkling fairies. Do you like fairies?" She laughed when London nodded again. "Seems like a fishy got your tongue today on the river. Open up. Let me see. Did a little fish get your tongue?"

London smiled and opened her mouth.

"Oh," Kenzie said with a gasp. "There's your tongue. A fishy didn't get it after all."

"Say good night, London."

Kenzie smoothed a lock of hair off London's forehead. "Sweet dreams. I'll see you tomorrow."

London puckered her cute little lips. As uncomfortable as she felt with Nick watching, how could she deny such innocence? Kenzie puckered up too, and gave London a smacking kiss, then Kenzie set her on her feet. "Good night, sweetie."

Nick picked up his daughter and started toward the Marshalls' RV, but turned back. "Hey, Kenz? Try F-sharp."

Because she knew he was right, Kenzie wanted to throw her guitar at him—and might have if London didn't have her arms wrapped around his neck.

Strangely, her own arms felt empty when London was gone.

Not good. She didn't need to lose her heart to an adorable two-year-old.

CHAPTER 5

*A*fter tucking London in bed, her stuffed rabbit wrapped securely in her arms, Nick went outside. The barbecue, delivered from the place Kenzie had recommended, turned out great. He'd ordered plenty, and Aaron's ego was sufficiently stroked by all the compliments and thanks he received.

He wasn't sure what to do about London's infatuation with Kenzie. Every time he turned around today, London was headed for her. He tried to put himself in Kenzie's shoes and knew his heart wasn't as big.

His mom had gone to another RV to play bridge with some of the other moms, while the dads sat around a picnic table playing poker. His generation and younger were line dancing to Mel McDaniel's "Louisiana Saturday Night" on the dance floor Jeremy built. The guy had strung patio lights between several trees and rigged a timer to a generator so they'd come on at dusk.

The stars were hidden by clouds that had rolled in during dinner, and the air was heavy with humidity and the smell of rain.

Kenzie, dancing next to his brother, laughed at something Griffin said. A memory of her in pigtails floated through his mind. She'd been about ten, sitting on the end of the dock, angry that her dad and Kyle had taken the boat out and left her behind. He sat down next to her and told her a joke he'd heard at school. She'd thrown her head back and laughed much as she was doing now. Then he told her to quit pouting and help him build a fire. And she did, smiling the whole time.

The music on someone's playlist changed to "When You Say Nothing at All" by Alison Krauss—one of Kenzie's favorites. Grif held out his hand and she walked into his arms.

A rumble of thunder moved over the camp, and Nick looked skyward. One night, much like this one, he'd been dancing with Kenzie when he suddenly realized he wanted more than the friendship they shared. And much like tonight, he realized he didn't want her dancing with anyone else.

That night, after the music stopped, he took her hand and they walked down to the creek—he said to cool off, but really he wanted to be away from watchful eyes. Rain began to fall, right before he kissed her for the very first time, with only night creatures and the distant flashes of lightning as witnesses.

He'd half expected her to haul off and smack him. Instead, she kissed him back.

For two years, they spent every minute they could together. His parents loved her. Her dad loved him. They shared the same friends.

But everything changed the night his mom innocently mentioned marriage. Kenzie had only laughed, but he became paralyzed with fear. He had a list of things he wanted to accomplish before he even thought about marriage.

A few days later a friend told him a new country singer

trying to move into the big leagues was auditioning bass players. He never thought he'd make it into Aaron Vance's band, so he hadn't told anyone about the audition, not even Kenzie. Why tell her about his hopes and dreams and then have to face her when nothing came of it? That was mistake number one.

Number two, he also didn't tell her when he got the call saying he was in. He didn't say anything until the night before he moved to Nashville. Knight Rivers was angry because he left them in a lurch with upcoming gigs and no bass player, which he understood. If the tables were turned, he'd be angry too. But he also knew if any of them had this chance, they would make the same decision.

That was the first time he hurt Kenzie. She wasn't upset that he was going out into the world of music, just that he hadn't told her. He'd seen the disappointment in her eyes, in the set line of her mouth.

He knew when he asked her to come with him, she wouldn't. She couldn't. Waylon had a stroke not long before, and she took care of him every day. She'd never leave her dad. Deep down he knew that when he asked. It took a while for him to acknowledge he'd chosen playing with a band over the woman he loved.

He'd heard a lot about the life of a musician on the road. Trying to make a name for himself, he wanted to experience everything that kind of life had to offer. He was almost twenty-seven years old, and he wanted it all—the fame, the glory, and the raw adulation. He didn't care if he was riding someone else's coattails. Aaron was just the beginning for him. Once his name got out there, other country stars—the ones who'd already made it—would want him playing for them.

His head had been in the clouds and stayed there until Juliette announced she was pregnant.

He left the Knight Rivers Band. He left home. And he left Kenzie.

Now he wished he had all those things back.

He stood on the dock in the dark watching everyone dance, watching her dance, wishing he could turn back the hands of time just the way Becky mentioned. But he made the choices and had only himself to blame.

How would things change in the coming months? Kyle told him earlier the band was on board with the tour. He'd already called Aaron's attorney to start working on the contract.

~

Thursday, Kenzie turned at the Marshalls' mailbox and followed the driveway past the house to the studio out back where Doug said they'd meet. Griffin walked out as she parked her car. He was as handsome as his dad and older brother, with an extra dash of humor.

"Hey, Kenz."

"Hey, yourself," she said, grabbing her guitar from the back seat. "Becky told me about your girlfriend. I'm so sorry, Grif. I wish you'd said something at the river."

"Naw. A long weekend out in nature was exactly what I needed."

"Some gorgeous woman will snatch you up before you know it."

His smile was sad. "Are you excited about the tour?"

"Yes," she said with wide eyes.

"Liar." Griffin opened the door to the studio.

Doug, Becky, and her fiancé, Brent, were waiting for them inside.

She hadn't been in the Marshall studio in over three years. Vicki was the only family member who didn't play an instrument, but she'd always joined their jam sessions, laughing, encouraging them, and singing along.

When Kenzie's mom left, Vicki had stepped in and helped Kenzie buy her first bra, and explained the birds and the bees before taking her out to shop for other necessities. When she needed a woman's advice, she'd head to the Marshall's house for help, and Vicki had always been there for her. At least until Nick left. Then Kenzie chose to stay away.

She glanced up at the loft where Vicki created gorgeous works of art. Huge windows allowed natural light to fill the space, and she could see blank canvasses stacked against one wall. Paints, boxes of chalk, and jars of paint brushes, along with other art supplies lined the shelves on the opposite wall. Kenzie had always been amazed by how easily Vicki was able to produce a scene that evoked emotions and touched hearts.

Seeing the leather sofa backed up to the railing reminded her of the times she spent in the loft with Nick when Vicki wasn't painting.

"Hope you don't mind me hanging with you guys, Kenzie," Brent said, bringing her back to the present.

"Not at all. I'd love your honest opinion. And I truly mean honest. I have pretty thick skin when it comes to my music. That goes for all of you," she said, pointing individually at Becky, Doug, and Griffin.

"We've all played through what you sent and like it already," Griffin said.

"Here's a better copy." Kenzie passed the sheet music to Doug, who'd be on bass guitar—which played a major part in this song. Griffin sat at the drums, and Becky moved over to the keyboard.

"Do we need to go through it, or do you feel comfortable enough to play right through?" she asked.

Doug looked from Becky to Griffin, who both nodded. "I

think we're ready. We played it through several times yesterday."

Kenzie didn't know why she was questioning herself about this song. Possibly because it was a little more rock than she usually wrote. Strapping on her guitar, she situated the music on the stand in front of her. "I think I'll be able to tell if I've got it right as soon as the bass comes in. Doug, I need your deep voice where I've made notes."

"You got it."

When everyone nodded that they were ready, she counted down. She and Griffin played four measures before the bass guitar joined in. They played two more measures before Kenzie held up her hand to stop them.

Closing her eyes, she took a moment to appreciate the doubt that was swept away by a sweet adrenaline rush.

Everyone was silent as the music faded away.

"Why'd you stop?" Brent asked. "That sounded great."

"That's why we stopped," Doug said with a grin. "Kenzie needs a minute to catch her breath."

Kenzie smiled as her heart rate slowed. The music was perfect, exactly what she'd aimed for when she wrote the words. Plus, the female artist who commissioned the song had a rusty voice that would blend with the music perfectly.

"I love it, Kenz," Becky said.

Doug played a bass riff, then put his hand over the strings. "Time to add the vocals, baby girl."

Vicki walked in with London on her hip. "Oh, Kenzie. I wondered whose car was out front."

"Mama!" London held out her index finger, pointing at Kenzie.

A look of horror crossed Vicki's face. "I'm so sorry."

"It's okay." It really wasn't, but what could she do? Nothing, except pretend it didn't bother her. When she came over this morning, she thought Nick and London would be back in Nashville by now. Seemed life had more fun in store for her.

"Would you rather we leave?"

"Of course not. It's your studio."

Hesitating a moment before taking a seat next to Brent, Vicki settled London on her lap.

Kenzie glanced at Griffin, who gave them another count. This time Kenzie didn't hold back. She sang it as she'd written it—with deep heart and soul feelings—knowing full well the artist might change the whole vibe with her own sound.

Halfway through she glanced at Becky, who was just as into the music as she was, which was exactly the reaction she hoped for—people losing themselves in the moment. Let the world with all its troubles fall away while they enjoyed the pulse of the rich bass. The keyboard and guitar blended seamlessly, and the drums brought it all together in perfection.

Eyes closed, she heard their small audience applauding as soon as the last note faded away.

"That's wonderful, Kenzie," Vicki said.

"So great," Brent added.

Kenzie lifted her guitar strap over her head, at the peak of a high she might not come down from for hours.

Becky came over and wrapped her in a hug. "That one's your best yet, girl."

"She's right." Doug pushed his guitar around to his back and hugged her too. "That song's a winner."

London ran to her and held out her arms. "Mama."

Kenzie scooped her up to avoid another awkward moment. She was too happy with how great the song sounded to let this pint-sized beauty confuse her emotions. "Hi, cute thing. How are you today?"

"I fine."

Kenzie tweaked London's nose. As much as she'd like to, London was too adorable to ignore.

"I don't know why she calls you that," Vicki said. "She was too young to know what the word meant before Juliette left."

Becky put her hands on Kenzie's shoulders. "I wish you'd written that kind of music when we were singing. We would have blown the other high school bands away."

"You should keep the song for yourself, Kenz."

Kenzie's stomach dropped at the sound of Nick's voice. She looked up. His hands were curled around the loft's railing as he looked down on them all. "I don't sing rock."

"You just did, and you sounded fantastic. Don't sell yourself short."

If she wasn't surrounded by his family she'd ask, *Is that what I did with you?* But she wouldn't hurt Doug and Vicki because of their son's actions.

London pointed with a grin. "Daddy."

"Hi, baby girl," he said, his voice filled with so much love for his daughter that Kenzie had to swallow back tears.

"We didn't know you were up there," Doug said.

"Mom gave me some space so I could work on the details of Aaron's upcoming tour."

Kenzie turned her attention to the little girl. "You have flour on your nose. Have you been helping grandma in the kitchen?"

London nodded, making her dark curls bob.

Anger threatened to envelop her. Anger that Nick or one of his family members didn't come and take London. Instead, they all stood, almost dumbstruck, and watched. She wouldn't hurt the little girl by rejecting her, so she sat down on a chair and perched London on her knee. "What were you making?"

"Cookies," Vicki said.

Oh good, one of them speaks.

Kenzie poked London's belly lightly. "That sounds yummy. Do you like cookies as much as I do?"

Another vigorous nod, then London pointed toward the door. "Es go."

Her anger grew. Didn't any of them understand how hard this was? To be looking into the piercing blue eyes of the little girl who should have been hers was torture. Yet they all just stood there like statues and watched. Swallowing down the hurt, she smiled at the innocent child, while hating Nick anew.

"Let's go inside, London," Vicki said, holding out her hand, finally saving Kenzie. "We'll get Kenzie some cookies to take home."

"Come, Mama," the little girl said, sliding off Kenzie's lap and taking her finger.

"We'll bring the cookies out here." Vicki picked up London and propped her on a hip.

After they left, Doug gathered the music she'd passed out while Kenzie put her guitar in the case.

"Thanks for helping me," she said, very aware Nick still stood at the railing, looking down on her.

"It's really a great song," Griffin said.

"Thanks, Grif." She gave him a hug. "I appreciate you playing with us."

"Anytime."

Doug handed her the copies of sheet music. "We were all just hanging out after the holiday weekend. Brent goes back to Atlanta tomorrow, and Becky leaves Sunday."

She hugged Becky's fiancé. "I probably won't see you again until the wedding."

"Fifty-one days and counting," he said when she stepped away.

"The song is great, Kenz," Doug said, giving her another tight squeeze.

"Thanks, Doug. And thanks for your help."

Becky looped her arm through Kenzie's as they walked out of the studio. "Since Nick is staying here, why don't I come over to the ranch tomorrow after Brent leaves for the airport so we can go over the songs the band will sing at the wedding?"

"Sounds good. I'll talk to Kyle and give you a call. How are the wedding plans coming?"

"Almost done. Did you get to Nashville for your dress fitting?"

"I went yesterday. Love the design and the color. Thanks for picking something I can wear again."

Becky laughed. "Remember those hideous dresses we had to wear for Jane's wedding?"

"How can I forget? We looked like bananas."

They paused in the shade of a poplar tree. "Since all the girls will be at the wedding, I thought we could sing a couple of our old songs."

"Really?" Kenzie had fond memories of their all-girl high school band. "Are you sure you and Brent want to take the chance?" The five of them hadn't performed together since the summer they graduated from high school.

"It was Brent's suggestion. He wants to hear us. Are you in if I can get the girls to agree?"

"Sure, but I won't be here to practice with you."

"We can talk about the songs tomorrow. Maybe we could practice together before the rehearsal dinner. Nick said you'd be back by then." Becky kicked at some loose gravel at the side of the driveway. "Sorry about Nick. I didn't realize he was in the loft."

Kenzie gave a whatcha-gonna-do shrug.

"I'm glad you came over so we could play with you."

Before Kenzie could respond, the dark-haired cutie came

running toward them, holding up a plastic sandwich bag in one hand. "Mama!"

Becky winced. "Sorry about that, too. Still don't know where she learned that word because Juliette was no mother."

"Not a problem." Kenzie squatted down so she was eye level with London. "What have you got?"

London held out the bag full of what looked like chocolate chip cookies.

"I bet they're the best cookies ever."

London grinned and Kenzie's heart melted.

"Thank you, sweetie."

London puckered her lips, her eyes sparkling with the same happiness Kenzie used to see in Nick's.

Kenzie tapped her own lips. London leaned forward and gave her a sweet peck. "Bye, London."

"Bye, Mama."

She opened the back door and set her guitar on the seat. When she slid behind the wheel, her traitorous eyes were drawn toward the studio. Nick stood at the door watching.

～

A heavy hand landed on Nick's shoulder. "For two years, I thought Kenzie would be my daughter-in-law. For three years, I didn't. Now, when I watch her with London, I see her in that role again."

"You should stop." Nick glanced at his dad. "Cliché as it sounds, that ship has sailed."

He leaned against the doorframe and watched Kenzie turn her car around and head down the driveway. She sounded good today. Better than good. She could easily take that song and sing it straight to number one.

Knight Rivers had decided to use his managerial services for the tour. Though he'd be on Aaron's second bus with his band members for travel, he'd still be working closely with Kyle, which meant he'd be around Kenzie quite a bit.

"Are you sure that ship has sailed? Or could it still be in the harbor waiting to be re-boarded?" His dad patted his shoulder again, a little harder than necessary. "Just a thought," he added before walking outside.

London ran toward her grandpa with outstretched arms, her smile as bright as the sun. Knowing he was leaving London with his mom and dad while on this tour eased a heavy burden. He hated leaving his daughter behind, but knew she'd be safe, loved, and well looked after with his parents. He also planned to come home several times, and his parents had offered to bring London to a few of the nearby concert stops.

His dad swung London into the air and kissed her nose. Her giggle was heartbreakingly perfect. She was perfect. How could two such mismatched people create someone so absolutely flawless?

He hadn't talked to Juliette in over a year. She'd been in South America because her interest had moved from country music to Latin.

Once they decided to divorce, Juliette signed away her parental rights for a sizable chunk in the settlement. Bottom line, they married for the wrong reasons. He knew it soon after they got back from Vegas. Juliette expected a life of luxury, but he gave her a sensible house with a dishwasher and a bed that didn't make itself.

Nick went back upstairs to the loft to organize the mess he'd spread out on his mom's worktable while Kenzie's song ran through his head. It would be another hit for her as a writer. He could almost guarantee a number one hit as a singer if she recorded it herself. Though he felt compelled to make the suggestion again, he knew she was content to stay in the background.

After traveling with Aaron, he tended to agree with her.

He walked over to the window when his cell rang and Kyle's name popped up on the screen. "Hey, Kyle."

"The band will be here tonight practicing if you want to go over concert details."

Tonight might work. And he'd get to see Kenzie again. "Great. Let me call you back as soon as I know if I have someone to watch London."

"Would you rather talk before or after practice? We start at seven and wrap up about eight-thirty."

Knight Rivers had kept the same practice schedule. "Are the guys ready to get out of there by eight-thirty?"

"They usually hang around for a while."

They'd also maintained the same habits. "Eight-thirty might be better for me. That way I can get London to bed before I leave."

"It seems crazy—you talking about babysitters and getting your daughter to bed. When did we get so old?" Kyle asked with a chuckle.

Nick felt so much older than his years. He should probably warn the band that being on the road could be energy-pumping, yet more often was soul-sucking hard. It took you away from people and places you loved. Days seemed to merge into each other, and nights became your days until you lost not only track of time, but pieces of yourself.

"Seems like it happened overnight."

"We miss you playing with the band, Nick."

"Yeah, I miss it too." He cleared his throat. "Let me make sure Mom will be here if London wakes up, and I'll get back to you."

He disconnected the call with a skitter of anticipation at the thought of seeing Kenzie again while also fighting shame at what he'd done to break them apart.

CHAPTER 6

*N*ick sat high on the hill overlooking the Rivers' ranch, his Harley rumbling under him. This was one of the most beautiful spots in the county, maybe the whole state. A sizable creek ran down the middle, splitting the main ranch house and guest house from the practice studio and stables. Kyle had mentioned he and Jessi moved into the main house after they married. Sheets hung on the clothesline behind the guesthouse, and Kenzie's car sat by the side door, which meant she'd moved out there.

That little house held as many memories for him as the practice studio. He'd helped Waylon and Kyle build the house when Kyle graduated from high school. That way Waylon could keep his son close, yet Kyle could have his independence while attending college. He'd spent so many nights there—he, Kyle, and Jeremy—"becoming men," drinking until they couldn't stand up, then the next morning paying for every shot of whiskey.

After Jeremy's wife and unborn baby were killed by a drunk driver, the three of them vowed never to drink again. But like so many of his vows and promises, Nick broke that one too—at least until London's birth. He hadn't taken a sip since that night.

He glanced toward the stables. He missed Waylon and regretted leaving without saying goodbye before the gentle man's death. Waylon had taught him to ride a horse and to build a house. The man had worked hard to give his kids a balanced, happy life after his wife left him with an eight-year-old son and a four-year-old daughter.

The Rivers' manager, who Kyle introduced Nick to on Thursday night, came out of the barn and pulled the big door closed. He climbed into his truck and drove away, leaving a cloud of dust to settle in the golden glow of the setting sun.

A car sat under the carport of the main house, but Kyle's truck wasn't anywhere in sight.

He switched the Harley's motor off. The sound of crickets, tuning up for their nightly concert, soon filled the silence that was as heavy as the humid air. Pastures stretched out behind the stables, and green trees dotted the creek and provided shade around the houses and studio. The pool lights flicked on, illuminating the surrounding area.

Nick had been here long enough that he'd seen Kenzie ride away on her beautiful Appaloosa Poco. Waylon gave her the horse on her eighteenth birthday, and she named him after her dad's favorite band. Once the sun disappeared behind the distant hills, dusk fell fast. Kenzie had gone out alone, but that horse was probably as protective of Kenzie as her brother. He'd get her home safely.

What would his dad say if he knew Nick was sitting up on this hill? He'd hinted a couple of times over the past few days that maybe this tour would be a good time for Nick to fix things between him and Kenzie. His mom, on the other hand, warned him to stay away from her—something he couldn't manage to do. Disappointment hit hard when he arrived for the Thursday night meeting with Knight Rivers and Kenzie had already ducked out—obviously to avoid him.

He spotted Poco cutting across a field, galloping at break-neck speed. Bent low over Poco's neck, Kenzie's hair streaming out behind her.

And Nick's breath caught.

He turned the key and the Harley's engine rumbled to life. He turned the bike and sped down the hill, hoping Kenzie was up for their old game of catch-me-if-you-can as they raced for the barn.

～

Kenzie spotted the Harley out of her peripheral vision and cursed under her breath, but spurred Poco on. "Tst. Come on, boy. You know you can beat that bike. You've done it before. Come on, handsome. Just a little farther. Tst. You'll get a nice rubdown and a tasty treat afterward."

To beat the bike, Poco would have to jump the fence, so Kenzie reined a hair to the left and pressed her left heel into Poco's side. The horse turned under her body as if they were one.

"That's it, boy, you've got this. Just a little farther. I don't know why he still insists on challenging you with that noisy thing because you've always been faster."

Poco jumped the fence effortlessly.

"You are beautiful, baby. You just earned two treats for that jump. We're almost there. Tst." Poco rounded the corral fence seconds before the Harley pulled up.

Kenzie slowed Poco and they cantered around the corral twice, slowing their heaving breaths while the horizon changed to vermillion with rays of gold reaching skyward.

Though she knew Nick was standing at the gate, arms on

the top rail and one foot on the lower one, she didn't look his way.

Why was he here? Did he know Kyle and his wife had gone to Chattanooga to celebrate Jessi's birthday?

After twice around, she swung her leg over the saddle, slipped the reins over Poco's head, and led him around once more, patting his neck and whispering sweet words in his ear.

When they reached the gate, Nicked stepped down.

"You beat me." Nick patted Poco's neck and took the reins from Kenzie.

"We always do," she said, closing the gate, then walking ahead to open the stable door.

He led Poco inside to the grooming area and tied him off, and while Kenzie grabbed a bucket of brushes, Nick unsaddled the horse.

When he picked up a brush and moved to Poco's other side, she didn't waste her time protesting. He was free to groom Poco until his fingers fell off.

"Why are you here?" she asked when he didn't say anything.

He looked over Poco's neck, eyebrow quirked. "That's not very friendly."

"I didn't mean it to be," she said, quirking an eyebrow right back. As if she'd ever want to be friendly with him. She'd rather talk to a baboon.

They continued to stroke the horse through long minutes of silence. "You didn't answer my question," she finally said. "Why are you here?"

He set the brush aside and scooped a bucket of oats from a bin, while she stood with arms crossed, waiting for his answer. Last, he picked an apple out of a nearby basket and held it out to her. "I figure you promised Poco a treat for beating me."

"I promised him two." She accepted his pocket knife and sliced the apple into quarters, feeding Poco from her palm.

"I came by to ask if you'd like to drive into town for dinner."

Time stopped as a million emotions raced through her. Was he asking her out? And did he think she'd actually say yes? "I-I have plans," she said, despising her stutter.

"It's almost nine o'clock. What plans do you have?"

White-hot anger flared. She locked eyes with him in an unblinking stare "That's none of your business. Ten months before your daughter's birth, you lost the right to ask."

Something moved over his face, an expression she couldn't quite read. Not that long ago she might have been able to guess what he was thinking. Not anymore.

Unhooking Poco, she led him into his stall and closed the door.

"Speaking of my daughter, she likes you."

Quick as a flash, she doubled her fist and slugged him in the chest. "Don't you dare use your daughter to manipulate me, Nick Marshall."

"I'm not using my daughter for anything," he growled, putting a hand over the spot she punched. "I'm simply stating a fact, Kenz. London doesn't take to strangers, yet she took to you right away."

Without a thought, she slammed her fist into his stomach and delivered it with enough force that he bent forward and groaned.

The sound was more satisfying than anything she'd experienced in a very long time. In fact, it felt so good she doubled up her fist to take another shot, but he caught her hand mid-swing and backed her up against the stable wall.

"You wildcat," he ground out. "I was paying you a compliment."

"I don't want your compliments. I don't want anything

from you, except for you to leave." More than anything, she wanted him to understand how badly he'd hurt her. And she wanted to hurt him back. "I hate you, Nicholas Marshall. I hate—"

His mouth covered hers, swallowing the rest of her sentence. She suppressed her moan of longing. For three years, she believed she'd pushed her desire for Nick too deep to resurrect, but she'd also missed him. Missed this. For a split second, she let her guard down before common sense kicked in with a vengeance. Instead of pushing him away, she opened her mouth enough that he thought she was surrendering, then she clamped her teeth down on his bottom lip.

"Yeow!" He jerked away and glared at her, holding the back of his hand to his mouth.

"You also lost the right to kiss me, Nick." Tears threatened. Tears she didn't want him to see. "You lost that right when you cheated."

"Fine. But how about you explain the kiss I walked in on between one of my best friends and my girlfriend?"

"Your girlfriend," she scoffed, leaning forward so they were nose to nose. "Juliette was already pregnant when you walked in that day."

To her embarrassment, tears filled her eyes and coursed down her cheeks before she could swipe them away. She wasn't about to explain that there was nothing between her and Jeremy and never had been. They'd shared one kiss. In a grief-stricken moment. If it hadn't been for Nick walking in on them, they would have laughed it off five seconds after it happened.

Nick lowered his hand and took a step back. "I'm sorry." Shaking his head, he looked away. "I came here tonight to apologize for everything I put you through. Obviously, I've screwed it up. I am truly sorry I hurt you, Kenz. I'm sorry I left when you needed me, and I'm sorry I didn't make it back in time for Waylon's funeral. I should have been here."

He ran fingers through his hair, standing it on end, and took another step back. "I'm sorry for everything."

She stood still, shaking with anger. Hurt because not only had he slept with another woman while they were still together, but he had a child with her. Yet her most over-whelming emotion was confusion. After what he'd done, she really wanted to hate him. But she didn't.

"Please don't cry. I'm leaving." He turned and walked out the door.

Kenzie didn't move until she heard the Harley's engine fade into the distance. Poco whinnied and stuck his head over the stall door.

She ran a hand down his silky nose. "Thanks again for winning, boy."

Inside her little house, she rushed through a shower, added a quick swipe of mascara and lip gloss before running a blow dryer over her hair. At the knock on her door, she slipped on her sandals and rushed through the living room. Pasting on a smile, she swung the door open. "Hi, Jason."

"Hey, Kenzie. You look beautiful."

"Thank you."

"Sorry I'm a little later than I said. I got stuck helping my sister move today, and it took longer than we expected."

"Not a problem. I was running a little late myself, so let's agree we're both right on time."

"Sounds good," he said, flashing a smile. "Are you ready to go?"

"Let me get my purse." She walked into the kitchen, locked the back door, and grabbed her purse off the kitchen counter.

After locking the front door, she let Jason take her hand

on the way to his car. The night was dark, the sky full of stars, but no moon. Still, she felt eyes on her.

She glanced toward the hill overlooking the ranch. Though she couldn't see him, she knew Nick was up there watching.

~

*T*he next morning Kenzie tiptoed into the chapel late, hoping to be inconspicuous. Kyle and Jessi usually saved her a seat, but they were still out of town, so she glanced around for a seat and spotted one next to a neighboring family about halfway down one of the aisles. Walking quickly, she kept her eyes strictly on her goal because she'd noticed the Marshalls' SUV in the parking lot, so she figured Nick was here with them.

Two more rows and she could slide into the empty space.

"Mama!"

Every eye turned to the little girl standing on the seat of a pew on the other side of the chapel, then turned to see who she was pointing toward. The preacher paused and looked over the top of the glasses perched on the tip of his nose.

Kenzie would feel less exposed if a bolt of lightning had struck right next to her.

London waved, a grin lighting her face, while Kenzie's attention shifted to Nick. The rat didn't even look apologetic as he settled London on his lap. His parents, on the other hand, appeared ready to crawl under their pew in embarrassment.

She wiggled her fingers at London and slipped into the vacant seat before the preacher continued.

She'd cut out of practice early to miss the meeting with Nick on Thursday night. For the third time, she told the band members she'd go along with whatever they decided, which saved her from sitting around a table with Nick going over details. A lot of good that did her. Instead, she ended up facing off with him in the stable last night.

She tried to get excited about singing new songs while traveling the country, seeing new places.

Waylon, always busy with the ranch, hadn't taken them many places when they were kids. They'd visited Gatlinburg and made a trip to Atlanta. The best was the time they drove to Alabama's Gulf Coast and spent four whole days lazing on the beach and splashing around in the warm water. That was so many years ago, her memories were faded around the edges, leaving soft, Easter egg-colored images of blue sky and pink sunrises.

For four months of her life, she could deal with living in close quarters with the guys. As long as she had a bed and a place to write, she could deal with the rest. But suddenly she was starting to wonder if she could deal with Nick.

While she listened to the preacher talk about the dangers of allowing old wounds to fester, she tried to justify her reason for holding onto the hurt Nick inflicted. In truth, she didn't like the person she'd become since her father's funeral. She'd allowed her heart to shrivel to the point where she couldn't remember the last time she truly felt joy. Constant bitterness always lay just under the surface.

"Resentment is a choice," the preacher said. "Anger is a choice. Forgiveness is a choice. How we live our life is a choice. My message today—choose wisely."

Her thoughts turned to her father. Though she and Kyle had encouraged him to date and even remarry, he never did. There were times when he seemed sad, but they never lasted long. If he were here today, he'd tell her life was too short to hold onto grudges or regrets. She could almost hear his voice whispering, *"Make forgiveness and happiness your choice, baby girl,"* in her ear.

But she'd been holding onto the hurt for so long, she wasn't sure she knew how to let go.

After the meeting was over, the neighbors she sat next to waylaid her plans for a quick escape, and before she could get away, London wrapped her arms around Kenzie's knee and looked up with big eyes and an adorable grin.

"Mama."

Heaving an internal sigh, Kenzie sank down into the pew bench and settled London on her knee. "Hi, sweetie. How are you today?"

"I fine."

Kenzie couldn't help but smile. She loved London's answer and her happy grin. "Your dress is pretty."

"Is bwoo," London said, bunching the skirt up around her waist.

She laughed and smoothed the skirt back down. "It is blue, like your eyes." *And your daddy's.* "Guess what? I ate the cookies you gave me. They were so yummy."

London giggled.

Vicki appeared next to them and held out her hands. "I'm sorry, Kenzie. She got away from us."

The girl leaned against Kenzie.

"We're going to the park before lunch," Vicki bribed.

"Mama, come."

"I can't come to the park today, sweetie," Kenzie said. "You go with Grandma and have lots of fun."

Vicki picked up London and offered another "Sorry."

As if she hadn't heard a thing the preacher said, Kenzie stood and offered a closed mouth smile without offering her usual *it's okay*, because it wasn't. As the resentment settled deeper into her soul, her heartfelt wish was that Nick and his adorable daughter would move far, far away after this tour.

CHAPTER 7

*N*ick stood backstage watching Kyle and Jeremy pump up the audience. Kenzie, who hadn't looked his way once, was on the drums. This new song had the audience on their feet. He took a step back and glanced around for Aaron. The guy was nowhere to be seen. He should be here in the wings watching Knight Rivers, which he'd insisted on having as his opening band. Aaron had pushed Nick to the point of insanity when he insisted Knight Rivers could only have a day to decide whether they'd go on tour.

"Don't they understand that opening for me will shoot them from unknown to a household name? This is an opportunity no other artist will give them."

Nick tried to explain that the band members had responsibilities and families to consider, and Kyle and Kenzie owned a horse ranch that would have to be managed while they were away. Two of them had wives, and they all had other jobs. Nick told Aaron they deserved more than twenty-four hours to discuss the logistics and make arrangements.

"If they want fame and fortune, there's nothing to discuss."

Aaron had stalked away in a huff, unused to being on the waiting end of anything. People had cooked and cleaned for him his whole life. He wasn't cold or unfeeling. He just expected instant gratification—which didn't happen in this business. Unless you were Aaron Vance.

Aaron had been livid when Nick quit as bass player. Juliette made the decision to stay with the band impossible when she left. He wouldn't leave his daughter with nannies for months on end or dump the responsibility of London's care on his parents. He had no choice.

Two days later Aaron's disgruntled manager walked, and suddenly Nick had a choice. He pitched his idea to Aaron. His major in music business with a minor in finance opened an opportunity he'd never considered as an option until London's birth.

With his uncle's approval, Aaron agreed to hire Nick as his manager on a one-year trial basis. In under a week, Nick had hired a new bass player, set up some publicity opportunities, and started firming up the schedule for this tour. Aaron's popularity jumped so exponentially in the first two months, his uncle told Aaron he'd be stupid not to hire Nick permanently.

And when Aaron's popularity continued to boom over that year, Nick's job became permanent. This tour was to get his feet wet and alert him about what to expect as a manager. Next tour, he could do the promo work for Aaron from home and the on-the-road, day-to-day headaches could be handled by someone else.

He glanced out at the audience. Since the tour started in Nashville, his family had driven up, along with girlfriends, wives, and long-time Knight Rivers fans. No one in Dove

Hill wanted to miss their hometown band opening for Aaron Vance.

They were all watching history in the making. Knight Rivers would become a big name in the music world. Sadly, Aaron would never let them forget the role he played in giving them a leg up. Somehow, the arrogant singer would spin that role to his advantage.

Knight Rivers would need help managing their affairs, and Nick would love to work with them, but he doubted Kyle or Jeremy would be willing to hire him past this four-month tour.

Someone nudged his hip. He looked down into Cara's smiling face. He didn't know Jeremy's wife well, but what he did know, he liked. She was personable and sweet and nothing like Jeremy's first wife, who'd been tall, willowy, and quiet. A petite blond, Cara had thoughtful eyes and a perpetual smile.

Nick had been with Jeremy the night his wife was hit by a drunk driver. That accident had nearly killed Jeremy too. He'd lost his wife and unborn baby all because someone decided to get behind the wheel while intoxicated. At the time Nick's heart hurt for his friend, but he hadn't truly understood the enormity until he became a parent himself.

"They sound great tonight, don't they?" Cara asked, lifting the camera looped around her neck and snapping a couple of pictures.

"Yeah, they do." Knight Rivers had fine-tuned their sound. Maybe it was Kenzie's voice that helped them achieve this higher level. Even though she used to sing with them occasionally back in his day, her being part of the band melded their performance like never before.

Cara turned her camera on him and snapped a shot. Then held it out so he could see the screen. She'd actually taken a decent picture. "Do you ever wish you were onstage with them?"

"Sometimes. To be honest, I miss being a part of the band more than I miss performing."

Jeremy took Kenzie's place, and she moved front and center. Her white dress and cowboy boots sparkled under the lights, and her dark hair fell in waves down her back. Within thirty seconds she had the audience on their feet again.

The night he'd kissed Kenzie, he sat on the hill overlooking the ranch long after she got in a car with a guy he didn't know and drove away. He waited for two days, thinking Kyle or Jeremy or both would show up and pound him into the ground. He wouldn't have even put up a fight. What he did was wrong and he deserved a good pounding, but they never showed, which meant Kenzie hadn't said anything to them.

"If you could turn back time—"

"I wouldn't have my daughter. A million nights onstage couldn't make up for that." He nodded toward Knight Rivers. "They might not be up there right now if I wasn't Aaron's manager, and I wouldn't be his manager if I'd stayed in town. Things worked out this way for a reason. They deserve to be on stage wowing the audience. This is their time." He smiled down at Cara. "All that said, I do miss playing with the band. We had a lot of good times together."

When he looked back toward Kenzie, she was rolling her shoulders, a movement he always found very sexy. He looked away.

Cara lifted her camera and fidgeted with the lens. "I saw your family in the audience. Is your daughter here?"

"My grandma lives in Nashville, so she's babysitting tonight. I got to spend time with London before the concert."

"You said you missed the guys. Do you miss Kenzie?"

Nick was both surprised and irritated that someone who didn't know him well would ask such a personal question. He was sure Jeremy told his wife everything, which would likely be the truth with a biased twist.

He watched Kenzie under the spotlight while the rest of the band seemed to fade into the background. *Yes, I definitely miss Kenzie.*

"I miss all of them," he admitted. "At the time I convinced myself I was doing the right thing. Knight Rivers was playing at rundown bars, high school dances, a few local festivals, and weddings. I didn't see us going anywhere. When the opportunity to audition for Aaron came up, I took it. Any of the guys would have done the same."

"You're right. They would have," she said, aiming the camera at Kenzie. "You know they don't hold your choice to leave against you."

He wasn't sure he believed that.

"Why did you quit playing for Aaron?"

He pulled out the speech he'd given so often. "When my wife left and gave me full custody of London, I decided I wanted to be home for her as much as possible. I want to be a hands-on dad. And, selfish on my part, I don't want to miss her firsts. First words, then first full sentences, first lost tooth, first day of school, first kiss. Those are moments I can't get back. Since this is Aaron's first time as a headliner, I'll be on hand for most of this tour. Next time around I can hire someone to be the tour manager."

He shifted his weight and looked over his shoulder for Aaron. Still no sign of the guy. "And I can manage bands until I'm old and gray. There will always be a band or an artist looking for a manager. Music will always be popular, but my daughter will only be three, four, and five once."

"You're a good father."

He sure hadn't started out the right way. "I'm trying."

Cara lowered her camera. "You know there was never anything between Jeremy and Kenzie, right? Jeremy told me what happened and that you assumed they were together."

"It wouldn't have mattered if they were." He'd already told this semi-stranger more than he should have. Might as well finish. "Juliette was already pregnant. I went that day, not only to pay my respects to Kenzie's dad but to admit what I'd done." He hadn't made the decision to marry Juliette yet, but seeing Kenzie in Jeremy's arms had pushed him to act immediately. "Double whammy, her dad dies, and I drop a bomb. I can't believe I was so tactless and self-absorbed. But Kenzie and Jeremy whammied me first."

"You led her to believe you were hurt because of what you'd seen."

"Sure." He shoved his hands into his pockets. "A way of easing my own guilty conscience that worked until I woke up in Vegas with a wife."

Cara smiled and returned her attention to Kenzie, who had the crowd cheering. She was truly amazing, so natural, born for the stage. Too bad that wasn't where she wanted to be. Except now she was in the big leagues. Maybe being onstage for four months would change her mind. Kyle would be ecstatic if that were the case. He'd already voiced his concern about finding someone to fill Kenzie's place after Bonnie told him yesterday that she wouldn't be back.

He turned to Cara. "Does it bother you that they're so close? Kenzie and Jeremy?"

"No, they kissed once, and it didn't mean anything. The band pulled me into their family. That's what Kyle and Kenzie are to Jeremy. Family." She flashed a quick, sad smile. "You were part of that family not so very long ago." You might not believe it, but they miss you as much as you miss them."

I doubt that.

Kenzie swiveled her hips while Jeremy fiddled next to her. The audience jumped to their feet again.

"Excuse me, Cara. I have to find out what's keeping Aaron."

She raised her eyebrows, then aimed her camera at Jeremy. "Probably the buxom blond I saw go into his dressing room."

Yep.

He walked down the short hallway and hammered on Aaron's door. "Come on, Aaron. We've got a full house out there. You need to get ready."

Aaron opened the door with a grin. His makeup artist stood behind him, buttoning her blouse.

"Gotta go, honey." He grabbed his hat and patted the woman's behind on her way out.

Nick glared. "Your eyes are glassy."

Aaron rolled those glassy eyes. "I'm fine."

He didn't look fine. "You pushed to have Knight Rivers, yet you can't be bothered to watch their first performance?" Nick asked on their way toward the stage.

"You expect me to hold their hands?"

"You could have at least shown your support rather than feeding your habit right before a show. This is a big deal for them."

"So I'll go onstage and sing a number with them." He looped his arm around Nick's neck. "Did Kenzie agree?"

"I haven't talked to her yet."

"I want her every night."

Nick moved out from under Aaron's arm. "You don't always get what you want."

"If you can't get it done, I will."

Aaron jogged up the stairs and walked onto stage in the middle of a Knight Rivers number which was drowned out by shouts and thunderous applause. He bowed dramatically and stopped next to Kenzie.

Nick followed him up the stairs.

Kyle grabbed a microphone. "Aaron Vance, folks." Then he backed away.

Aaron unhooked a microphone and put an arm around Kenzie's waist to keep her close. "Hello, Nashville! Wow! What'd'ya think of Knight Rivers? They're great, aren't they? I came across them a month ago and decided they deserve a chance."

Idiot. Nick leaned out enough to see his dad's look of disgust. Doug was not a fan of Aaron Vance.

Aaron turned to Knight Rivers. "What do you say we sing 'Rocking Lights' for the crowd?"

This song was sitting at number five in the charts and would get the audience dancing. Luckily, Knight Rivers had practiced a few of Aaron's top songs before the tour started, so Jeremy gave them a lead-in. They rocked the crowd until Kyle strummed the last note, Aaron gave the crowd a wave and walked off stage.

"There. You happy now?" Aaron sniped as he passed Nick.

～

*A*fter Aaron left the stage, they sang one more song and gave a bow. Big crowd or small, the smiles and cheers told Kenzie the audience appreciated their music. All she'd ever wanted was to give joy through music, and that's exactly what they accomplished tonight.

They exited the stage, ran down the stairs, and fell into each other's arms, hugging and high-fiving. Kenzie shrieked when Jeremy lifted her up and swung her around.

"Y'all sounded fantastic out there," said the sound

manager for the venue. "Even better than at your sound check."

"Thanks, Deke," Kyle said, patting the man on the shoulder.

Bodhi and Tripp's girlfriends joined them, along with Jessi and Cara.

They were in Nashville, not far from home, but Kenzie felt like she was worlds away from the ranch. They were spending the night in town, then leaving in the morning for the three-hour drive to Louisville, Kentucky, the second destination on the tour schedule.

Kenzie, still reeling a little from when Aaron joined them on the stage, didn't want him to get the idea she might be interested. She tried to move away while singing with him, but he kept a tight arm around her waist. To jerk away would have looked terrible to the audience.

He came out to give the concert-goers an early glimpse and reminder of who they'd really come to see, and she understood but hoped he didn't make a habit of hanging onto her that way. The others might feel like they had to walk on glass to keep Aaron happy, but she wasn't afraid to have a little chat with the guy about what was acceptable to her.

Nick whistled low and long. She looked over to see if Kyle had heard. The whistle was distinct and unique, a sound the three friends had started using as teens to get each other's attention. When Kyle looked up, Nick beckoned him over. He was standing near a man in jeans and a suede vest.

"Give me a minute," Kyle said, leaving their circle. "Then we can head out to dinner."

"Wonder what that's about," Jeremy said as Cara joined them. He pulled his wife close, and they exchanged a sweet kiss.

"That's Aaron's uncle, Marc Vance," Kenzie said.

Jeremy turned wide eyes on her. "The music producer?"

Kenzie watched her brother shake hands with Marc when Nick made introductions.

"My curiosity is aroused." Jessi looped her hand over Kenzie's arm.

"What do you think it's about?"

"Maybe we should go check," Ryder countered.

"No." Kenzie shook her head. "Kyle will let us know when he's finished."

"By the way, the Marshalls said to tell you hi and that you sounded fantastic," Jessi said. "And they're right, Kenz. You really should think about staying with Knight Rivers."

She gave Jessi a side-eye. "Did my brother tell you to say that?"

"Nope. That's all me, sweet sister-in-law. And I mean every word."

Nick shook hands with Marc and walked over to their group. This was the first time she'd been so close to him since their kiss in the barn. She hated that his blue eyes directed at her set her heart racing.

She turned away and noticed a man wearing a press badge around his neck watching. He gave a nod and she smiled.

"Y'all sounded amazing," Nick said to their group.

"Thanks." Tripp thumbed over his shoulder. "What's going on over there with Kyle?"

"Marc asked to meet Kyle and Jeremy."

A frown puckered the skin between Jeremy's eyebrows. "Why didn't you tell me?"

"I whistled. You ignored."

"Is Marc Vance interested in Knight Rivers?" Ryder asked.

"I'll let Kyle tell you." Nick looked at her, and Jeremy moved closer. "Kenzie, Aaron wants you to sing a song with him."

Jeremy put a protective arm around her shoulders.

"Just me?"

"Just you."

"Is this something he's going to want her to do at every concert?" Tripp asked.

Nick nodded.

Jeremy slashed a hand in front of his chest. "No. We already know our bus will leave before his."

"She can ride on Aaron's bus those nights."

"No," Jeremy repeated.

"I'll be there with her, so she'll never be alone."

"Oh, well, that makes me feel so much better," Jeremy said with saccharine sarcasm.

"There's a separate bedroom she can use."

All the band members' heads were turning back and forth between Nick and Jeremy. If Kenzie wasn't so nervous about the suggestion, she'd laugh.

"First, would you both quit talking like I'm not standing right here? And second, I can't sing with him tonight. We haven't practiced anything together."

"All you have to do is sing harmony during the chorus. I can give you a cheat sheet of the words."

"Oh, that'll look real professional," Tripp interjected.

"He just wants a pretty face on the stage with him," Bodhi said. "Pumps his ego."

Suddenly Aaron stopped next to Kenzie. "I want you onstage for my fifth number." He winked like that would seal the deal, then he ran up the stage stairs two at a time. Applause and cheering followed.

His demand didn't sit well with her. At all. She glanced at Nick. "What's his fifth number?"

By his expression, she could tell she wouldn't like the answer. Kenzie had always been very particular about the content of the songs she sang. She wanted her songs to set a good example for young boys and girls who might be in the audience.

"'Before Nightfall,'" Nick shouted over the noise of the crowd.

"Come on, Nick," Jeremy shouted back.

"I didn't know what song Aaron was going to pick. He hit me up with this right before y'all went onstage."

"And you didn't think to ask?"

"No, Jeremy. I was more concerned about the bus situation than I was about the song. I don't want Kenzie to be stuck alone with Aaron any more than you do. Don't forget I know the guy. I traveled with him for a year before London was born."

"Yeah, you learned from the master," Jeremy threw back. "To be clear, I don't want Kenz alone on a bus with you either."

"Jeremy," Cara said, pulling his arm. "Nick's doing the best he can under the circumstances."

"Send him a message," Kenzie said. "If he wants me onstage, I'll sing 'Help For Me' with him.

"Hey, gang, let's head out," Kyle said, joining their group. "Marc Vance invited us to a private dinner."

"Cool," Ryder said.

"We need to go now, though." Kyle took Jessi's hand and pulled her close. "He has a limo waiting. Wives and girl-friends are included."

"Go," Nick said to Kenzie. "Marc is the guy to go with for a recording deal."

She knew about Marc and his tremendously successful history, but she didn't want a recording deal.

"I'll get a note to Aaron that you had to leave. Maybe you two can sit down tomorrow and decide on a song that you'd be willing to sing with him."

Kenzie nodded.

"What's going on?" Kyle asked.

Jessi tugged Kyle's arm. "I'll fill you in on the way to dinner."

Jeremy put his arm around Kenzie and Cara's waists and steered them toward the exit. Kenzie glanced back before going out of the door. Nick stood alone, hands in his pockets. For a moment, she felt sorry for him. Would he lose his job because they were defying Aaron?

She disagreed with Jeremy about one thing. If Nick was with them, she'd feel safe on Aaron's bus.

CHAPTER 8

$\mathcal{T}$hough the bus wasn't leaving until eleven, Kenzie couldn't sleep past six. Ranch living meant a lifetime of early mornings. She changed into workout clothes and headed to the hotel gym for some exercise. Afterward, she'd order breakfast, grab a quick shower, and possibly squeeze in some writing time.

Despite being tired after their late-night dinner with Marc Vance, she'd tossed and turned most of the night. The more she thought about staying behind to perform with Aaron, the more nervous she got. At least until Kyle assured her Knight Rivers would hold their bus rather than leave her behind. The others agreed.

Marc said if all went well with the tour, he wanted to discuss a recording deal with the band in September.

Kenzie needed to talk to Kyle about that. She needed to make him understand she was only singing with Knight Rivers as a placeholder until they could find someone to fill Bonnie's position, which meant Kyle would have to find her replacement before the tour was over.

She took the elevator down nine floors and followed the

signs to the gym. Holding her room card against the lock, she opened the door, popped in her earbuds, and headed for a treadmill.

The place was empty until Bodhi joined her ten minutes later. They ran into each other at the gym in Dove Hill a couple of times a week. He greeted her smile with a wink before he climbed onto a treadmill and started jogging at a moderate pace. Within ten minutes, he'd have the machine pushed almost to the max. Bodhi ran marathons and was on a team that participated in a couple of Ironman Triathlons around the country every year.

Tripp, Kyle, and Jessi trickled in ten minutes or so apart. Ryder worked out on the dance floor rather than a gym, and Cara and Jeremy would hit the pool for their exercise. She wasn't sure about Jeff. He was a loner and, no matter how often he was invited, he chose to do his own thing.

When Nick came in, his gaze locked on hers before he went to a corner holding weights. She decided to give a rowing machine a chance since it was in the opposite corner and didn't face any mirrors.

The next four months would be the longest of her life if she didn't get used to being around Nick. *Baby steps, Kenz.*

*T*he bus ride to Louisville, Kentucky was actually kind of fun. Knight Rivers passed the time picking guitars and singing. Jeremy played a couple of goofy songs on his banjo and they laughed and sang along. Even Jeff joined in.

This was the beginning, the first leg, so of course, it was fun. Things would change, though. They would get tired and cranky and sick of each other's company. What was funny now would become irritating and grate on everyone's nerves in a few weeks. Today was for singing and joking.

She hoped they would be doing the same a month from now.

Kyle had taken the month of June to renovate the interior of Aaron's hand-me-down bus. The front lounge held seating for ten with two twenty-five-foot slides on each side. The kitchen had a decent-sized fridge, a four-burner stove, and a microwave that doubled as a convection oven. Her brother took out a broom closet and installed a stackable washer and dryer. Aaron already had nine bunks—slightly larger than a twin bed—for his band members, with mini televisions, privacy curtains, and separate controls for heating, air, and lighting.

Beyond the bunks, six narrow closets stood on one side and three on the other—plus a bathroom—lined the walls. Kyle turned the one big bedroom, bathroom, and back salon into two bedrooms with queen beds, making the second bathroom accessible to everyone.

He insisted Kenzie take one of the bedrooms with a closing door. The second bedroom was for visiting spouses or girlfriends.

Jeremy started singing "Norma Jean Riley" by Diamond Rio, and they all joined in. They hadn't done this kind of goofing around in a long time, and the downtime was much needed since they were usually practicing or entertaining others.

And bonus—Raymond, their bus driver, proved to have a fantastic voice when he started singing along.

Cara and Jessi were following the bus to Louisville. They'd head back to Tennessee tomorrow while the band traveled on to Columbus, Ohio. Cleveland and a Fourth of July concert followed, then on to Pittsburgh, Philadelphia for two nights, and Scranton the first of next week.

The bus would be the only downtime they got. She packed several decks of cards and a couple of board games.

Since storage space was an issue, she'd only been able to pack a couple of books in her suitcase, so her e-reader would be put to good use.

They arrived in Louisville early, got checked into the hotel, and headed to the auditorium for a sound check. She braced herself for another Nick moment, knowing he would already be there.

~

*N*ick was surprised when Aaron walked into the auditorium at the time they agreed upon. Then again, he wasn't. Kenzie should be here any minute.

Last night, when Nick passed him the note about Kenzie leaving with his uncle, Aaron pulled a woman out of the audience to serenade, and she thoroughly enjoyed the limelight, the parting kiss, and the backstage passes before leaving the stage.

Aaron wasn't a yeller when things didn't go his way. He pouted. On their bus ride to Kentucky, Aaron locked himself in his room, which was fine with Nick.

Aaron pulled his guitar out of its case and sat in the row behind Nick, propping the heels of his boots on the chair in front of him. "Tell me what you think of this."

Nick listened to the melody. Catchy. Something that would encourage concertgoers to jump up and dance. "Nice. Where'd you get it?"

"I've been working on the music for a month. The words came to me today."

Writing music while pouting could be a great combination.

Aaron pulled a sheet of music from his back pocket and passed it forward.

Nick unfolded and smoothed the paper out, reading over

the lyrics while Aaron continued to strum the tune. He glanced at Aaron. "This is a duet."

"Yep."

Nick knew the answer before asking, "Who's going to sing it with you?"

Aaron looked at him like he was an idiot. "Kenzie."

Nick handed the pages back to Aaron. "She won't sing these lyrics."

The scowl Nick had talked to Aaron about appeared. Too many pictures and memes were showing up on social media with the now-famous Aaron Vance scowl. "You told me last night she agreed to sing with me."

"She will, but she won't sing this."

They both turned at the sound of the door.

"Hey, Kyle," Aaron called as Kyle made his way down the aisle followed by the rest of the band members. Kenzie stayed in the back of the auditorium talking to Carl, the sound manager with a chip on his shoulder the size of Kentucky. She actually had the guy smiling.

"Yeah?" Kyle asked when he got closer.

Aaron grabbed the sheets of music from Nick and held them out. "I wrote this for Kenzie and me to sing together. I finished the lyrics this morning."

Nick saw the concern on Kyle's face at the mention of his sister singing with Aaron.

"Let's hear it." Kyle listened to Aaron play as he scanned the words. He frowned and glanced at Nick.

Nick shrugged. "I told him Kenzie wouldn't sing those lyrics."

"Why?" Aaron stopped playing and dropped his feet to the floor.

"Nick's right," Kyle said. "She won't sing this."

Jeremy, who'd paused behind Kyle, looked over his

shoulder and shook his head with a smirk. "Not gonna happen."

"I spent three hours writing this," Aaron barked. "Nick, you promised Kenzie would sing with me."

Nick held up a hand when Knight Rivers' members turned to him. "I never promised. I said I would ask her, and she agreed. And she will sing with you, but not this song. You need to come up with something both of you agree on."

"Here she comes. Ask her," Bodhi, who now held the sheet of lyrics, said.

Aaron started playing again, and Kenzie smiled as she approached. "That sounds great. New song?"

"Yeah, I wrote a duet for us to sing," Aaron said with a smug grin. "So you like it?"

"I do." She glanced around at everyone watching her. "What's going on?"

Bodhi handed her the lyrics. Nick watched her eyes move back and forth as she read. Then she raised her brows. "Yeah, you're going to have to sing this with someone else."

Aaron stood up. "You just said you liked it!"

Nick could tell she was taken back by Aaron's anger.

"That was before I read the lyrics."

"You agreed to sing with me."

"I will sing with you, but I won't sing this song."

"What's wrong with the words?" Aaron got a little too close to Kenzie, and Knight Rivers closed ranks. "I wrote them for us."

Instead of shrinking back, Kenzie stepped even closer. "Aaron, I am *not* going to sing about the thrill of a one-night stand. I don't believe in them, and I'm not going to stand onstage and pretend I do by singing these lyrics. The music is beautiful, but—"

"You think you can do better?" Aaron challenged.

Nick could almost see the steam rising off Aaron's red

face—not from embarrassment but anger. The guy refused to accept rejection.

"I can write lyrics I'd be willing to sing to your music." A slight smile played over Kenzie's face as she handed the lyrics to Nick, opened the case she carried, and pulled out her guitar. Slipping the strap over her head, she looked down at the music Aaron had left on a chair. She started picking out the melody before she even sat down. "Are you sure you want me to change your words? You can always find someone else to sing this with you."

"Let's go," called cranky Carl.

Nick gestured for Aaron to go onstage.

"Let's see what you come up with." Aaron stalked away to join his band.

Kenzie propped the music up and sang the first line the way Aaron wrote it.

"Do you think you can change the words enough?" Nick asked.

She nodded without looking at him. "Can you write this down, please?"

Nick turned the page of lyrics over and fumbled through his briefcase for a pen. "Start over."

She smiled at him—At him!—for the first time in . . . He couldn't remember the last time she directed her pearly whites in his direction.

He smiled back. "And sing slowly. You know I don't write fast."

"Let me play the song all the way through first."

He picked up the sheets, held them up for her to see, and she played the song like she'd written the music herself. Kenzie had always been able to pick up a song after hearing it once or twice. Which was why he was surprised when she struggled with a note when writing over Memorial Day weekend. "Did you ever try F-sharp like I suggested?"

She gave him a don't-mess-with-me look, which meant she'd tried F-sharp and it worked.

Nick bit back a smile.

After Aaron and his band started the sound check, Nick sat next to Kenzie so he could hear her—close enough that he could smell her perfume. He scribbled as fast as he could while Kenzie tried out new phrases and reworked some of Aaron's original sentences by changing the meaning. Twice she got stuck and looked at him for help. *Just like old times.* He offered several suggestions. Some she accepted and wrinkled her nose at others.

Aaron kept a sharp eye on them, as did Kyle and Jeremy. Nick felt like they were in a fishbowl, but he didn't care. Being this close to a smiling Kenzie was an unexpected gift.

～

The next four concerts came off without a hitch. Since the bus trips between locations were short, Kenzie spent time on Aaron's bus practicing the song they co-wrote. He kept insisting his words fit the music better, which was a crock. The truth was, she'd bruised his ego and he couldn't let it go. She told him repeatedly if he wasn't happy with the results, he could change the words back and find another duet partner. He didn't.

They finally agreed on one of his songs that she'd come out and sing with him at each concert. Again, he was unhappy that she refused to sing the first song he picked. Her answer was the same. "You can always ask someone else to sing with you. Jeremy would be happy to step out there with his fiddle and get the crowd dancing in the aisles."

"I can get the crowd dancing on my own." He stalked toward the bedroom in the middle of the bus and shut the door.

"You have a way of getting under his skin," Nick said without looking up from the book he was reading.

Kenzie hadn't realized he was paying attention to her and Aaron's conversation from where he sat at the kitchen table. The rest of Aaron's band members were playing poker in the back salon of the bus.

"Just telling it like it is."

"And that's how you get under his skin. Most people tell him what he wants to hear. You, on the other hand, are straightforward. You intimidate him."

She scoffed at the idea. Aaron was so full of arrogance she had a hard time believing he'd be intimidated by anyone. "Do you?"

Nick looked up from his book. "Do I intimidate him?"

"No. Do you tell him what he wants to hear?"

Nick inhaled, his chest expanding, and held the breath for a long moment before exhaling. "Sometimes."

"Because it's easier?"

He raised his arms and rested them along the back of the bench seat, stretching his T-shirt over his chest muscles and accentuating his biceps. "Sometimes."

"How do I intimidate him?"

"You challenge him. And he doesn't like that, but he thinks you're hot and would look good on his arm, so he's trying to figure out how to work around the challenge." Nick set his book on the table. "Aaron doesn't like to lose, Kenz."

She turned sideways on the bench seat and pulled her knees up. "No one *likes* to lose."

"Let me rephrase, the people around him capitulate to Aaron because he's such a sore loser. He knows if he repeats himself enough, the people opposing him will give in."

Okay, good to know. "Why didn't you tell me all this before I agreed to sing with him?"

"You weren't exactly talking to me."

True. "So what would you suggest?"

"Keep doing what you're doing." He flashed a grin. "Especially if you want him to get frustrated enough to *forget*"—he used air quotes—"he ever asked you to sing with him."

She couldn't stop her smile from making a brief appearance. If he was right, she'd owe him . . . something. Like a donut. Maybe.

Since their second concert in Philadelphia was in the afternoon, Knight Rivers agreed to sing at a benefit for a children's hospital in Philadelphia. Nick had warned them to bring black-tie attire for a few occasions that might crop up. Kenzie was a jeans and T-shirt kinda girl but loved to get gussied up—as her dad would say—for an occasional event.

The benefit was held at the Mill House on the Schuylkill River. Fragrant white bouquets were everywhere, and music floated through the air from hidden speakers. Tables were set up around a large dance floor, and a light dinner was served buffet style from long tables lit by more candles than Kenzie had ever seen at an event.

After she and the band went through the buffet line, they sat at several different tables, mingling with the crowd before they hit the stage.

Kenzie was glad Aaron had another event to attend. He asked her to accompany him, and she was relieved to have a reason why she couldn't. She'd had enough of his company in the past few days. They'd perfected two songs they could perform together, so she saw no reason to continue riding on his bus. Yay!

Because of their early concert, Nick flew home to see his daughter this morning, giving her a double reprieve. Though, after rewriting Aaron's song together and their talk on his bus, the tension between them had ratcheted down from teeth-grinding anger to swatting at a fly annoyance.

After dinner, Knight Rivers entertained the crowd for

about forty minutes before another band took the stage. Before she could sit, Ryder grabbed her hand.

"Let's dance."

"Only if you promise to tone down your moves."

"Why?" He pulled her close. "You think these Philadelphians will be shocked by our sexy moves?"

She pushed him back a half-step. "This isn't exactly the venue for that kind of dancing. We'll save our sexy moves for another night."

Ryder could still move her around the floor like no other. As they danced, he scanned the room. There was almost always one woman, but usually, three or four, who leaned forward on her chair or barstool and watched Ryder with interest.

One day Ryder would find life's perfect partner, and she would miss him while he was dancing with his ladylove.

"Oh, there she is," Kenzie said when a woman moved closer, drink in hand. "She's in a blue dress, late twenties."

Ryder turned Kenzie and glanced past her shoulder. "I don't know. She's got big hair."

"And a beautiful face." When the song ended, Kenzie straightened his already straight tie, patted his chest, and said, "Go see if she's ready for a twirl around the dance floor, handsome. Just remember we have to leave early tomorrow, so no hanky-panky."

"Yes, Mom."

Before she made it to a chair, Jeremy took her arm. "Take a turn around the floor with me. I'm missing Cara."

"I hate to break the news to you, but I look nothing like Cara."

"No, you don't, but you smell good."

Kenzie laughed. "You're such a dork."

"So, you homesick yet?" he asked after they circled the floor once.

Ryder was smiling at something the woman in blue was saying. "Always."

"How are things between you and Nick?"

She glanced up at Jeremy. "I haven't strangled him yet."

"That good, huh?" he asked with a grin.

"We're fine. I stay away from him. He stays away from me."

Jeremy raised a brow. "You've been traveling on Aaron's bus. Isn't Nick around then?"

"Yes, but if we're in the kitchen, he's sitting near the front. If we're on the couches, he's at the kitchen table or in the back."

Jeremy laughed.

"I know the bus isn't that big, but it's sectioned off by a wall or a door. He's not *right there* with us."

"But he *is* close enough if you need help," Jeremy stated rather than asked.

"Yes. He's close." *And he warned me to be careful around Aaron.* "Nick said I intimidate Aaron. Do you think that's true?"

Jeremy didn't answer, so she looked up. "What are you looking at?"

He gave a slight shake of his head. "Kyle and Jeff are having a talk."

Jeremy turned her so she could see.

Jeff was quiet compared to the rest of the band members, but he was also the new guy, not yet privy to inside jokes. But he didn't seem interested in changing that. He gave the impression he liked being on the outside, which seemed strange since the rest of them were so close. He'd been with the band for four months, plenty of time for them to get to know him, but every time she tried asking questions about himself or his family, he closed the door.

Jeff waved his hands around and actually laughed. "I don't

think I've ever seen Jeff so animated. He looks happy for a change."

Jeremy nodded with an unconvincing expression. "Yeah, maybe a little too happy."

"Too happy? What do you mean?"

Jeremy turned her away. "I don't think his happiness comes naturally."

CHAPTER 9

*K*enzie dabbed at her laugh-tears with a napkin. After a two-concert day, she felt punch drunk tired. They had a concert tomorrow in Syracuse, New York, and then they'd be able to enjoy their first day off.

She could hardly wait. Since they missed Fourth of July weekend at the Tennessee River, they were going to make Monday night a mini celebration. They actually had a campsite near a lake and were looking forward to a swim and cooking dinner around a fire.

Rather than take the stairs, Jeremy jumped off the karaoke stage with a grin. People patted his back and shook his hand as he headed for their table. He'd entertained the packed bar with three songs because, at the end of each, the crowd shouted for more.

Knight Rivers made a habit of finding karaoke bars and picking songs for each other. They always chose music that would entertain the crowd if their name got called. This bar happened to be in their hotel's basement, and very few patrons were here when they came down.

The DJ leaned toward his microphone. "Next up we have Kenzie Rivers. Let's give her a big hand. She'll be singing Gretchen Wilson's "Redneck Woman.""

Kenzie stood and looked around the table. When Bodhi couldn't keep a straight face, she knew he'd put her name down. Fair was fair—she'd done it to him more than once.

She made her way to the stage and took the mic. Life behind one was becoming so commonplace, the nervous jitters that used to make her sick before she hit the stage were a thing of the past. So, one good thing for her had come from this tour.

Eleven days on the road and no catastrophes. Eleven days of putting up with Aaron pulling her close and kissing her with his alcohol-laden breath after they performed the song they wrote together. Her name was on it only because Nick threatened Aaron with a lawsuit if he didn't include her. She didn't care enough to sue Aaron, but it was nice to know Nick was looking out for her. She told Aaron Nick's name should be added as well. He helped her that afternoon and deserved his share of credit.

She caught sight of him now, sitting at the bar next to a guy she'd noticed backstage several times. He appeared to be about Nick and Kyle's age, and always wore a press badge around his neck.

"Let's see your moves, Kenz!" Ryder shouted from their table.

From the time the music started until it ended, she performed like she was in front of any other audience. She had to change a cuss word to heck, which always made the band members laugh. Encouraging the crowd to stand and dance to the upbeat tune, she finished with a dramatic bow and a standing ovation.

The next name called was Nick Marshall. She glanced around the table, wondering who'd put his name in the hat.

Jeremy was suddenly very busy with the napkin under his drink.

Nick made his way to the stage, bopping Jeremy on the back of the head as he passed.

"How'd he know?" Jeremy asked.

"You look as guilty as you did when you put that fake head in Mr. Hooper's car in high school," Kyle said with a laugh.

Nick got up and sang "Ticks," by Brad Paisley, just like he had when it first came out, and he was great at urging the crowd to sing along.

"I'll get you next time, Jer," he said when he passed their table after his performance.

The exchange reminded Kenzie of how things used to be. It seemed like maybe the tension between them and Nick was lifting. She knew she was the catalyst, and that she alone held the key to restoring the friendship they used to share.

"Seems like we have a roomful of talented people tonight," the DJ said. "I just heard that the band opening for Aaron Vance is here. Think we can get them up to do a song together?"

The crowd clapped and shouted their approval.

"Might as well get a little publicity while we're here," Kyle said, standing.

Jeff stayed in his seat with a shake of his head. "Not my scene."

"The stage isn't big enough for all of us anyway," Tripp said.

"Lean on Me," Club Nouveau style, was the song the DJ chose. They overplayed it as much as possible, then followed up with Lynyrd Skynyrd's "Sweet Home Alabama." Ryder jumped off the stage and swung Kenzie down. While the rest of the band sang, the two of them danced. Kenzie wasn't sure who was having more fun, Knight Rivers or the audience.

～

*T*hough the crowd loved it, Nick would forever hate watching Kenzie dance with Ryder. He turned to face the bar instead of the stage.

He'd acted put out with Jeremy when truly he was glad his name had been entered into the hat. Getting up to sing was fun and reminded him of old times. He couldn't count on fingers and toes how many times he'd gotten up on a karaoke stage with Kenzie, one of the guys, or by himself. They had an unspoken rule that they couldn't get up of their own accord or put their own name in to sing. The fun of getting called was finding out the song that had been chosen for you.

"You're quite the singer yourself."

"Not anymore," Nick said. The reporter sitting next to him was writing an article on Aaron Vance for *Rolling Stone* magazine.

"How long have you known her?"

Nick didn't have to ask who to know Travis Sprenger was asking about Kenzie. "Since she was a baby. Her family and mine have been friends since before I was born."

"I heard the song she wrote with Aaron. Did she have a hard time getting credit?"

Nick chuckled, shaking his head, not about to admit Aaron was an egotistical buffoon. Besides, Travis already knew the answer. Nick had to remind Aaron repeatedly that Kenzie wrote the majority of the lyrics, and if he refused to give her credit, he could go back to his original copy or face a possible lawsuit. Kenzie hit him with a surprise when she insisted Aaron also include Nick's name. He almost declined but changed his mind. Aaron needed to man up and give the people around him credit when it was due.

"Don't interview her without me or Kyle present."

"Afraid she'll tell the truth?" Travis asked with a smirk before taking a swig of his beer.

"If you want an interview, tell me. I'll set something up when Kyle can be with her."

Travis set his glass on the bar. "Fair enough. Can I get an interview with the whole band?"

"I'll talk to Kyle."

"How well does Knight Rivers get along with Aaron?"

"Fine. They don't see much of each other. Very seldom do they leave a town at the same time. Knight Rivers usually waits for Kenzie to sing her duet with Aaron and then they hit the road."

"Where is Aaron tonight?"

"He had a radio interview," Nick said while watching Kenzie cheer Ryder on while he was onstage.

"Do his band members hang out with Knight Rivers?"

"Not much."

"But there aren't any bad feelings or fights over territory?"

Nick scoffed. "You know how concerts work. Aaron's band is onstage for two hours after Knight Rivers gets off. If Knight Rivers doesn't have to hit the road right away, they find a place like this to unwind."

"Another band is scheduled to open for Aaron a couple of nights at the end of the month."

"Knight Rivers is singing at my sister's wedding."

Nick swiveled to face the stage. A guy was performing one of Aaron's songs. And not doing well. Nick was glad Aaron wasn't here to witness the sad performance.

He glanced at the table where Knight Rivers sat. Of course, Kenzie cheered on the terrible singer, because that's what she did. The rest of the band followed suit, making the guy feel like a rock star.

Jeff got up and walked out of the bar. Nick wished he

could follow because he was increasingly curious about where Jeff spent his time.

Since that day on Aaron's bus, he hadn't really had much chance to talk to Kenzie again. When he went home for a couple of days, his sister was in town and asked how things were going. He didn't know how to answer.

Were they civil? Sure. Did they talk? Only when forced to. Had she accepted his apology? No. Would she ever trust him again? Probably not. Where did he go from here? He had no idea. Did he want her back? Yes.

Time to head to his room, where regrets and longings would keep him awake most of the night.

He'd talked to London earlier, and heard all about how she was having fun with Grandma and Grandpa. His dad was showing her how to kick a ball, and his mom was spoiling her with clothes and dolls. Every time they talked, her sweet little voice squeezed his heart. Those three days he was in Tennessee only made him miss her more now. He was constantly amazed at how much London changed in just a week, and how much she changed his life for the better. Which was funny, because he'd thought he had a pretty great life before her birth.

He was constantly amazed how much a tiny being could change hopes and dreams, uprooting everything you thought you wanted and showing you the truth.

"Knight Rivers looks like they're leaving. Think you can swing an introduction now?" Travis asked. "I'm not sure when my schedule will coincide with another concert."

Nick nodded and walked over to their table and patted Kyle on the shoulder. "Can I introduce you to someone before you leave?"

"I'll see you in the morning," Kyle said to the rest of the band.

Travis stood as he and Kyle approached.

"Travis Sprenger, this is Kyle Rivers. Travis is a freelance journalist doing an article about Aaron for *Rolling Stone*."

Kyle stuck out his hand. "I've seen you backstage a couple of times. Nice to finally meet you, Travis."

"Yeah, you too," Travis said to Kyle while his attention stayed riveted on Kenzie.

"Travis has asked of he can interview Knight Rivers members," Nick said.

Kyle nodded. "We can make that happen. Do you want to talk to everyone?"

"If possible, yes. If not, then you and your sister."

Nick watched a lightbulb go off behind Kyle's eyes. He'd been afraid he'd have to actually spell out that Travis wanted to meet Kenzie.

Kyle glanced at Nick, then nodded. "I'm sure the *whole* band would love to sit down for an interview."

~

*G*rateful to be home, Kenzie sat at her piano and looked out over the green pastures. Horses grazed just beyond the stables, their coats glistening in the sun. The sweet scent of jasmine hung heavy in the air. From here, she could see purple coneflowers lining the path to the main house, and the branches of hydrangea bushes bent heavy under the weight of the huge flowers along the backside of the pool.

Their brief camping trip had been fun and a nice break. Jeff, the only one who didn't join them, caught a ride on Aaron's bus. She thought that was weird, but the others shrugged it off. That he seemed to spend so much time with the other band made her wonder if he was hoping to get a job with Aaron.

After leaving New York, Aaron's tour took them through Connecticut, Vermont, and Maine before heading south to Virginia, North Carolina, and then South Carolina. They'd spent nights on the first part of the tour in hotels, and the past week they slept on the bus while they traveled. She thought she'd have a hard time sleeping, but the movement, the sound of the wheels on the pavement lulled her to sleep pretty quickly . . . when she wasn't thinking about Nick.

They'd seen so many beautiful places she wished she could explore, yet there was no place like home.

She turned back to the piano. Kyle and Jessi went into Nashville for the afternoon, just to spend time together. Though he didn't moan about it, her brother had been missing his wife and based on Jessi's welcome-home kiss and their prompt disappearance, his wife had missed him too.

Kenzie pressed F-sharp and listened to the sound echo through her quiet house—making her think of Nick again. The lyrics to the song she was working on weren't coming as easily as the tune, and she needed to finish it before going back on the road two days from now. The song would be part of a soundtrack for a new movie and she was on a tight deadline to finish.

Time was running short. At five she was scheduled to be at Brent and Becky's rehearsal dinner. Afterwards, she and their girl-band planned to practice here at the ranch. She'd be busy with the wedding most of the day tomorrow. Luckily, Becky seemed to be taking everything in stride. She would laugh the minor hiccups off because that was her personality.

Kenzie sang what she'd come up with so far, playing along with the piano. Like painting herself into a corner, she didn't know where to go from the word "crack." Aloud, she started trying to find a word or phrase that rhymed.

"Still hung up on F-sharp?"

She whipped around with a hand to her heart to see Nick leaning against the doorjamb leading to the kitchen. If he'd made the comment, of course, he'd heard her lonely F-sharp. "You scared me to death."

"Sorry." Nick pushed away with a shoulder.

"Most people knock." She turned back to the piano.

"Try *and just like that*," he said, ignoring her comment.

Running the lyrics through her mind, she rolled her eyes. Of course, his suggestion worked perfectly. Again.

He picked up a wooden rocker and moved it close to the piano, making no attempt to hide his smirk.

"You don't have to be so smug about it."

"I'm not smug. Just enjoying the fact that you know I'm right, but don't want to admit it."

"The exact definition of smug."

He leaned over her shoulder and looked at the music. "Want to hear the harmony?"

As much as she wanted to yell NO, she did want to hear it. And he knew it because he knew her writing process. She nodded toward her bedroom door where she kept another guitar, and he left the room.

Nick hadn't been in this house since she moved in, and she wondered what he thought—not that his opinion mattered. And she'd keep telling herself that until she believed it.

Nick helped her dad build this place for Kyle. He'd also helped Kyle decorate. The scheme—pure bachelor pad.

He carried her guitar and a music stand into the living room. "Is that the only music you have?" he asked, pointing to the sheet music in front of her.

She could play the song from memory, so she turned the sheets over to him. He sat on the edge of the rocker, arranged the music on the stand, and perched her guitar on his thigh.

She waited while he played through the song once. Watching the fingers of his left hand move along the neck of the guitar, she remembered the day he helped her rewrite Aaron's song. The walls of her anger and hurt were crumbling and she wasn't sure how she felt about that.

At the last note, he looked up and smiled. "I like it."

She smiled back before she could stop herself.

His grin grew. "Did that hurt?"

"What?"

"Smiling. That's only the second time you've smiled at me. Though I got an almost-smile on Aaron's bus that day he stalked off in a huff."

Quick as a flash her anger raised its ugly head. "You're the one who wiped the smile away, so yeah, it did hurt a little."

His grin dropped away and he nodded. "Fair enough."

It was fair, but her comment didn't make her feel better. In fact, she felt petty for bringing up the past. She imagined her dad shaking his head.

"You ready?" he asked.

No. "Yes."

He strummed the opening notes and she joined in, singing the lyrics while she played along with him. At the chorus, his voice coupled with hers just like it did when they dated, and even before. She filled in the phrase he provided. Which worked perfectly. *The rat.*

As the last notes faded away, he glanced up and smiled. "That's good, Kenz."

"Thank you. And thanks for your help." She stood up from the piano. "As much as I hate to admit it, your suggestion worked."

He also stood, his smirk back in place. "That hurt as much as the smile, didn't it?"

She held up her thumb and index finger about two inches apart.

He laughed as he carried her guitar and the music stand back into the bedroom. When he returned, he settled on her sofa.

What do you think you're doing? she wanted to ask. He'd come inside without being invited, offered his opinion—which worked—and now he sat down like he intended to stay. Instead, she raised her eyebrows.

"I like what you did with this place. It reflects your personality."

She glanced around, quite happy with the transformation. A fresh coat of cream paint had covered Kyle's choice of brown walls. She'd used muted blues and greens to further brighten the little house.

"Have you talked to Becky?"

"We talked last night." She sat on the edge of a chair. "She's extremely calm about the wedding tomorrow."

Nick shrugged. "She says something going wrong will add to the memories."

"That's a great attitude to have." She paused a moment. *Watch, Dad. I can be nice.* "Would you like something to drink?"

"No. Thank you. I just want to talk."

"About?"

He leaned forward, resting his forearms on his knees, and laced his fingers together. "How do you feel about the tour?"

"What do you mean?"

"Do you feel comfortable? Overwhelmed?"

"As long as I can find time to write, I'm fine." She pulled a throw pillow out from behind her back and settled it on her lap, feeling the need for a shield, but her guitar was back in the bedroom.

"What are your plans after the tour? Will you continue to sing with Knight Rivers?"

"No. The band will have to find someone else."

"Bonnie isn't coming back?"

"No, she's decided to stay home with the baby. She told Kyle she's afraid this tour will put Knight Rivers on the road way more than she wants to be gone."

"Would you consider going solo?"

She scoffed. "No. I don't want to be on the stage. I just want to write."

He tipped his head and studied her for an uncomfortable moment. "Want to go for a swim?"

"With you?" she asked, shifting the pillow to cover her chest.

He smiled. "Yes."

"No. I want you to leave." *Sorry, Daddy.*

"Again with the unfriendly," he chuckled. "How about a horseback ride?"

Didn't he get how badly he'd hurt her? He had no idea how painful being around him was. She wasn't interested in being friends or anything else he might have in mind. "No."

"Okay." He pushed to his feet. "I guess I'll see you tonight at the rehearsal dinner."

She walked him to the door, disappointed to see him leave. Yet, wasn't him leaving exactly what she wanted? She hated the swirl of confusing emotions—her mind set on one thing and her heart suggesting something else.

Her feelings for him were changing, which muddled everything. Emotions could be so fickle and unkind. Hate and love could be intertwined in a web sticky with memories —both good and bad—which surfaced when you least expected. Some of the good memories were so sweet they softened the heart, smoothing out the sharp edges of hurt. Only to be crowded out by the bad.

That he still had such a strong hold over her was even more confusing. After what he did, she should be long over him. Yet here she was, gazing into the electric blue of his eyes while butterflies stirred deep within.

She didn't want to love him anymore. She didn't even want to like him. Where was neutral ground, and why couldn't she find it?

"Bye, Kenz."

He left by the front door, and she stood on the porch watching him walk back to the main house, where he must have left his car. Why had he come? She hadn't even thought to ask.

She walked through the house to the back door, out into the heat, and looked over the pastures and the grazing horses.

She couldn't avoid being up close and personal with Nick for the next two days. When she found out Becky and Brent had quite the lineup of attendants—eight friends and relatives for each, sixteen people standing at the front of the chapel during the ceremony—she'd begged Becky to match her with anyone but Nick when it came to walking down the aisle. Her friend took pity and paired her with Griffin instead.

Eight attendants each!

Kenzie's idea of a wedding was small and simple. A greenery-covered arbor by the pool behind the main house with the pastures and horses as a backdrop. A small ceremony with just a few close friends, followed by a nice barbecue and lots of music afterward. Her dad would have appreciated modest with music.

Kyle and Jessi had kept their wedding simple, choosing to get married at the courthouse with only her and Jeremy as witnesses.

She didn't want a big wedding, but she did want something more memorable than standing in front of a judge at the courthouse.

Enough thinking about weddings. Tonight would be hard.

Tomorrow would be harder. But she'd get through it, just the way she was getting through the tour. Being friends with the Marshall family meant Nick would always be around. The sooner she got used to that, the better for her heart.

CHAPTER 10

*a*nybody watching Nick at the wedding rehearsal would know he couldn't keep his eyes off Kenzie. She was wearing gold sandals with a light blue dress that tied on the side. It was covered in happy little yellow flowers. While his gaze zeroed in on her, she was looking everywhere but at him. Which told him she wanted to look but kept up a vigilant defense instead. That was all he needed to know.

After a quick meet and greet with everyone who'd be involved, the wedding planner lined them up for their rehearsal walk down the aisle. He and Brent's sister were right behind Kenzie and Griffin. From where he stood, he could smell Kenzie's perfume—light and flowery, a summer scent. Griffin pointed at something and Kenzie turned just enough that he could see her eyes light up in delight.

Every time he was near her, Nick spent the next thirty minutes beating himself up.

When he went over earlier today, he knew Kyle and his wife had gone to Nashville, leaving Kenzie alone at the ranch. So he parked by the main house, then walked to her place.

When he reached her back door, he could hear her playing the piano, so he let himself in, which he shouldn't have done. The Rivers' door had always been open to Kyle and Kenzie's friends—except he wasn't a friend anymore.

Walking in without her permission had been rude and presumptuous, but her music was irresistible. And so was she. Not wise on his part, but he couldn't seem to stay away from her.

He heard her stumble over a phrase, changing the words a couple of times. When she sang it through one more time, the solution popped into his mind. Before thinking, he blurted out the suggestion.

Now he smiled at the memory of her holding up the two-inch space between her finger and thumb to acknowledge that his phrase worked. He knew having him in her house hurt much more than that.

They walked through the rehearsal twice with much laughter and joking. Becky and Brent were good sports and loved having fun, even though they probably should have been serious or worried about everything running smoothly. Both sets of parents did their best to rein in the group enough that they could finish and get to dinner.

Brent's parents had rented the back room of a steakhouse, where the tables were set up in a big square, so all thirty guests could see each other. Before she sat, Kenzie made her way over to his grandparents. Grandpa Marshall passed when Nick was ten, but the other three had loved Kenzie—still did, judging by the way they hugged her. Proving they still had good taste. Grandma Marshall had pulled him aside and read him the riot act the first time he brought Juliette to a family function.

Kenzie finally took a seat directly across from him. He watched her look up and realize her mistake, but too late. Everyone else had taken the remaining seats.

Nick was pretty sure Kenzie had asked Becky to let her walk down the aisle with Griffin instead of him. Or maybe it was his mom's idea to make sure they didn't walk together. He was a little disappointed about that detail. He would have liked to have her on his arm again.

Dinner was the choice of steak or chicken, baked or mashed potatoes, salad, and one of the steak house's decadent desserts. He knew before she ordered that Kenzie would choose a filet, baked potato, a salad with ranch dressing, and the chocolate cake. She didn't disappoint. A creature of habit when it came to food, she very seldom tried new things. He used to tease her about her stubbornness to experiment beyond her palate preferences. Now he found it comforting to know how unwavering she remained. *Not a bad thing.*

He kept up a conversation with the people around him while stealing glances at Kenzie as often as possible. She was sitting next to his little brother, who was paying way more attention to her than he should be. At least in Nick's opinion.

Brent's dad stood and tapped his glass with the side of a spoon. "I'd like to propose a toast."

He waited a moment for everyone to pick up their glasses. "First, my wife and I would like to thank y'all for coming. I love seeing all your smiling faces and knowing you're here for our son and soon-to-be daughter. Sorry, Doug and Vicki, we're stealing her from you."

He paused while the group laughed. "In all seriousness, Natalie and I would like to thank you for raising such a beautiful, talented, loving woman. Becky, you have brought out the very best in our son. The first time he brought you home to meet us, we saw a difference in him. His happiness was palpable. Son, we love you and are delighted with the choice you've made in a forever companion. We believe you will make a wonderful husband and, dare I say, father"—the group laughed again—"in the near future. Let us raise a glass to the groom and his lovely bride."

Becky and Brent sipped from their glasses, then shared a kiss.

How his sister and Brent found each other was a story for the books and one they could tell their children and grandchildren. Two years ago, while visiting Ireland for different reasons, they were both in line to kiss the Blarney Stone and struck up a conversation. Apparently, they did just fine even before kissing the stone and gaining the supposed gift of eloquence. Becky accepted Brent's invitation to lunch, and the rest was history.

Next, Nick's dad stood. "First, Vicki and I would like to thank Natalie and Sean for this wonderful dinner. Dove Hill doesn't have a lot of places to choose from, but we do have one of the best places." Doug waited while a few in the group voiced their approval. "I'm not going to stand here and tell you Becky was the perfect child because there were times— Sorry, Brent." He put a hand on Vicki's shoulder. "We kept her pranks and rowdy ways to ourselves while you were dating. And now it's too late for takebacks."

Laughter filled the room.

When Becky picked up a dinner roll and threw it at her father, the laughter grew.

"Sorry, honey," he said to Becky. "She told me I was forbidden to embarrass her tonight, so I won't tell you about the time she tried to climb over a fence and ripped her jeans from crotch to ankle or how she painted her butt cheeks and sat on a poster paper to make a *butt*-erfly picture for school."

"Dad!"

"In her defense, the teacher did tell the class to be creative," Vicki added.

"Our daughter expressed her personality perfectly when,

at six, she dressed up as a princess carrying a scythe for Halloween."

Kenzie, who'd probably been present for most of the moments mentioned, laughed along with everyone else.

"In all seriousness, we love Becky more than words. She has been a joy. I was more than honored to give my and Vicki's blessing when Brent asked us for Becky's hand in marriage. We can't think of a better man for our beautiful daughter." He turned to the couple and held up his glass. "Here is wishing you a forever filled with happiness, love, *and children*," he emphasized, to more laughter.

After the toast, Nick glanced at Kenzie. She was wiping tears away. He hadn't thought about how hard tonight might be for her. And not just because of him. Waylon wouldn't be here to toast his daughter or walk her down the aisle. She was very careful not to look around, instead busying herself with buttering a roll.

He was glad he and Juliette eloped. Not that he wouldn't like a nice wedding, but running off to Vegas was the right choice for his less-than-a-year marriage.

Griffin's laugh drew his attention to the other side of the room. His eyes connected with Kenzie's.

He winked.

She looked away.

~

The wedding planner came into the bride's room of the church and clapped her hands. "Becky, you look lovely. You all do," she added, scanning each of Becky's attendants from head to toe. "Your dresses are perfect."

Becky had given them fifteen styles of dresses to choose from, and colors that ranged from blush to iris, and the seamstress made sure they each chose a different style and color. Kenzie was wearing a crisscross off-the-shoulder, floor-length dress in lavender haze—the most modest of the fifteen styles. She could easily adjust the hem to tea-length and wear it again.

"It's time to go outside for photos."

All eight of Becky's attendants gathered around the bride to make sure every hair was in place. Unnecessary, since she already looked stunning.

As they filed out of the room, the florist handed each a bouquet. As soon as they were outside, the photographer arranged them in different poses. Luckily, Becky and the photographer were both very laid-back about the whole thing, so the poses were fun rather than stiff and fake.

Halfway through, she noticed they had an audience of groomsmen, sans the groom. Nick looked devastatingly handsome in his soft gray tux.

When their gazes met, he winked—and her heart stuttered. Just as she did last night at the rehearsal dinner, she looked away before a smile crept free, carefully giving Becky, the photographer, and the other attendants her full attention.

They went back into the bride's room after the session to freshen up while the groom and his men took their turn in front of the camera. She stood at the window, gazing through the blurred view the gauzy sheers had to offer while thoughts of her father moved front and center.

Doug's toast to Becky and Brent last night triggered memories she'd tucked away. As he lay dying, her dad took her hand. "One regret will be not walking you down the aisle on your wedding day. I can picture you so clearly in my mind. You'll make the most beautiful bride Dove Hill has ever seen."

Kyle took their dad's other hand. "Dad, I'll put a picture of you in my breast pocket when I walk her down the aisle—if she'll have me," he added with a smile.

"Thank you, son. I sure would like to see you both married and settled in a happy life."

"We don't have to be married to be happy, Daddy," she said.

"I just wish your mother—"

"Stop, Dad," Kyle said. "Kenz and I couldn't have asked for a better parent than you. Even alone, you gave us all the tools, all the love we could ask for, or will ever need, to build happy lives."

"Kyle's right. We never needed anyone but you," Kenzie said, wiping away her tears.

Arms circled her from behind. "You seem a million miles away," Becky said. Are you thinking of your dad?"

"Just for a minute." Kenzie turned around to face her friend. "Have I told you how gorgeous you look?"

"At least twice," Becky said with a smile. "But go ahead and tell me again. You know I love attention and adoration."

Kenzie laughed, grateful Becky knew just what she needed. "You look absolutely amazing. I can't wait to see Brent's face when you walk down the aisle."

"I love this dress." Becky held out her delicately beaded skirt.

"It's perfect. Are you nervous?"

"Only in a please-don't-let-me-fall-on-my-face kind of way. I'm not suffering cold feet or having second thoughts— Golly! I hope Brent isn't either. Go check," she said, pushing Kenzie toward the door. "Make sure he's still here. Or even here in the first place. Did you see him come in?"

"He and the groomsmen are outside having their pictures taken. I'm sure one of your brothers would have come in to warn you if Brent took off."

Becky's shoulders relaxed and she heaved out a breath. "You're right. Though they can be so annoying, having brothers can come in handy every once in a while."

"You don't have to count on your brothers today. Brent is crazy about you."

"Promise me I can be a part of your wedding when the day comes."

"*If* the day comes, of course, you will. Why would you think otherwise?"

"Who knows where we'll end up once Brent finishes his residency?" She took Kenzie's hands in hers. "You are my oldest friend. I just don't want to lose touch."

"We'll never lose touch. One day you and Brent will end up back here, and we'll get together every Sunday afternoon to watch our grandchildren play in the yard and ride horses. We'll give them all the chocolate they can eat before sending them home to their parents. We'll take them to the river for holiday weekends and sing around the fire before bed. They'll laugh when we tell them we used to sing in a band together. And if I never get married, I'll be the old auntie who spoils your kids and grandkids rotten."

This time Becky laughed. "Do you promise?"

Time to be serious. Kenzie placed a hand on her heart. "I can't promise that, but I can promise that any time you visit or call or email or text, I'll be there for you."

"Pinky swear," Becky said, holding up her baby finger.

Kenzie curled her baby finger around Becky's, then they laughed and hugged tight.

"Thanks for your friendship."

"Right back at you, girlfriend," Kenzie said.

Becky hadn't lived in Dove Hill since she left for college, but Kenzie knew they would always be friends. She loved that part of living in their small town. People stayed in touch.

The wedding planner entered the room and clapped her hands again. "Okay, ladies, time to line up."

"Best wishes for a fabulous life, sweet friend," Kenzie said.

"Kenz." Becky caught her arm when she turned for the door. "Nick regrets his choices."

She opened her mouth . . . but wasn't sure how to respond.

Becky took both Kenzie's hands without making eye contact. "You might not want to hear this, but he still loves you." Becky met her gaze. "I don't think he ever stopped. You should think about giving him a second chance."

A lump tightened her throat. Had Nick talked to Becky? Did she know this for a fact, or was she just hoping? "If the tables were turned, would you?"

"Nope."

Though it was a serious moment, Becky still made her smile. "I don't think I can, Beck."

"You can if you try. We both know you're a much bigger person than I am. Just open your heart. You won't regret it."

"Kenzie, we need you," the wedding planner said.

Kenzie escaped Becky's pleading eyes.

Griffin was already in his place, waiting. He smiled down at her. "I thought you stood me up. By the way, you look gorgeous."

She pretended to straighten his tie, trying to keep her attention on Griffin. "You look pretty dapper yourself."

"I thought wedding rules stated the attendants shouldn't outshine the bride on her wedding day."

"Oh, Grif, you haven't seen your sister. She looks . . ." She waved a hand. "There are no words to describe how gorgeous she looks. She'll out-dazzle everyone in the room."

The music started, and the wedding planner opened the double doors leading into the chapel.

While Brent's sister and brother—serving as the maid of honor and best man—moved down the aisle, she and Griffin paused at the threshold. Since they were the second attendants in line, she'd have to stand at the front while Nick and then five other couples took their places before Becky appeared.

"Mama!"

Griffin chuckled. "The little munchkin spotted you."

A ripple of laughter moved through the guests as they turned toward the back as one.

"Mama!"

"If you wave, she might be appeased enough to stop," Nick said near her ear, generating a ripple of goose bumps over her shoulders and down her arms.

Kenzie raised her hand and gave a little wave, all the while wanting to elbow Nick in the gut. Hard.

After making her way up front, still determined not to look Nick's way, she searched the wedding guests for familiar faces and paused on Kyle and Jessi. She wished she was sitting next to them instead of spotlighted up front.

When the music changed, the guests stood, and Becky appeared at the door. Kenzie glanced at Brent. The overwhelming look of love on his face took her breath away. She hoped the photographer caught that moment for Becky. Her soon-to-be husband wore his feelings in plain sight for all to see.

With Becky's comment still running through her mind, she glanced at Nick, who was staring at her. Is that why he came to the ranch yesterday? Had he planned to tell her something?

She looked away, hoping everyone's attention was on the bride or groom and not on the two people up front staring at each other.

Halfway through the ceremony, London broke free of her grandma's grip and ran up the steps to Kenzie. She held up her arms. "Mama."

What could she do but pick her up? Another round of laughter erupted from the guests. Why couldn't London want her aunt to pick her up? Now that would be funny—the preacher being interrupted while Becky held her niece until Grandpa or Grandma or Nick took her. She glanced at all three, but none of them made a move to rescue her. Instead, Vicki gave her a tiny shrug and mouthed, *Sorry*.

Kenzie plastered on a smile, hoping it didn't look too fake.

London held her leg high, twisting her foot so Kenzie could see her purple shoe. "Pretty."

"They are so pretty, but we need to be really quiet so we can watch Aunt Becky get married," Kenzie whispered near London's ear.

The little cutie put a finger to her lips, hissed a loud *Shhh*, and the guests laughed again. Fortunately, Brent and Becky were getting a kick out of London's cuteness.

The photographer turned her lens their way and London waved. That wasn't the photo Becky would want. She pointed to London's aunt to discourage any more picture-taking of the two of them, while seriously considering the idea of strangling Nick when the wedding was over.

She clapped one of her hands against London's when the preacher pronounced the happy couple husband and wife. As the attendants walked back down the aisle with their partner, Griffin tried to take London, but she clung to Kenzie's neck. Nick met them at the door and peeled London away with the promise of cake at the reception. Kenzie didn't dare glare for fear the photographer would freeze the moment forever.

She waited her turn to tell her friends congratulations, then made her way back outside for more pictures. The photographer lined them up in combinations different from when they walked down the aisle. In one, Nick was right behind her.

He leaned forward. "Hey, Kenz."

She felt his breath on her neck. Without thinking, she elbowed him, rather pleased with herself when he grunted.

"What was that for?" he asked under his breath.

"What do you think?"

"Everybody, smile!" the photographer called.

Kenzie grinned.

CHAPTER 11

$\mathcal{N}$ ick took the front seat in his dad's car while his mom sat in the back with London. Griffin volunteered to drive the grandparents to the reception.

"Mama," London said pointing out the window.

Kenzie was getting into her car on the other side of the parking lot.

"I just about died of embarrassment for Kenzie during the wedding," his mom said.

"Mama," London said with a grin.

Nick glanced over the seat. "More embarrassed than at church?"

"Don't remind me," she said with a roll of her eyes. How are we going to handle this?"

"Kenzie handled the situation just fine." His dad shifted into reverse and backed out of the parking space. "L-O-N-D-O-N might make things worse if the grownups cause a ruckus."

Nick chuckled. "I'm pretty sure you don't have to spell her name yet, Dad."

"I'm just saying—"

"I think you're wrong, Doug. I don't think this little smarty pants is going to forget. She sees Kenzie and . . ." His mom shrugged. "I know she doesn't understand what the word M-A-M-A means, but for some reason, she's attached it to Kenzie. We need to think of something."

Nick didn't miss the eye-daggers his mom shot over the seat. "I can skip the reception."

"Absolutely not." His dad turned out of the parking lot. "Becky will be hurt if you don't show. Is it too late to find a babysitter?"

"Everyone we know—including babysitters—will be at the reception," his mom said.

"We'll keep an eye on her—"

"We were keeping an eye on her at the wedding and she got away from us, Doug."

"*I'll* keep an eye on her," Nick said.

His dad pulled into the parking lot of the reception center. "The adorable little ham stole the show for a moment, but Becky and Brent were cool about the whole thing. I just hope the photographer got some good pictures of London and Kenzie together. It was good of Kenz to roll with the punches."

"At some point, Kenzie is going to get very tired of being punched," his mom countered.

Nick turned in his seat as his dad parked the car. "Mom, could you please just get all *your* punches out now? I know I hurt Kenz. If I could turn back time without losing London, I'd do it in a heartbeat. I'm more than sorry. I regret my actions. I regret taking the job with Aaron in the first place. Except for London, the past three years are one huge regret."

He opened the car door, then paused. "I've apologized to Kenzie. She may never forgive me, but I'll continue apologizing because I—" He almost said he still loved her, but that would be like announcing his feelings with a bullhorn. He wasn't brave enough to show his vulnerability. "Because I'm truly sorry."

Brent and Becky didn't have assigned seating for dinner, so he chose a table on the opposite side of the room from Kenzie. Or perhaps it was she who picked the table away from him. Either way, he made sure his chair faced her. He put London in a high chair facing away from Kenzie so she wouldn't interrupt the reception too.

After dinner and toasts, Knight Rivers took the stage and the dancing began. While the bride and groom danced, he and London watched Kenzie. London picked up a spoon and mimicked her heroine's moves while still sitting in her high chair.

Next, the bride and her father danced, followed by Brent dancing with his mom. Once the floor opened to couples, he picked London up and danced around the outskirts of the floor, to her great delight. Though his daughter pointed at Kenzie and said Mama several times, she didn't yell it out like she did during the wedding.

Kenzie and the guys looked like they were having fun, and Nick wished he could join them. He missed their practices even more. They used to have lots of laughs. Touring with them had allowed him to experience a hint of the friendship they used to share and made him feel even lonelier at the same time.

Becky and Brent cut the cake, and London squealed with joy all the way back to her high chair. Even with the bib he brought, he knew she'd be a mess when she finished.

His mom, careful to stay out of reach, watched London while he went to the kitchen to beg a wet rag to wipe her down.

Kenzie walked out of the restroom at the same time he left the kitchen. He smiled, she looked toward the reception hall.

"Knight Rivers sounds great tonight."

"Thank you." Her eyes dropped to the wet rag in his hand.

"London made a huge mess with her piece of cake."

"I can imagine."

"Griffin was right earlier. You do look beautiful."

"Nick."

"What? I'm just stating a fact."

"Well, don't."

He stopped her before she could disappear into the crowded reception. "That's not the response Griffin got when he complimented you earlier."

"Thank you," she said like he was threatening to pull her nails out.

He wished he knew how to break through her barriers. Maybe it was too late. But what if it wasn't? He wasn't ready to show his vulnerability to his mom, but he wasn't too proud to try anything with Kenzie. "I'm sorry about London earlier."

Kenzie shrugged a shoulder. "It's a good thing she's so adorable."

The little pipsqueak had him—along with every other adult around—wrapped around her pinky.

"I have to get back in," she said.

He followed her through the door, pleased with their short but half-pleasant conversation.

Becky sidled up to him while he was wiping down London. "Where've you been, big brother?"

"I went to the kitchen to get—"

"And came back with Kenzie," she said with a smirk.

"Don't read anything into it. We just happened to meet in the hall, and she barely spoke to me."

"Fix this, Nick," she said pointing at his nose.

"I can't fix it if I can't get her to talk to me. But I'm open to ideas."

A wicked grin spread across his sister's face, reminding him of the bratty little kid she used to be. "I do have an idea, and if it works, you'll owe me big time—like being my personal babysitter whenever I come to town to visit, and some of your homemade caramel corn shipped to me once a month," she said, before walking away.

"You don't have any kids," he called after her.

She turned with a smile. "But I will. Possibly a dozen."

A small price to pay if you can make things happen, Sis.

London struggled to get out of her chair.

"Want to dance?"

"Yes."

"Yes, what?"

"Yes, pwease."

He leaned down to her. "Give daddy a kiss, pwease."

She puckered her little bow lips.

After a quick kiss, he lifted her out of her high chair and danced her around to more delighted giggles. She loved dancing, and could actually move to the rhythm of the music pretty well. When she squirmed to get out of his arms, he set her down but took her hands while she twisted and turned and wiggled her little fanny. After a few minutes, her Aunt Becky swooped in, picked up her niece, and danced away with her.

When the song ended, Kyle announced Knight Rivers would be taking a short break, but to give it up for The Pink Dragonflies.

This was a surprise to Nick. He didn't know Becky and Kenzie's old high school band planned to play tonight.

All the girls took their places onstage with Kenzie on the drums and Becky in front with a guitar. They started with "Pontoon" by Little Big Town, then moved to Sugarland's "Stuck Like Glue." For their third number, Jeremy took over at the drums while Kenzie and Becky ruled the stage with

Christina Aguilera and Missy Elliott's version of Rose Royce's "Car Wash."

Everyone—including both grandmas—was clapping and dancing. His dad picked up London and danced right in front of the stage. Nick wasn't sure who was having more fun, his daughter or his dad.

Their last song was Dolly Parton's "I Will Always Love You." Becky and Kenzie had voices that blended like angels and hearing them sing together after so many years sent goose bumps across the back of his neck and down his arms.

When the song ended, Becky glanced around until she spotted him, then leaned into the microphone. "Since this is my day, I have a special request. Nick, will you come up here and sing "Perfect" with Kenzie?"

He glanced at Kenzie, who showed only a moment of surprise, which disappeared as quickly as it appeared. She nodded toward him, and he walked through the crowd and climbed the stage steps.

He hugged Becky as she passed him. "It's a good thing you're leaving on your honeymoon tonight, or you might not make it out of town alive," he said in her ear.

"Because of you or her?"

"Kenz all the way. I, on the other hand, plan to bequeath you my kingdom."

Becky laughed and walked down the stairs to her waiting husband.

"Kyle, Ryder, can you come up and play for us?" Kenzie asked.

While he moved the microphone he'd be using close to Kenzie's, Kyle and Ryder came up onstage to play the guitar and keyboard for them.

They'd never sung this song together, but after yesterday he knew they'd have no problem harmonizing.

"You sing the first verse and I'll come in on the second," she said to him.

"Okay."

He nodded to Ryder, who played the first few notes before Kyle joined in.

Becky and Brent danced in front of the stage. Though others joined in, they let the newlyweds have the spotlight. Most guests watched the bride and groom, but a few eyes were riveted on the stage where he and Kenzie stood close together while they sang.

His mom wiped away tears while she danced with his dad, London between them.

The song ended, and she smiled at him.

~

"*D*ance with me."

Kenzie turned to look at the hand Nick held out. "That sounds more like a demand than a request."

"It was actually a question."

"I guess I missed the question mark."

"Will you please dance with me? See there, I added a please *and* a question mark."

Knight Rivers had been back on the road for a week since the wedding. After their concert in Palm Beach, Florida tonight, they'd crossed the street to a dance club. Tomorrow they were going to hit the beach before heading to Miami for a concert at a big street festival. The weather was hot, and the air heavy with humidity, so a little water time would be refreshing.

Nick took her hand. "I'll take your non-answer as a yes."

She stood, trying hard to convince herself it was just his

hand, skin on skin, no big deal, and let him lead her to the dance floor.

She hadn't forgiven Nick, but they were talking more like they used to before they started dating. Friends—yes, while singing with him at Becky's wedding, she'd decided they could be friends.

When she walked in tonight, she noticed him sitting with Jeremy and Kyle. He usually joined their after-concert decompressions about once a week, but since the wedding, he'd been showing up more often.

If Ryder hadn't decided to take a swim in the hotel pool instead, she'd already be dancing with him, which would save her the jittery anxiety that twisted her stomach now.

Nick was always jealous of Ryder's ability to dance. But being in Ryder's arms didn't evoke the emotions she felt when she was anywhere near Nick. Though most people who watched them dance thought she and Ryder were a couple, they'd never felt anything but friendship for each other.

Nick took her in his arms but kept a safe distance between them.

When he turned her, she noticed Jeff sitting with a man she hadn't met yet, but who'd been spending a lot of time with the members of Aaron's band during the past week.

What caught your attention?" Nick asked.

"Jeff Davidson."

"Do you know much about Jeff?"

She glanced up at him. She'd missed this view, being eye level with his Adam's apple. "I don't know anything about him. He keeps to himself most of the time."

Nick nodded like she'd confirmed something for him.

"Do you know who he's with?" she asked.

"He introduced him to Aaron as a relative, but I wasn't paying enough attention to remember."

Jeff and the man stood. She glanced at Kyle, who turned in his chair to watch both men walk out of the club.

Nick turned her again, and she noticed the man who was usually wearing a press badge sitting at the bar. He nodded.

"Kenz, I'm not an enemy."

"I never said you were."

"You treat me like I am."

She didn't like where this conversation was headed. "I didn't realize I was treating you as anything but Knight Rivers' manager."

"Actually, you look through me like I don't exist most of the time."

Defense mechanism. "Sorry. I have a hard time acting like the past didn't happen. I'll try to be friendlier."

"Then you'd be fake."

"How should I act, Nick?" she asked, noticing the sharpness in her tone.

"Normal."

"Under the circumstances, this is normal."

"I'm sorry about what happened, Kenz."

"You say that like you had no control over the circumstances, but you did."

He turned her again. "I'm one hundred percent responsible, and I'm sorry."

"Oh, well, if you're sorry, then I guess everything's okay."

"I'm trying to apologize to you Kenz. Again. I messed up, and I am truly sorry. Can't we get past this?"

"I'm not sure I can. What you did—"

"If memory serves, I walked in on a pretty heated kiss between you and Jeremy."

She looked up at him, incredulous that he would compare that kiss to what he'd done. "My dad had just died, and *you weren't there.*" She stepped out of his arms and drove her index finger into his chest. "I needed you"—she sucked in a shaky breath, on the verge of tears—"and you weren't there."

She narrowed her eyes at him. "Not that it mattered. Your girlfriend was already pregnant."

He dropped his chin to his chest. "I wish I could erase what happened, but I can't." He looked into her eyes. "And I know there's nothing I can do to make that up to you, but can we at least go someplace and talk? Just talk."

"About what?"

"Let me try to expla—"

"Do you really think I want to discuss you and your ex-wife? I'm here for the band and nothing else. When this tour is over, I don't have to see you ever again. Then you can quit worrying about me acting like you don't exist."

CHAPTER 12

*K*enzie stalked off the dance floor, not quite sure where to go. If she went back to her hotel room, some of the band members would follow. And she couldn't go to their table because they'd start badgering her with questions, so she headed for the bar.

The press-pass man who'd been watching cocked his head when she stopped next to him. "Looks like you could use a drink."

"I'd rather you ask me to dance."

He chuckled and rubbed the back of his neck. "I'm not much of a dancer. Two left feet."

"You can't wrap an arm around me and sway to the music?"

He set his glass down and slid off the barstool. "I can try."

She put a hand on his chest to stop him. "Are you married?"

"Nope."

"Are you dating someone? Have a serious girlfriend?"

"Nope."

She took his hand and led him to the dance floor.

"I just want to be very clear. I can't do what you and that guy from your band do."

"Nobody can dance like Ryder."

"I can't even do what you and Nick were just doing."

She looked at him in surprise. "You know Nick?"

"I know his name and that he manages Aaron Vance's band."

"Do you need me to lead?"

"If we're doing more than swaying, you'll have to. By the way, I'm Travis Sprenger."

"It's nice to meet you, Travis. I'm Kenzie Rivers," she said shaking his extended hand. "I've seen you backstage at a couple of Aaron's concerts with a press pass."

She placed the hand she held on her waist and took his other hand in hers.

"Sorry."

"For what?"

"For stepping on your toes."

Kenzie smiled. "We haven't started dancing yet."

"No, but I will when we do."

She started moving, and he looked down at his feet and shuffled along.

"Don't look down," she said, touching his chin. "Look at me."

"Not a hardship."

She spotted Nick watching and turned them so he was out of her line of sight.

"Uh," he stammered looking down at his feet. "I'm not sure I should be talking, dancing, and turning at the same time."

"You're doing fine." She'd never met a guy who was so uncomfortable on a dance floor. "Do you write for a specific publication, or are you freelance?"

"Oops. Sorry. Can't say I didn't warn you." He glanced down after he kicked her foot.

She lifted his chin again. "Eyes here," she said pointing two fingers at his eyes, then hers. "Publication or freelance?"

"Both. I'm doing an article about Aaron Vance for *Rolling Stone*."

"That's impressive."

"Is it?"

"I think so." She could write music from sunup to sundown, but couldn't imagine writing an article for a magazine that millions of people would read. "Are you focused on a specific topic or Aaron in general?"

"Specifically, what's it's like to already have a leg up."

"Really?" Kenzie knew her shock showed because he laughed.

"No, but I should."

He had a nice laugh and a unique color of amber-yellow eyes that reminded her of a wolf. "You're going to leave me wondering?"

"I'll let you read the article, but I'll warn you against it if you're really close to Aaron."

"Why? Are you going to be mean?"

"Truthful. I heard you two wrote a song together."

The music stopped and so did they. "He wrote a song with lyrics I refused to sing, so I rewrote most of the words to fit his music."

"Lyrics you refused to sing?"

"I changed his R rating to sweet PG."

"Ah." He nodded toward the bar. "How about that drink I offered earlier?"

"Sure." She could tell he wasn't comfortable dancing, but she was enjoying their conversation.

"I'm also submitting a review of Knight Rivers."

"I don't read reviews."

He raised both brows. "You'll like this one."

"I don't read reviews," she repeated.

"What'll you have?" the bartender asked when they stepped up.

Travis nodded toward her.

"Ginger ale, please."

"And I'll have a beer," Travis said.

Kenzie chanced a glance at her brother. He, Jeremy, and Nick were all seated at a table watching.

"Seems your brother and friends are nervous about you talking to me."

"Just protective."

He picked up their drinks and led her to a table away from watchful eyes. "How did you get started singing with Knight Rivers?"

"I'm not answering any of your questions." She took a seat and then a sip of her drink.

He honestly looked surprised. "Why?"

"I don't want to be misquoted."

"Kenzie, I'm not a reporter, I'm a journalist."

"There's a difference?"

"Reporters tend to have a narrower scope than a journalist. I have time to do a little more fact-checking. And I've checked a few facts about you."

She held up a hand, afraid to know what he might be referring to. Probably the drama between her and Nick. "I'm still not answering any questions."

"How am I supposed to get to know you if you won't answer any questions?"

"You could ask about my favorite food."

"Okay." He sat back in his chair. "What's your favorite food?"

"Anything that tastes good."

He chuckled. "Chinese or Italian?"

"Oh," she moaned, crossing her arms on the table. "You ask really hard questions. I'm going with Chinese. No, Italian. But I love Chinese. And Mexican. Ask me something easier."

He laughed out loud. "That's the question you wanted me to ask. Okay, favorite band."

"Easy. Knight Rivers."

"Besides Knight Rivers."

She swirled the liquid around in her glass. "Too many to narrow down to just one. Come up with an easier question."

Travis shook his head. "Would you rather be writing or singing songs?"

"Writing."

He raised his brows again. "You don't like singing?"

"Writing."

He chuckled again. "Okay. How do you like touring with Aaron Vance?"

She took a last sip of her drink and stood. "Thank you for the dance and the drink, but I'm going to leave you here regretting your lack of judgment for asking that last question."

"Wait." He stood. "I was asking out of curiosity, not for an article."

"Good night, Travis."

"Would you let me take you to dinner sometime?"

She waved over her shoulder before walking away.

~

*N*ick didn't think Kenzie would talk to a reporter knowingly, but had Travis been up-front enough to tell her who he was? Most reporters didn't, at least not right away. Especially when they were angling for a story.

Kenzie would never forgive him if he kept bringing up

that stupid kiss between her and Jeremy. He knew nothing happened, so why did it still bother him so much? Especially after what he'd done.

Pleased when Kenzie pushed back from the table and stood, Nick still felt a jolt of jealousy ricochet through his body when she grinned down at the guy.

"Does Kenzie know Travis is a reporter?" Kyle asked.

Nick turned toward Kyle and Jeremy. "I'm sure she's seen the press badge he wears around his neck."

"You didn't tell her?"

"Kyle, I introduced Travis to you so *you* could tell her."

"As manager for Knight Rivers, you should have told her she couldn't talk to him," Jeremy said.

Nick laughed. "I don't think so. I learned *not* to tell Kenzie who she can and can't talk to during a jealous moment a couple of years ago, Jer."

Jeremy stood. "Well, I can tell him not to talk to her."

Nick and Kyle followed him to the table. Travis glanced up with a grin. "Hey, guys. I'm surprised it took you so long to get over here."

"Jeremy Knight, this is Travis Sprenger."

"Ah, the Knight of Knight Rivers. You're a talented man, Jeremy." Travis nodded toward the empty chairs at his table. "Would you like to join me?"

Jeremy folded his long body into a chair. "Does Kenzie know you're a reporter?"

"I'm not a reporter. I'm a journalist," Travis said in a tone that told Nick he explained that a lot. "I'm doing a story for *Rolling Stone*. I don't work for tabloids, so I'm not into stretching the truth or fabricating stories to sell more magazines. I asked her one question, which she refused to answer. After I asked the second question, she left."

Jeremy drummed the table. "What did you ask her?"

"How she got started with the band. Just a simple getting-to-know-you question. I had no intention of printing her answer."

"I told you I'd set up an interview with Kenzie when Kyle could be there," Nick said.

"I wasn't interviewing. I was sitting at the bar having a drink, and she came up and asked me to dance." Travis smirked. "After she left you on the dance floor. Alone."

"The same way she left you sitting here. Alone," Nick said.

Travis gave Nick a salute. "Touché."

"Ha! I like this guy," Jeremy said, resting a hand on Travis's shoulder. "Let me buy you a drink."

"Let me ask you some questions," Travis countered.

Jeremy glanced at Nick, and Nick shrugged. Kyle and Jeremy were big boys. They could take care of themselves. In truth, Kenzie could take care of herself, too. He just worried she might say something that would hurt her writing career. Aaron could be vindictive when he wanted. "Ask away."

Nick leaned back in his chair and listened while Jeremy and Kyle answered questions about how the band got started. Travis looked at him when they revealed Nick was one of the original members. "Why'd you quit?"

"I started playing for Aaron's band."

"Are you sorry?"

Nick looked at his two oldest friends. A wall of his making stood between them now. Though crumbling, it would stand until Kenzie knocked it down. Which wasn't looking so good after tonight. He needed to remember to enter the fight zone as a docile sheep, rather than a raging wolverine.

"Sometimes."

"Is that why you agreed to be their manager for this tour?"

"No. I offered because they're friends, and I knew they'd

need a manager who wouldn't charge them more than they'd make on the road."

"We knew we could trust him," Jeremy said.

The comment shocked Nick. Maybe the wall had more missing bricks than he realized.

~

*K*enzie spent a long, sleepless night being mad at herself for getting mad at Nick.

She hated what he'd done to their relationship, but she could see the honesty of his apology in his blue eyes.

Plus her negativity and anger were eating her up inside. She kept thinking that if her dad was alive, he'd tell her to let the toxic emotions go. Had he done that with his feelings for her mom—just let it all go? He'd seemed sad at times, but never angry.

She wished he was here to talk her through this confusing time. A time she thought she would never face. Never in a million years did she think Nick would come back or be divorced. She wanted to forgive him. Every time she thought she could, she remembered how badly she'd needed him during her dad's illness, but he'd been with someone else. And that someone else had given him a child.

Adorable London.

She and Nick had talked about having children. She wanted four. He said three. She'd argued that their family would be lopsided. He said okay, two. She said she'd find someone else to marry.

He'd hooked an arm around her neck and pulled her close. "Wrong, sweet pea. It's you and me all the way."

In the wee hours of the morning, she finally sat up, grabbed her laptop, and search for sites about forgiveness until she came across one that suggested seven steps.

The first step was acknowledging the hurt—which she'd done a gazillion times over the past three-plus years.

Number two was to consider how she'd been affected by the negative feelings acquired since the incident. She'd also accomplished that one by realizing she didn't like the person she'd become, but to be thorough, she made a *long* list.

Step three said to accept that she couldn't change the past. Her anger toward Nick wouldn't change or redeem what he'd done. He'd apologized more than once—which was all he could do.

In the fourth step, she had to determine whether she could forgive him. After much thought, she realized her answer was yes. She wanted—No—she *needed* this is order to restore her capacity for joy.

Step five advised repairing—not restoring—her relationship with Nick. Suggested acts of repairing were kind words and simple gestures.

Number six, learn what forgiveness would mean to her. She decided on possible closure and a lighter heart for starters.

And step number seven was to forgive, which maybe she'd already done. She just didn't want to admit it to herself. Or Nick.

That vindictiveness had to go.

Morning arrived too soon, and Knight Rivers hit the beach. They usually reserved their relaxing times for after a concert, but who could visit beautiful Palm Beach, Florida without a trip to the ocean? Kenzie spread a towel and lay soaking up the sun while the guys grabbed boogie boards and a football.

Even Raymond, their bus driver, joined in the fun. Only Jeff stayed behind with the excuse that he didn't feel well. She could tell Kyle and Jeremy didn't believe him. Kenzie was surprised they were keeping Jeff with the band if they suspected he was dealing with drugs. Knight Rivers had always maintained a no-tolerance policy.

A shadow fell over her and she opened an eye. Nick stood above her.

"You're not going swimming?"

She took a deep breath, determined to follow through with the seven-step plan. "Eventually. Aren't you supposed to be on your way to Miami?"

He sat down on her quilt, so she scooted over, reminding herself to be nice.

"Aaron is, but Kyle said I can catch a ride with Knight Rivers."

She'd have to remind Kyle to give her a heads-up from now on when there was a change of plans.

"I wanted to talk to you about Trav—"

"Stop."

"I just want—"

"I know he's a journalist, and I know he wants a story. He's not going to trick me into telling him something I don't want him to know, *but* if I did want to talk to him, there's nothing you could say that would stop me." *Be nice.* "Thank you for your concern, though."

Nick pulled his T-shirt over his head and lay back. "Fair enough. As long as you're aware."

"I don't remember inviting you onto my quilt," she said, as sweetly as possible, trying to keep her eyes above his chin. Or maybe his neck. Okay, his shoulders were fair game.

"I forgot to bring a towel, and I don't want to lie on the sand. You've got more space than you need. Plus, I like the smell of your . . . fabric softener. Suntan lotion with a hint of citrus."

Why did his almost-slip make her smile? The forgiveness stuff conjured feelings she didn't want to deal with. Being mad at him was easier.

"You're smiling."

"Shut up." She stood up and walked down to the water, which was warm. At hip depth, she let the waves splash over her, knocking her back a step or two with each surge.

A big ship crept south along the horizon. From here, she couldn't tell if it was passenger or freight. She took a moment to wonder where the boat might be going. Somewhere colorful? Or just moving freight from one port to another? Perhaps it was a cruise ship, carrying a few honeymooning couples to a fun location.

She'd always wanted to take a cruise to some exotic, faraway place, but she knew once she got there she'd only want to be home again. Back in her little house writing music while the horses grazed in green pastures.

Looking down the beach, she watched the guys throwing the football, diving into the waves to catch it, laughing and shouting good-natured insults.

"The ocean always makes me feel small and insignificant."

She didn't need to turn to know Nick was right behind her. The Marshall family always spent a week on the Florida Gulf Coast every summer. She'd gone with Becky twice before she and Nick started dating. They spent hours on the beach, walking the shoreline, ogling the cute boys, and giggling over the six-packs those boys liked to show off.

"The ocean makes me feel free. Makes me want to give thanks for the things I take for granted." She turned to him and skimmed her hand through the water, so clear she could see the bottom. Nick was close enough she could see the navy that ringed the outside of his blue-blue iris. "Like the soft sand, the warm sun on my skin. Friends," she added after a pause.

Nick's mouth quirked up on one side right before his eyes widened. Suddenly she was hit from behind by a truck. She tried to gulp air before her feet were swept out from under her, and she tumbled like a rag doll, scraping both knees on the sand she just said was so soft.

An arm wrapped around her middle and lifted her up. She coughed and sputtered and opened her eyes to find she was nose-to-nose with Nick. "You could have warned me," she wheezed out.

"Ah, but this is so much more fun."

She lifted one knee to see the damage right before another wave hit, strong enough to push her hard against him. She grabbed his shoulders as he struggled to stay upright.

Once he got them both on firm sand, he grinned. "It wasn't the fabric softener that smells so good after all."

With his arm still around her, Nick's gaze dropped to her mouth.

"You're awful."

"Yes, I am. And you're smiling again."

"Shut up."

CHAPTER 13

*T*he week passed quickly with concerts every night. Kenzie kept a journal and noted each place they visited with a few pictures of the venue and a favorite moment—spotting a fan in the audience singing along or a young girl with the promise of possibilities shining in her eyes.

Things were changing between her and Nick. She caught him watching her, but only because she was watching him. They didn't talk much, but he seemed to be around Knight Rivers more often. Even Jeremy seemed more accepting of Nick's company.

Coming off the stage at a Mississippi Fair, she smiled at the man standing backstage. "Hi, Travis Sprenger."

"Hi yourself, Kenzie Rivers. Great performance."

"Thank you." She pulled her guitar strap over her head and settled the instrument in the case one of the stage crew handed her. "What brings you to the great state of Mississippi?"

"Besides writing a story for *Rolling Stone*, I'm visiting my parents."

That news astonished her, though why she wasn't sure. She knew nothing about Travis. "How are you from Mississippi? You don't have an accent."

"I haven't lived in the South since I graduated from high school."

"How's the *Rolling Stone* article coming?"

"I actually got to interview Aaron this afternoon."

"So, you must be wrapping things up."

"Close." Travis pushed away from the wall he was standing against. "I hoped you might like to take a walk around the fair."

Kenzie loved fairs. While they were singing, she'd watched the Ferris wheel in the distance. She loved the music and the barkers and the animals. "I'd love to."

"Hey, sweet pea, I thought you were coming with us," Jeremy said, narrowing his eyes at Travis.

"I'm sure we'll run into each other during the evening," Kenzie replied, patting Jeremy's chest. Sometimes he could be a little overly protective. She and Travis would be surrounded by people at the fair.

When she loaded her guitar on the instrument cart, she noticed Nick standing behind Jeremy, hands on hips, staring at her. She turned away. "See you guys later."

Kyle pulled her aside from the others. "You need to be careful, baby girl."

"I'll be very careful and stay in well-lit areas, big brother."

After they walked away, she felt Travis's gaze on her and glanced over. "What?"

"I didn't expect you to say yes."

"Want me to say no?"

"No. I like that you agreed. I just didn't expect it." They'd reached the Midway. "What would you like to do first?"

"Let's go see the animals." She could tell by his raised brows that looking at animals wasn't what he had in mind when inviting her to the fair. She tugged him toward the barns. "I promise you'll love them."

"I doubt that."

"When Kyle and I were little, we always started with the animals first. I loved the goats and rabbits, Kyle always wanted to see the horses and pigs."

As soon as she entered, a longing for home settled over her. She loved seeing the country, but Dove Hill was always calling to her in the background. Tomorrow they would start week eight of sixteen in New Orleans. Eight more weeks, and then she could go home for good. She loved going home for Becky's wedding. The break had been a nice reprieve, but touring hadn't been bad so far either.

She looked over a metal fence. "Isn't he beautiful?"

Travis leaned past her shoulder. "He's a black sheep. Literally."

She squatted down and made a sound. The sheep walked over to her and bleated loudly. Travis laughed. "Do you still think he's beautiful?"

"Don't you like animals?" she asked.

"Cats and dogs, yes. I guess your love comes from growing up on a ranch."

She glanced up at him. "You've been doing your homework."

"I had to. You wouldn't answer my questions. Even after that, I didn't discover a whole lot. I know you grew up on a horse ranch in Tennessee. Besides the guitar, you play the drums and keyboard. You've won several awards for songs you've written, and you're eleven years younger than I am. Now I can add that you like black sheep."

"You *have* done your homework." She let herself into a pen across the aisle where baby goats were jumping around. Picking up an adorable one, she carried it over to the gate. "Look at this cute little guy."

Travis tipped his head, looking at the goat. "Are you sure it's a guy?"

"Positive."

He laughed. "I'll have to take your word for it."

As they wandered up and down the aisles, she stopped at different pens every few yards, Travis asked her questions about her childhood, careful to stay on safe ground, so she answered.

"I read your dad's obituary from three years ago. I'm sorry."

"Thanks." A little melancholy crept through the fissures that remained open. "My dad loved music and encouraged us to play. He didn't push, just offered opportunities to develop things that interested us. Kyle and I wouldn't be here without him."

"What about your mom?"

"When I was four, she decided she didn't want to be a wife or mother and left."

"Sorry. Again."

"We did okay. My dad raised us with tons of love." She rested her forearms on the top rail of a pen and wiggled her fingers, hoping the pony inside would come over to her.

"Do you know where your mom is?"

"Nope." She decided to shift the conversation onto him. "Tell me about your family, Travis. Do they live in Brandon?"

He mimicked her position so their elbows touched. "Less than an hour west in Vicksburg."

"You grew up on the Louisiana-Mississippi border."

"I did."

"Tell me more."

"My parents just celebrated their fortieth wedding anniversary, and still live in the same house I grew up in. My fraternal grandparents live down the street. My maternal grandparents are in Florida. I have a married sister who settled in Atlanta and a married brother living in St. Louis. Both have three kids."

Kenzie was surprised he'd offered so much information. Maybe it was the journalist in him—get as much info out as possible with few words. "Have you ever been married?"

"And divorced. My wife decided she liked my best friend better."

She glanced at him. "Ouch. Sorry."

"It was a long time ago."

"Do you have any children?"

"No kids."

Kenzie turned toward him. "Said wistfully. Do you hope to have kids?"

"Maybe. Someday. I'm not sure I'm cut out to be a dad. I have six nieces and nephews that I can spoil when the mood strikes." He looked down at his boots. "I enjoying traveling too much to settle down permanently. I like being in a new city every couple of days."

"Really?"

"Said like you think I'm crazy. Don't you like traveling?"

"I can't wait—" She glanced at him and mimed pulling a zipper across her lips.

He laughed. "Sorry. I didn't mean to step over the line with my simple travel question."

"Let's circle the conversation back to you. Do you have a home base?"

"Los Angeles."

"Oh, wow, you're a long way from home. How did you end up on the West Coast?"

"I attended UCLA and never left."

"You must like it."

"I do. You can't beat the weather." He pointed toward the door. "Ready for some fresh air?"

It was her turn to laugh as he led her outside. "Did the

smell get to you?"

Travis took an exaggerated breath. "From the moment we walked in there."

Animals were definitely not his thing.

"Are you hungry?" he asked.

"Starving."

They passed numerous choices, from deep-fried turkey legs to tacos on a stick to bacon-wrapped corn on the cob.

"How about some waffle fry nachos?"

"Sounds like a perfectly balanced, nutritional meal to me," she said. "And some strawberry lemonade."

"Lemonade for you, beer for me."

After they got their food and drinks, Travis found an available picnic table not too far away, where they shared the nachos.

"What made you want to be a journalist?"

"My grandfather was editor of the paper in Vicksburg. My brother, sister, and I worked there through high school. Guess it's in our blood. My sister and brother both work for magazines, and my mom is a freelance editor."

"Did you ever consider doing something else?"

"Sure, I wanted to be a cowboy, but I didn't have a horse. Then I thought superhero, but I don't have the legs for tights."

Kenzie enjoyed his easy sense of humor.

"Still hungry?" he asked after they polished off the nachos.

"No, but I have to try that pizza on a stick. Want to share one with me?"

"Anything that comes on a stick has to be great, right?"

She tipped her head. "Do I detect a hint of sarcasm?"

"Sarcasm from me? Never." He stood. "You wait here, and I'll get that pizza on a stick. Want more strawberry lemonade?"

"Water, please."

Kenzie looked around. People-watching was a favorite pastime. A little girl tugged her mom's hand while pointing at a game with Kewpie dolls as prizes. A little boy sitting on his dad's shoulders flashed a toothless grin. "Barbeque Stain" by Tim McGraw popped into her mind—the perfect county fair song.

When a group of teenagers walked past, memories collided with real life. How many times had she gone to fairs with her dad, a group of friends, or Nick? Too many times to count.

After their pizza on a stick, they made their way down the brightly lit midway, waving off the carnival barkers. Travis stopped in front of a ticket booth.

"How about a ride on the Ferris wheel?"

"Yes, please."

While he waited in line, she bought a bag of cotton candy. A pinch of the fluffy confection melted on her tongue and she closed her eyes and savored the sugary sweetness.

"You look like you're experiencing nirvana."

"Total bliss." She opened her eyes and held out the pink cloud for him to taste.

"No, thanks. I can't eat that stuff," he said.

She stared at him while he led her to the line for the Ferris wheel.

"What?" he asked.

"Not eating cotton candy is just . . . wrong. It's un-American. You can't go to a festival or fair and not eat cotton candy."

Kenzie noticed Jeff walking with the man who was supposedly a relative and another she didn't recognize. He seemed agitated and was gesturing wildly.

Travis laughed. "I've been to many fairs and festivals, and I'm very American, but just the thought of cotton candy makes my teeth ache."

"Un-American," she muttered, as they climbed aboard the ride.

"Very American," he muttered back, resting his arm along the back of the seat.

When they lifted into the air, she spotted Nick buying a bag of cotton candy. They used to get sick on the stuff when they were together. He turned and their gazes locked.

He didn't smile, just watched while she and Travis rose into the air. She stared at him until the Ferris wheel went all the way to the top and he was lost from sight. When they started back down, Jeff was standing with him. Nick pulled something out of his front pocket and handed it to Jeff. Jeff did the same, handing something to Nick.

For a split second her heart stopped, then she shook her head at her silliness. Nick would never do drugs. Their exchange had to be about something else.

Travis asked a question about the horses on the ranch. She answered as they circled around to the top. When they came back down, Nick and Jeff were gone.

At the top again, she looked out over the fairgrounds, listening to the sounds of the midway while scanning for Nick's dark hair.

How ironic. She was at a fair—something she looked forward to every year—with a nice man, and she was searching for Nick.

~

*K*enzie walked to the front of the bus and sat next to Kyle on one of the bench seats and looked out the window at the passing landscape.

"What's up, baby girl?" Kyle asked.

"Did you spend much time at the fair last night?"

"Not much. Did you have fun with Travis?"

"Don't worry. I didn't give him any information he hadn't already looked up online." She glanced from the scenery to him. "Except about Mom. When he asked about her, I told him she left when we were young."

"I don't see any harm in that," Kyle said, lifting a shoulder. "Do you like him?"

"Sure, but not the way you mean. He's nice, but I'm not interested."

"Why?"

"First of all, I barely know the guy, and second, he lives in California. I live in Tennessee. I'm pretty sure neither of us has any intention of relocating."

"I don't know, it might be kind of nice to have a journalist in the family."

"Oh, my gosh, Kyle, we didn't buy a house together. We went to a fair."

"I met Jessi at a fair."

Kenzie laughed. "You did not. You met her at the McCarthy's barbecue."

"Which is like a fair."

Kenzie rolled her eyes. "I came up here to tell you I saw Jeff last night. He was with a guy from the dance club a few nights before and another man."

"Yeah, I saw him too. Jeff introduced the one man as a distant cousin."

She leaned forward. When she came to the front of the bus, she'd noticed Jeff slumped in a seat chair in the back salon, baseball hat pulled over his eyes. "Do you think he's trying to get a job on Aaron's band?"

"If he wants to go, I won't stop him."

"What aren't you telling me?" she asked, studying his face.

"Nothing."

"Kyle, I know when you're keeping something from me."

He looked her in the eye. "Let it go, Kenzie. Everything's fine."

Everything wasn't fine. She could hear it in her brother's voice, see it on his face. Not only was everything *not* fine, but the situation seemed serious. "I also saw him with Nick. They exchanged something small. Something really small . . . like money for a little baggie of drugs."

Kyle glanced across the bus at Jeremy, who was wearing headphones while reading a book. "It's none of our business."

"It's none of our business if Jeff is dealing and our band's manager is a junkie?"

Kyle snorted. "Nick is not a junkie."

"But it's okay if Jeff is dealing," she said, adding as much sarcasm as possible.

"It's none of our business," he repeated.

"How can you say that? If Jeff's got drugs in his luggage and the police pull the bus over, we all go to jail. Is that when *it* becomes our business?"

"Kenz," Kyle said, his voice hard. "Let it go."

"Have you lost your mind?" She fell back against the cushions. This was so unlike her brother. "This is serious, Kyle."

She tried to get Jeremy to look this way by staring. He didn't. *Come on, Jer, look over here.*

"Quit trying to telepathically send Jeremy an I-need-help message."

She stared harder.

"Do you trust me, Kenz?"

This was Kyle, who at eight years old, got up every morning and helped her get breakfast, who packed her lunch, who taught her how to make a bed and load the dishwasher. She trusted him with her life. "You know I do. More than anyone."

"Then trust me now." He took her hand and squeezed.

"Everything is going to be okay."

She glanced across at Jeremy. *Oh, sure, now he looks over.*

"Do you know what's going on?" she asked him.

He lifted one side of his headphones and glanced between her and Kyle. "What?"

Again, there had to be a song in this situation. Kyle wanted new material before the tour was over. She'd give him new material. She pushed up out of her seat and headed to her bedroom, where she kept her notebook and pencil. Ryder was stretched out on her bed, so she sat beside him and started jotting down words like betrayal and misplaced trust.

"What inspired this one?" Ryder asked, his eyes closed.

"A brother."

"My brother inspires all kinds of phrases, but they wouldn't be something I could sing aloud."

"Tripp is a sweetheart."

Ryder snorted. "Sweetheart. You must be talking about someone else's brother."

He jumped when she pinched his side. "Yeow!"

"Be nice," she said.

"No pinching, Kenz." He rubbed his side. "That hurt."

"Quit being a baby. I barely squeezed that flab."

"Flab?" Ryder yanked up his T-shirt and flexed his abs. "There's not an ounce of flab here, baby. That's pure muscle. You can touch if you want."

"I think I'll pass," Kenzie said. "I have to go somewhere else to write. You're interrupting me." She climbed off the bed.

"I was here first," he mumbled, closing his eyes.

"On my bed."

"It was closer than mine. Hey! Save me a dance later tonight," he said when she reached the door.

"Always."

CHAPTER 14

*N*ick followed one of Aaron's band members into a bar down the street from the hotel. It was dark and seedy, and a place where not many would recognize the country singer. Aaron sat in a corner booth with three women, all vying for his attention. At least he'd given up on Kenzie. He was so used to women falling all over him that when she didn't, he lost interest—but that took him longer than normal.

Aaron told Nick he didn't want Kenzie onstage with him anymore—right before Knight Rivers performed tonight. Nick suspected the real reason for this decision had to do with the hoots and hollers Kenzie received when she left the stage each night. Kenzie did a little happy dance when Nick broke the news.

Nick took a seat at the bar, where he could watch what was going on in the mirror behind the bartender.

Jeff walked in and noticed Nick. He lifted a brow in question. Nick shook his head. He had the gram he bought last night tucked deep in his pants pocket.

Aaron's band members were sitting nearby with a few women of their own. They weren't the same guys Nick had played with. Those men had been fired and replaced, one by one, as Aaron Vance's popularity grew and more experienced guitarists and drummers came calling. Nick expected to be replaced as soon as the tour was over, if not before. And he was completely okay with that. More than okay. He'd had about enough of Aaron's privileged expectations. Having an uncle in the business made Aaron think he could skip even more rites of passage than he'd already floated over.

Seemed obvious Aaron was tired of Nick telling him no or contradicting him, so they'd part ways amicably. Or not. He'd have to wait and see how things played out.

Nick watched Jeff pull a couple of clear baggies out of his jeans pocket and pass them around before money changed hands.

Nick placed a few bills on the bar and slid off the stool. Time to find more pleasant company. Since he couldn't seem to go five minutes without thinking about Kenzie, he went looking and found her dancing with Ryder. He took a place at the bar and, again, watched via the mirror behind the bartender.

They danced to Maroon 5's "Girls Like You." The two of them could make any song look fun to dance to. They moved on to "Down at the Twist and Shout" by Mary Chapin Carpenter, followed by LANCO's "Greatest Love Story."

What did it say about him that he was keeping such close tabs? Luckily, the mirror behind the bar gave him the perfect opportunity to watch without anyone knowing. Except Kenzie, whose eyes met his several times.

Though she'd put up a good fight, her feelings toward him were changing.

Or maybe he didn't have a clue. Just weeks ago, she said she hated him.

The music changed to "In Case You Didn't Know" by Brett Young, and Ryder pulled Kenzie close. Too close. In the mirror, their eyes met, then she looked away, only to meet his gaze again moments later.

Kyle took the stool next to his. "Hey."

"Hey, yourself."

"What's going on?"

"Nothing new," Nick said, swirling his drink around in his glass.

"No?"

Nick shook his head. "Nope."

"Hi, guys," Kenzie said, sliding onto the stool next to Kyle.

"Did Ryder finally find another dance partner?" Kyle asked.

"You know him. He's been using me to pick up girls since we were teenagers. Ginger ale, please," she said when the bartender stopped in front of her.

Kenzie turned on her stool. "The blonde he's dancing with has been eyeing him since he walked in the door."

"Too bad she won't last long," Nick said, deciding to get into the conversation. "She can't follow his lead."

"He doesn't need to find someone so far from home anyway." Kenzie smiled at the bartender when he set her drink down next to her elbow. "There are plenty of good dancers in Tennessee, he just hasn't found the right one yet."

Kyle slung his arm around her shoulders. "My sister, always looking for a happy ending."

"Nothing wrong with that. You found yours. So did Bodhi," Kenzie said.

Nick assumed she was referring to Bodhi's onstage proposal to his girlfriend tonight.

"Ryder deserves the same," she added.

"True. And on that note, I'm going to bed." Kyle set some

bills on the bar. "For all three drinks," he said to the bartender, gesturing to Nick and Kenzie.

"Thanks, Kyle."

"Yeah, thanks, big brother," Kenzie added.

After Kyle left, Nick slid over next to Kenzie. "So, I haven't talked to you for a few days. How are you?"

"Good. How many more weeks are left?"

"Too many." He wanted to go home as badly as Kenzie. He missed his daughter, and talking to her over the phone just wasn't cutting it anymore.

She turned to him. "I bet it's hard being away from London."

"It is. We had a lot of fun when I went home last week, but three days aren't enough. I'm looking forward to seeing her again tomorrow."

"Another trip home?" she asked, centering her ginger ale on the napkin the bartender provided.

He nodded.

"Now that you're managing, you plan to stay home more?"

"Yeah. I'll hire someone else to do the traveling. I'm ready to settle London in one place."

"In Nashville?"

He noted her curiosity while she tried not to let it show. And he liked that she felt comfortable enough to ask questions. Though their conversation still felt a little stilted, at least they were talking. "No, somewhere closer to Dove Hill. I want London to grow up near my parents."

"What about Juliette's family?"

Two weeks ago, she said she didn't want to discuss his ex-wife. Now, she was bringing Juliette into their conversation. "I'm embarrassed to admit I don't know much about them. Juliette said her parents were older and not interested in grandchildren. She told me they live in Rhode Island, and she's an only child, so London doesn't have any aunts or uncles on that side."

"I guess you didn't spend much time talking about family."

Nick noticed the change in her tone, so he covered her hand with his. "Don't, Kenz. Let's not go there tonight."

She withdrew her hand and gave a jerky nod. "Right. Okay."

"Will you dance with me?"

She shook her head.

"Please, Kenz. Come dance with me."

He stood up, and tugged her off her stool, not giving her a chance to say no. And she didn't pull back while he led her to a spot on the dance floor. "Perfect" by Ed Sheeran came on, and, after them singing it together at Becky's wedding, the song was *perfect* for this moment.

*K*enzie and Nick rode the elevator up to her floor together. It was after midnight, and the halls of the hotel were quiet. She put enough distance between them that their arms or shoulders didn't brush. Still feeling the magic she always felt when dancing in Nick's arms, she didn't need to add another zing of torture to her night.

When the elevator doors opened, she stepped out. He started to follow, but she put out a hand to keep him inside. He leaned against the threshold so the elevator door wouldn't shut.

"I'd like to walk you to your room."

She looked away. "I'd rather you stay right here."

He turned her face back to him with fingertips on her jaw. "You saying that tells me you're afraid."

She took a step back and he let his arm drop to his side. "Afraid of what?"

"You're smart enough that I don't have to spell it out, sweet pea. I miss you, Kenz. I miss us."

His comments stopped her. Saying that opened a door she wasn't ready to step through. She put a hand on his chest and pushed him back a step. "Good night, Nick."

He raised a brow before the elevator doors closed.

Just being around him was tension overload. She was well aware of the battle she was losing even though she'd put up a good fight. Or had she? Once she decided to forgive him, there was very little fight left in her.

Nick occupied her thoughts more than he didn't. She'd received a few *Are you crazy?* looks from Jeremy, but Kyle's glances told her he wasn't surprised.

She slipped her card key into the slot and opened her door, feeling the chill in the air. The room was hot when she first got here, so she'd turned the air way down. She adjusted the thermostat, washed her face, and pulled on an old T-shirt and a pair of athletic shorts. Then she unpacked a book she picked up two days earlier because sleep wasn't going to come easily—if at all.

Just as she settled against the propped-up pillows, the hotel phone rang, making her jump out of her skin.

"Hello?"

"Can't sleep?"

The sound of Nick's voice over the line made her pulse skitter. It had been years since they'd talked over the phone. "What makes you think you didn't wake me up?"

"'Cause I know your I-just-woke-up voice. So, what were you doing?"

"If you must know, I just started a new book."

"Your favorite pastime when you're not writing music."

He knew her well. Even before they started dating, he

teased her about her reading habit. "So, you called because . . . ?"

"Because I can't sleep either. Remember how we used to say good night and then I'd call you as soon as I got home."

"Yes." Sometimes they'd talk for hours. One thing about her and Nick, they didn't fight. They might bicker back and forth, but they never had a raised-voice argument. Even after she found out about him and Juliette, they didn't exchange angry words. They just stopped speaking. Well, they actually stopped speaking before she found out, but that was a given.

The night he came to the ranch on his Harley was the first time she'd ever spoken in pure anger. She was generally an upbeat person, and it took a lot to get her mad. Same with Nick, but his indiscretion had changed them both. She just wasn't sure yet if the changes were good or bad.

"I heard you working on something new before the concert. Is it for someone?"

Kenzie set her book aside and snuggled down under the sheet. "Kyle asked for a couple of new pieces. It's easy writing for Knight Rivers since I know their vocal ranges. I can actually imagine them onstage while I'm writing."

"Do you know what you'd write for me if I was still singing?"

What would she write? Something about an attentive, sweet daddy and his adorable little daughter. "Do you think you'll ever sing again?"

"I don't think so. Believe it or not, I like what I'm doing. When I was home last week, I picked up two more clients. They'll be a lot easier to work with than Aaron."

"No way," she said with a laugh. "Easier than Aaron?"

"Despite Aaron, I really do like the job."

She ran a hand over the down comforter. "I'm glad you found something you enjoy."

178 | TINA NEWCOMB

"If you told me three years ago that I'd be managing, I would have said you were crazy."

"Having a great ear for music has to help."

"You think I have a great ear?"

"I know you do. And you know too, so quit fishing for compliments."

He laughed.

Kenzie hesitated a moment before she said, "Can I ask you a personal question?"

"You can ask me anything."

Her stomach twisted in a knot, but she had to know. "Do you promise to answer honestly?"

"You sound pretty serious."

She noticed his slight hesitation. They used to talk about everything, but she was nervous about what his answer might be. "Are you doing drugs?"

He snorted. "No. Why would you ever think that?"

"At the fair in Mississippi, I saw you buy something from Jeff."

There was a moment of silence. "I didn't buy anything from him. I barely know the guy."

Lie.

"I'll let you get some sleep. Good night, sweet pea."

"Good night, Nick."

~

*K*enzie walked out of the hotel with the rest of the band members and climbed aboard the bus. Thanks to Nick, she only got about five hours of sleep. They had a three-and-a-half-hour drive to their next destination, and she headed toward her bed in the back. Ryder was stretched out across the whole mattress.

"Scoot," she said, pushing him over with a hip.

He turned on his side, making room. "You kept me out too late."

"You're the one who chose to stay out last night."

"I saw you leave with someone," he sing-songed to the music of "Perfect." "No wonder you're so tired."

"We rode up the elevator together. The end." No reason to tell Ryder about the phone call after she got to her room.

She turned her back to him, hoping he'd drop off soon. Instead, he hooked an arm over her hip. "Something going on with you and Nick?"

"Nope."

"Come on, you can tell me. Something's going on, isn't it? Does he want a second chance?"

"I'm going to sleep now, so be quiet."

"Maybe you should consider it, Kenz. He really is a good guy who just lost his way for a while."

"He has a child, Ryder."

"Who seems to adore you."

"Shush," she said. "I'm going to sleep now."

Kenzie awoke with a start, new lyrics running through her mind. Pushing up in bed, she grabbed her notebook and pencil and quickly wrote the words down, adding to or changing some as she went. All the while, Ryder continued to snore softly beside her.

Nick's words to her last night *Do you know what you would write for me if I was still singing?* must have inspired the thoughts.

The words came easily, faster than with any song she'd ever written. A tune also played through her head. She jumped off the bed and ran for her guitar.

She darted past Tripp, Jeremy, Bodhi, and Kyle, who were trying to come up with a tune for the lyrics she'd given Kyle yesterday, and then Jeff, who sat alone with his hat pulled over his eyes, showing no sign of interest. Big surprise.

Her thoughts turned to the night at the fair. Jeff and Nick exchanging something, which Nick denied. During the hours of no sleep, she'd convinced herself that Nick wouldn't be involved with drugs, but in the light of day, she wondered if she was completely wrong. Although she couldn't believe he'd put his job or his daughter at risk.

"Are we almost there?" she asked, pulling her guitar out of the case.

"About thirty minutes." Kyle pulled her down next to him and held up a page of sheet music. "I think we'll change the lyrics here."

"I told you I'm okay with you changing whatever you want."

"You'll still get full cred—"

"Kyle, you know I don't care about that where Knight Rivers is concerned." She wasn't emotionally tied to the lyrics she'd written for them.

"You should care, Kenz," Bodhi said. "Take the credit."

"If it'll make y'all happy, put my name all over it. By the way, congrats again on the engagement, Bodhi. Did your fiancée leave this morning?"

"I took her to the airport while everyone was in the gym."

Ryder came out of the backroom rubbing his eyes. "Yeah, congrats. Imagine how embarrassing it would have been if she'd turned you down in front of all those people."

"Stay out too late last night, little bro?" Tripp asked.

"It's Kenzie's fault. I was just babysitting," he said, pointing at her.

"Whatever." Kenzie stood up. She wanted to get this tune plunked out before it slipped away.

Jeremy grabbed her arm but looked at Ryder. "What do you mean you were babysitting?"

"I couldn't leave her alone with Nick."

"Oh, for Pete's sake. You could have gone to your room at

any time but you were too busy looking for Mrs. Ryder Cross to even notice when I left."

"Did you leave with Nick?" Tripp asked with a grin.

"Oh! My! Gosh! Nick and I rode the elevator together. When it stopped on my floor, I got off. He didn't."

CHAPTER 15

From the back of the concert hall in Springfield, Missouri, Nick watched Knight Rivers go through their sound check while trying to calm his crying daughter over the phone. She'd eaten the Froot Loop necklace he'd made for her the last time he was home and wanted him to make another one immediately. "It's okay, baby girl. Daddy will make you a new necklace when I get home tonight."

"No, Dada," she said, hiccupping between sobs. "Now!"

London always reverted from daddy to dada when she was upset.

"Please, don't cry, baby. I'll be home tonight. I can tuck you into bed and read a story."

"Now."

His life had been one big improvisation since London's birth. "Once upon a time, there was a little girl named London, who lived in a big castle painted pink and purple, your favorite colors."

While making up a story, he glanced around for Aaron, who was late, as usual. Knight Rivers had just finished up, and Aaron was nowhere in sight. He got up and walked to the back doors. Pushing one open, he looked out into the corridor. Aaron and Jeff—who should have been onstage with Knight Rivers—were arguing in low voices.

"Aaron!"

When Aaron glanced up, Nick waved a hand, then shut the door. The guy was worse than a petulant child. If he didn't fire Nick, or Nick didn't quit, Nick would find someone with the ability to herd the country singer along while appeasing his ego.

Nick sat on the back row and continued his story. London's sobs had subsided, with just the occasional hiccup now.

"Princess London looked out of the tower window and saw a pretty yellow dragonfly past."

"No, Dada. Pink."

The door banged open, and Aaron stalked in, casting a glare Nick's way.

Sorry, buddy, but I shouldn't have to tell you where you need to be every minute of every day. He was as tired of Aaron as Aaron was of him. Ten weeks into this tour and he was ready to be done. "But as soon as the dragon landed on the ground, her scales turned pink with purple flowers!"

London's giggle was music to his ears. He ached to hold her in his arms and kiss her soft little cheeks.

"The beautiful princess climbed out the window and down a vine so she could pet the dragon." He probably shouldn't encourage any climbing out of windows. Surely his two-and-a-half-year-old daughter was too young to remember this moment when she was able to climb out windows. "But she only climbed out the window after she asked her Daddy, and he made sure it was very safe," he added as a disclaimer.

"Princess London climbed on the dragon's back, and he

whisked her away to a beautiful flower garden where she chased butterflies until she snuggled down and took a nap."

"No nap."

He chuckled and glanced at his watch. One o'clock in Dove Hill—his mom was probably ready for London to take a nap. "I'll be home when you're eating dinner, baby girl. Can you let me talk to Grandma?"

"Bye."

And she hung up. Oh well, Nick had emailed his parents with flight details. He'd catch an Uber and be home before London's bedtime.

Kyle walked down the aisle and took a chair in front of him. "Jeff didn't make it to our sound check."

"He was in the hall with Aaron."

"Do I need to start looking for another bass player?"

"I can give you a couple of names. You could do a virtual audition unless they can meet you at one of our stops."

"Do you have a timeline?" Kyle asked.

"Nope. Just playing it day by day. I'm flying to Nashville later this afternoon, so not for the next couple of days."

Kyle rubbed a hand over his jaw. "What will happen to you?"

Nick chuckled without humor. "I'm new to this, so I'm not sure. I've got some reassurances from the Tennessee DA, but that won't help me in another state.

"Thanks for filling me in on what's going on. I know you probably shouldn't have."

"Not a problem. Anyone asking questions?"

"Just my sister."

"Yeah, she asked me if I was doing drugs a couple of weeks ago. She saw me with Jeff at that fair in Mississippi."

"Jeremy knows something is up but hasn't asked."

Raised voices turned his attention toward the stage. "I better go take care of a child."

"Yeah. Good luck with that. Hey," Kyle said when Nick stood. "What's going on with you and Kenz?"

Nick shook his head. "Don't know what you're talking about."

"Don't hurt her again, Nick."

He only nodded when he spotted Kenzie headed their way.

Up on stage, while the country singer ranted at the audio engineer, Nick noticed two of Aaron's band members' expressions. They were losing patience with their boss. Nick would be looking for a new lead guitarist and keyboardist before long.

Aaron cared more about them agreeing with his ideas than he did their ability to play music. Nick had talked to him numerous times, but Aaron wouldn't change until forced—or maybe never. Aaron was too blinded by ego to notice he was ruining his career.

After smoothing things over enough that Aaron's band could go through their sound check, he went to grab his bag and call a car to take him to the airport. The Knight Rivers bus was still in the parking lot with the door open.

He heard someone playing the guitar before he climbed the stairs and saw Kenzie with her back to him. No one else was around. He liked the tune she was strumming, something he hadn't heard yet.

"That's nice," he said when she stopped.

She whipped around, losing her grip on her guitar. He caught it just before it hit the floor.

"You scared me to death."

"You probably shouldn't leave the door open when you're alone."

"Right. I lost track of time when everyone left for lunch."

"You're not hungry?" he asked, propping the guitar next to her.

"This tune has been running through my head, and I wanted to get it down on paper."

He reached down, took her hands, and pulled her to her feet, looking her in the eye. "I am truly sorry for my choices, and for hurting you, Kenz. Do you think you can ever forgive me?"

"Yes."

Not the answer he'd expected, and his surprise joined a flood of unexpected warmth filling his chest. "Any time soon?"

"Yes."

Would her forgiveness finally give him a pass to forgive himself? He used to justify what he'd done with excuses. Though they were invalid, he'd talked himself into believing them, but it was time to own his mistakes and try to forgive himself.

He wanted Kenzie in the next chapter of his life, and he wanted that chapter to start soon. But he needed to be patient and work his way back into her heart.

The hitch was, would she be able to accept London? He hated that thought even running through his mind—almost like an ultimatum. He had no right, yet he had a daughter to consider. Kenzie was sweet with London, but she was sweet with puppies too.

"Do you think you can forgive me enough to . . . let me take you to dinner when I get back from Tennessee?"

"Yes."

"Really?"

Just then, his phone buzzed, informing him his car had arrived. He had no choice but to break the moment between them. "My ride to the airport is here. Hope you have a great concert tonight."

"Have a safe flight. Enjoy your time with London."

He studied her for a long moment, his heart pounding so

hard he could barely think straight. He bent, hovering his mouth just above hers, giving her an out. She closed the distance, pressing her lips to his for a sweet kiss that left him wanting more.

*K*enzie watched Nick disappear through the bus door. She wished she'd closed the door so he couldn't come in, and at the same time wished Uber had arrived later.

No, him coming aboard was a good thing. It gave her a chance to say she forgave him. Well, she hadn't actually said anything but "yes." Still, he asked, and she was able to voice her decision. Forgetting might take longer, but forgiving lifted a weight she knew she'd been carrying for too long.

She moved to the window and watched while Nick climbed into the back seat and the car pulled out of the parking lot.

Her dad wasn't around to witness what happened between her and Nick, but he experienced something similar. Had he carried the burden around for years, or had he forgiven his wife soon after she left? Somehow she knew Waylon had forgiven pretty quickly. Holding onto anger hadn't been her dad's style.

She touched her lips with her fingertips, shocked that she'd kissed Nick before he kissed her. His expression said he'd been just as surprised. They'd been dancing around that kiss ever since New Orleans—almost three weeks ago.

Him going to Dove Hill for three days was just what she needed to re-evaluate.

Picking up her guitar, she sat down and played the melody of the song she'd written for him and London. He could sing it to the little cutie at night when he was tucking her into bed—or possibly years down the road at London's wedding. She could imagine Nick throwing a major party for that event . . . if he ever gave a guy approval to marry his princess.

⁓

*N*ick entered the outdoor stadium in Minot, North Dakota, where Knight Rivers was on the stage running through a practice session before the state fair opened for the day. Of course, there was no sign of Aaron. Jeff was also missing.

He noticed the famous country rapper, Alabama Gray, who had a song on its way to number one, standing in front of the stage watching. He was on today's lineup, scheduled to sing right after Aaron. His sound was fresh, and he had a huge fan base.

Nick knew the minute Kenzie spotted him. Like a magnet, they were drawn to each other. He hadn't seen her since their kiss four days ago and was still a little shocked that she kissed him first—not that he was complaining.

When Knight Rivers hit the final notes, the rapper whistled and applauded. "That was great! Mind if I come up there with y'all?"

"You're more than welcome," Kyle said.

"Y'all have a great sound," he said, climbing the stairs.

Bodhi, closest to Alabama Gray, shook his hand. "It's great to meet you. We're big fans."

"Really?" Alabama said, sounding surprised.

Ryder was next to shake his hand. "We love your music. Kenzie over there is great at 'Alabama Screaming.'"

The rapper eyed Kenzie dubiously. "You think you can keep up with me?"

"Absolutely."

He looked around the group. "You guys have time to run through the song?"

"Sure," Kyle said. He moved over so Alabama Gray could have his mic. "Jeremy, grab your fiddle."

Nick took a seat about ten rows back, anxious to see if Kenzie could indeed keep up. She was talented, but this song would put any drummer to the test.

Kyle gave a count, and Kenzie took off with Knight Rivers coming in perfectly. He could tell by the rapper's expression that he was impressed. Kyle, Bodhi, and Tripp filled in the chorus. Even Nick was impressed by their ability to jump in and play the song just like Alabama Gray's band.

Aaron dropped into the chair next to him. "What's going on?"

"An impromptu jam fest. Is your band here?"

"Yeah, I need a new keyboardist. Jim wants to quit."

Big surprise. "He's under contract until the end of the tour."

"I want that guy," Aaron said, pointing at Ryder. "And I want Kenzie on drums. Not many bands have female drummers. She'll bring in the guy fans."

"First of all, Ryder won't leave Knight Rivers."

"You did."

And I wish I hadn't. "Ryder isn't me. And second, you don't need a female drummer to bring in fans, Aaron. If you'd get clean, be on time, and work on your craft, the stands and concert venues would be packed every night."

Aaron turned in his seat. "What do you mean work on my craft?"

"You forgot the words to a song *you* wrote last weekend in Cape Girardeau."

"I forgot the words once, and it was Jerry's fault. He came in late on the chorus. And I'm clean *and* on time today."

Nick would give Aaron the on-time part, but he looked

into Aaron's eyes, then rolled his own. "You haven't been clean this whole tour."

"Wow! You guys can play," the rapper said at the end of the song. "That was great."

Nick cupped his mouth. "Kyle, can you wrap things up so Aaron and his band can get a few songs in before the fair opens?"

Kyle nodded at Nick while shaking hands with Alabama Gray.

"Maybe I should start rapping," Aaron said.

"A line here and there, like Jason Aldean, would be fine."

"No, I mean like full-out."

"Yeah, no," Nick shook his head.

"Why? Darius Rucker changed the genre of music he sings."

You're not Darius Rucker. "Time to hit the stage."

~

*T*he second Kenzie spotted Nick coming down the aisle, her heartbeat kicked up into her throat. She'd spent the past four days and nights regretting that she'd kissed Nick—so dumb on her part. He seemed to have changed, but what did she really know about him anymore? He was divorced, wasn't singing, but managing. And he had a child.

Could she trust him?

Did she even want to try?

Yes. As always, the answer was yes.

Luckily, Alabama Gray took her mind off Nick when he almost challenged her to play "Alabama Screaming." Could she keep up with the country rapper? Yeah, buddy. Once Kyle gave the count, she was lost in the world of music, unaware of anything but what was happening between her and the rest of the Knight Rivers band members. Yes, she would miss this once the tour was over. For about ten minutes.

Alabama Gray walked toward her at the end of the song. "If you ever decide to leave Knight Rivers, let me know. I can set you up with a dozen bands in a heartbeat."

"She's already spoken for," Aaron said from behind the rapper. "I've got a job waiting for her when she's ready."

Kenzie looked from Aaron to his drummer, who threw his sticks down on the stage and stalked off. Nick jumped out of his chair and rushed toward the man walking away. She glanced back at Aaron, who seemed oblivious.

"I appreciate the offers, but I'm done after this tour," she told them both.

"I'll change her mind," Aaron said, moving to her side.

She moved a step away but looked at Alabama Gray. "I truly enjoyed playing for you just now. Knight Rivers loves your music."

He shook her hand. "The pleasure was all mine. And if you do change your mind, let me know."

As Alabama walked down the stage stairs, Nick walked up with Aaron's drummer, probably having threatened him with breach of contract. The guy didn't look happy, and Kenzie couldn't blame him. She wondered how Nick could take on new clients while dealing with Aaron. The guy was a full-time job.

She decided this was the perfect time to escape by following Knight Rivers down the stairs. Tomorrow, a rare day off, they were going to visit Mount Rushmore and Crazy Horse before heading to Sturgis for their next concert.

Travis Sprenger stood at the bottom of the stairs. "Hi."

"Hey. Heard you playing with Alabama Gray. Sounded great."

"Thanks. You haven't been around for a couple of weeks."

"I was on another story. I have a final interview with Aaron as soon as he's done here."

"Good luck."

"Can I take you to dinner?"

"Sure. As long as we can make it early."

"It's a date."

Except it wouldn't be. Travis was nice, but she didn't feel anything for him. Maybe under different circumstances, but she was interested in someone else. Possibly a mistake, but sometimes the heart chose to ignore rational thought.

CHAPTER 16

*K*night Rivers piled out of the bus at Mt. Rushmore the next day. A storm was supposed to move in later that afternoon, so they wanted to see as much as possible before it hit. Nick came with them while Jeff stayed behind with Aaron's bus. They'd been jolly on the way here, singing old songs and harmonizing with each other. Jeremy grabbed his fiddle and entertained in his usual crazy way.

She was careful to stay away from Nick, to act like nothing had happened between them, but it was hard when he kept looking at her in a way that made her heart hammer. She was certain the whole band knew something was going on.

After walking through the Avenue of the Flags and the Lincoln Borglum Visitor Center, they got a close look at Mt. Rushmore from the viewing terrace. Kenzie had seen a lot of beautiful sights over the last twelve weeks, but this one set her emotions on edge. She declined the guys' offer to take the Presidential Trail closer in lieu of just sitting on a bench in the amphitheater and gazing at the majesty of the mountain before her.

"That sight is amazing, isn't it?"

She'd felt Nick behind her before he spoke. Like the north-seeking and south-seeking poles of magnets, they were drawn together. Before Nick made his move all those years ago, she'd been attracted to him, watching him from the corner of her eye whenever possible. Since he was four years older, she never thought he'd notice her. She was just Kyle's little sister, Kenz, sweet pea, or baby girl, always hanging around with the big boys. Always in the way when they were playing music. Always imitating them or trying to sing along.

When they danced that long-ago night, even before they walked down to the Tennessee River and shared their first kiss, she felt the shift in his feelings for her. She wasn't sure what caused the change, and she didn't care. She loved Nick long before he even *saw* her.

"It is amazing. I can't imagine looking at the mountain and being struck with the idea to stick four presidents' faces up there."

He sat beside her. "So, you went to dinner with Travis last night."

"I did."

"And?"

And after dinner, Travis moved to kiss her, but she stopped him.

"No?" he'd asked.

"Tell me the truth." She moved her hand between them. "Are you feeling anything here?"

"Maybe I would be if we were kissing."

She shook her head, smiling. "I don't think kissing is going to change anything."

"Trying wouldn't hurt," he said with a frown.

They'd parted as friends. At least she hoped they did. Travis was a nice guy, and hopefully, he'd find someone who would make him happy.

She knew what Nick wanted and couldn't help but tease. "And we had a nice dinner."

"And?"

"I'm going to look through the gift shop while I wait for the guys to get back," she said, standing up.

He jumped up and followed her. "Tell me what happened."

"We had dinner."

Backing her against a wall, he leaned close. "And?"

She couldn't let this continue if she wasn't sure. Sure about him, and sure about London. She was losing her heart to him, but did she dare let him know, exposing herself to the possibility of being hurt all over again?

The biggest question; was she ready to be a mom? Could she accept London as her own if things progressed forward? The little girl was a doll, but holding London on her lap and tucking her into bed every night were two very different things. And what if Juliette came back?

"And nothing."

"So . . . there's nothing between you and Travis?"

"Is there anything between you and Juliette?" She wanted to bite her tongue off as soon as the question left her mouth.

"No," he said, wide-eyed like the question surprised him.

"What if she comes back?"

"It wouldn't matter. We're divorced, Kenz."

Wanting to escape, she pushed away from the wall. "I'm going to look through the gift shop."

She took her time, browsing through the T-shirts and mugs for sale. If her dad was alive, she'd buy him a baseball hat. He would have gotten a kick out of a hat from so far away. Thinking of her dad made her miss him so much her heart ached. She wished he were here because she needed someone to give her advice.

She picked up a pair of turquoise earrings, held them next to her ears, and looked in a small countertop mirror. Nick was standing behind her, so she turned. "What do you think?"

"I think you should wear them to dinner with me tonight."

They would look nice with her white dress.

*K*enzie was nervous, and Jeremy wasn't helping. She told Nick she'd meet him in the lobby of the hotel, and when she walked out of her room, Jeremy stood against the opposite wall waiting.

"Do you have any mace on you?"

She snorted. "I don't need mace."

"You might," he said, falling into step with her.

"I won't."

"Where's he taking you?"

"To dinner."

"Where?" he demanded, with an edge of irritation.

"He didn't tell me, but if he had, I wouldn't tell you." She looked at him out of the corner of her eye. "You might show up with mace."

She pushed the down button for the elevator and Jeremy stopped next to her. "What? You're going to come downstairs and meet my date, Dad?"

The elevator doors opened, and she stepped inside. Again, he followed. She put her hand up to stop the door from closing. "Get out, Jer."

"I'm going to get something to eat."

"Y'all are getting something to eat at seven. I heard Kyle telling the other guys."

"I thought I'd go down early," Jeremy said.

She moved her hand and the door closed. "Nick isn't intimidated by you."

Jeremy leaned back, crossing one ankle over the other, and stuffed his hands in his jeans pockets. "Never said he was."

The doors opened on the first floor to reveal Nick standing against the opposite wall much as Jeremy had been. Just seeing him made her heart jump with happiness and her stomach churn with apprehension at the same time.

Was going to dinner with him the right decision? She knew Nick wouldn't want to be just friends. He'd want more, but was she ready?

His appreciative gaze moved from her to Jeremy as they stepped out, and his smile turned cynical. "Really, Jer?"

"I could ask you the same thing, Nick."

"Do you want to come with us?" Nick asked.

"No, he doesn't." Kenzie put her hand on Jeremy's chest. "Have a great dinner with the guys. I'll see you tomorrow, and you can grill me all the way to North Platte."

Nick didn't touch her while they walked through the lobby and out to the car he'd rented for the occasion. Traveling on a tour bus meant you had few transportation options. He opened the passenger door for her. One thing about Nick, he was a gentleman on dates.

"Where are we going?" she asked after he slid behind the wheel.

"It's a surprise."

They listened to the radio as Nick drove out of town. Now the storm had blown through, the air smelled fresh and the sky was a clear blue, and their surroundings became more rural.

"Have you been where we're going before?" she asked, suddenly wondering if he'd taken Juliette to the same place.

"Yes."

"When?" she asked, not completely sure she wanted to hear the answer.

"This afternoon." He reached over and squeezed her arm. "Now quit asking questions and enjoy the scenery."

She looked out the passenger window and watched the trees go by. It was a pretty area. She wasn't surprised Nick went to the trouble to plan something nice. When they were together, he did plan fun, unique dates.

Nick slowed down and a lake came into view.

"That's pretty," she said.

"I thought so."

"How'd you find this place?"

Nick ignored her question as he turned onto a dirt road, where she spotted a house or cabin up ahead with a huge wraparound porch and green metal roof. No other cars were around.

"Do you know the people who live here?" she asked when Nick pulled near the garage and put the car in park.

He turned toward her in his seat. "You sure ask a lot of questions. How about, just this once, you sit back and enjoy the evening without worrying about anything or anybody?"

"I'm just curious."

"All will be revealed shortly."

He climbed out of the car and came around to get her door. Then he went to the trunk and pulled out a picnic basket.

"You really planned this out."

"Does that earn me some brownie points?"

She couldn't help but smile. "Depends on what comes next. I wore a white dress, and you didn't bring a blanket to sit on. You might lose major brownie points if I get dirty."

He looked skyward and blew out a breath. "I forgot a blanket."

Shaking her head slowly. "One brownie point down."

He gestured to a path, and she walked ahead of him, around the side of the garage to a yard that ran down to the lake, which hadn't looked so very large from the road. When the path ended, Nick took her hand and led her around a stand of trees. A short dock came into view and on the end sat a table covered in a white cloth and two chairs.

She covered her mouth and glanced up at him. "You did this?"

"How are those brownie points looking now?"

"Plus three."

"Only three?" he asked with a chuckle.

She looked back at the house. "The people who live here are okay with this?"

"They're an older couple, and they were thrilled to lend us their dock."

"How'd you find this place?" The setting was absolutely gorgeous.

"I went door to door asking?"

She closed her gaping mouth, astonished at the trouble he'd gone to when a simple dinner out would have sufficed. "Okay, four more brownie points for effort."

He set the picnic basket on the dock and pulled out her chair. After she sat, he opened the basket, took out three votive candles, and lit them with a flourish. Next came two plates, silverware, glasses, and napkins. As he continued to remove things from the basket, she watched in dismay. Nick had gone to so much trouble. This had to have taken most of his day to set up.

Which reminded her, she hadn't seen him at their concert earlier. He'd started standing at the left corner of the stage to watch, right in her line of sight most of the time.

Out of the basket came a brown paper bag with the end rolled tight, two small tinfoil containers, and two large ones.

As soon as the smell of Italian seasonings hit her nose, her stomach growled. "That smells delicious."

"We have tossed salad with Italian dressing and bread-sticks for starters. Your choices for dinner are lasagna and lobster ravioli. Or both, because there's plenty," Nick said, taking his seat and spreading a napkin over his lap. He removed the top on one of the small containers and handed it across the table along with a small bottle of salad dressing.

"You outdid yourself, Nick. This is wonderful. Thank you so much."

"I'd say my brownie point count just went up by ten."

"Twenty," she countered. "Possibly thirty."

"Yay, me." He flashed one of his devastating grins.

She put salad on her plate and added some dressing, then passed it back to him while he took a couple of breadsticks out of the paper bag, handing her one.

"Mmm, this bread is so fresh."

They made small talk while they ate. Not uncomfortable, just inconsequential. She marveled at the view and Nick's thoughtful planning.

After they finished their salads, he opened the main dishes and immediately frowned.

"What?"

"I didn't bring anything to serve the lasagna." He glanced at her. "I guess that will cost me a few brownie points."

She returned the leftover salad to the picnic basket, moved the votive candles to one side of the table, and placed both main dish containers between them. "Problem solved. We'll just eat out of the containers."

"And I get to keep my points?" he asked.

After she took her seat, she smiled across the table. "Every one of them."

They both dug into the lasagna and the ravioli. Every-thing tasted so good.

Nick had planned the perfect night. She couldn't believe he'd gone door to door to find a spot where they could share dinner. Just the thought of all he'd done to make this possible astonished her.

When they finished, they packed everything away, then he pulled out his phone, started some music, and held out his hand. "Can I have this dance?"

She put her hand in his and stood. The sun had set behind the surrounding hills, and though the sky was still light, the moon was already up.

He tucked her close, and they danced slowly around the dock. His touch on her back was light, but not so much that she couldn't feel the heat of his skin through her cotton dress.

"You smell nice," he said close to her ear, sending goose bumps across her neck and down her arms.

"So do you."

"You also look beautiful. I wanted to tell you when you first stepped out of the elevator, but I was afraid Jeremy would minimize it somehow."

Probably true. Jeremy was allowed to forgive Nick for what he'd done, but he didn't seem to want her to. It was her responsibility to tell Jeremy she already had forgiven Nick. And it felt pretty wonderful. Carrying that hurt and anger around for three years had taken a lot out of her.

She glanced up. The tenderness and affection in his eyes made her heart skip a beat.

Nick touched her face, softly running his thumb over her cheek. "I'm sorry I kissed you that night at the ranch. I had no right to do that to you, Kenz."

"You could kiss me now."

He ran his thumb over her bottom lip before lowering his mouth to hers. Her breath caught in her throat as he reintroduced her to his lips. She hadn't really forgotten anything

202 | TINA NEWCOMB

about him, except now he seemed softer in his tone, and his patience had grown by leaps and bounds. How he dealt so calmly with Aaron and some of his antics was beyond Kenzie.

As he deepened their kiss, pulling her closer, all thoughts flitted from her mind. She wrapped her arms around his neck and leaned in closer still. Her body buzzed with the awareness of him. She didn't believe he'd do anything to hurt her again. Now everything that might follow was in her hands. For them to build a relationship, she'd have to be able to accept London as her own.

When he pulled back enough to take a deep breath.

She touched his cheek. "Your brownie point bin is full."

CHAPTER 17

The next day Kenzie felt like she was floating during their five-and-a-half-hour drive to North Platte, Nebraska. She responded to Jeremy's one million remarks with a smile. Of course, her thoughts were on Nick all day. She was glad he'd ridden on Aaron's bus, so she had time to come down off the cloud he left her on the night before.

She downloaded a book about toddlers to her e-reader. Definitely jumping the gun, but it wouldn't hurt to know a few things.

Just as she flipped to chapter two, Kyle plopped down next to her.

"Hey, baby girl. How was your date last night?"

"Did Jeremy send you?"

He stretched his arms along the back of the bench seat with a smile. "No, he didn't. I'm asking because I care."

"Aww," she said, pinching his cheek lightly. My date was . . . extremely nice."

"Where did Nick take you?"

"To a lake for a picnic."

"And you had a good time?"

"I did." She turned on her seat to face her brother. "Do you think I should give him a second chance?"

"Since you went out with him last night, I'd say you already have."

"It was only one date."

"Do you trust him?"

Did she? *Yes,* whispered softly through her mind. And her heart. Was that irresponsible on her part after what he'd done? "I do."

"Sounds like you have your answer." Kyle's expression turned thoughtful. She could see so much of their dad in his features. "We all make mistakes, Kenz. Nick's was pretty huge, but I think he regrets the choices he made. We've both known him forever, and we both know he's one of the good guys."

She agreed. Nick was a good guy and had so many qualities she admired. Despite what happened, over the years he'd proven to be dependable, kind, a hard worker, and honest, to name a few. Plus, he was devoted to family.

"Sometimes we have to trust our hearts rather than our fears."

"That's like stepping off a ledge in the dark and hoping there's a soft landing below."

He chuckled. "Sometimes the landing isn't so soft, but the rewards can be worth the fall. One thing to take into consideration, though, is he's a package deal. Are you ready to be a mom?"

"It was only one date, Kyle."

"That you shouldn't go beyond if you can't accept his daughter." Kyle leaned forward, elbows on knees, and looked back over his shoulder at her. "You seemed to be good with London, the few times I've seen you with her."

"She's a sweetheart, but I've never really been around children."

"Nick wasn't either before London was born."

True. "But he had a little sister and brother."

"Twenty years ago."

"Did you ask her?" Jeremy asked, joining them. He sat on the other side of Kenzie.

She looked from one to the other. "Ask me what?"

"Jessi and Cara are flying into Colorado tomorrow. We'll pick them up at the airport before we head to Red Rocks for the concert, and they'll travel with us until we reach Missoula."

"Of course, you can have both bedrooms."

"Thanks, sweet pea," Jeremy said.

"Anytime." Kenzie pushed up from her seat, afraid if she stayed Jeremy would start in on Nick all over again.

Jeremy grabbed her arm. "Let's talk about last night."

"Let's not."

"Kenz and I already had a talk, Jer. It's all good."

"How can you say that, Kyle? She went out—"

"Let it go. Kenz knows what she's doing."

Kenzie bent and kissed her brother's cheek. "Thanks for the talk and the confidence in me."

≈

*A*aron's tour bus arrived at the truly unique concert venue—Red Rocks, just outside of Morrison, Colorado, ahead of Knight Rivers band since their bus went to the Denver airport to pick up Kyle and Jeremy's wives first.

He hadn't spent much time with Kenzie since their picnic two days ago, because her watchdog—Jeremy—stuck close to her side. Hopefully, Cara's visit would keep him occupied for a few days so Nick could get Kenzie alone.

Their date went well, at least in his opinion. He could tell she was softening toward him, or she would never have agreed to their first date.

He knew he had a long way to go, but he'd gone from impatient to patient since London's birth, so he wouldn't push. Trust was fragile, and he'd shattered Kenzie's, so he planned to take his time building it back, stronger than before. He now trusted himself, something he didn't have when he started touring with Aaron. His future had become clear in his mind's eye, and he wanted Kenzie traveling that road with him.

Aaron was onstage, so Nick found a seat, taking time to appreciate his surroundings. Red Rocks was an open-air amphitheater nestled in among some of the area's unique red rock formations. A large, disc-shaped rock sat behind the stage. Another huge, vertical rock angled up along one side, and several outcroppings angled out from the other side. The amphitheater held a little over ninety-five hundred people, and the show was sold out.

Once this tour was over, life would settle into a new normal for him and London. He wanted to stay in Dove Hill, where London would grow up near her grandparents, so he planned to find some property and build a house close to town. His office was in Nashville, but he'd work things out so he didn't have to go into the city every day of the week.

He had researched preschools and enrolled London to start three days a week, beginning next month. Besides being fun, being around other children should be good for his daughter, since she needed to learn basic things like sharing and interacting with small people rather than just adults.

He turned when he heard Kenzie's laugh. She walked into the amphitheater with Ryder. As they climbed onto the stage,

Jessi and Cara made their way to where he sat. He stood and hugged them.

"It's good to see you. Kyle and Jeremy have been impatiently awaiting your arrival."

"We've been anxious to get here," Cara said.

Jessi nodded her agreement. "How's the tour going?"

"Smooth, so far." But that would change soon. A couple of Aaron's band members were miserable and ready to bolt. Their contract held them firm for four more weeks, but then Aaron's band would crumble.

"You say that like you expect trouble," Cara said.

He tried to laugh off his comment. "No, trouble just has a way of showing up. That's life, right?"

Cara lifted her camera out of its case and hung the strap around her neck. "This place is incredible. I'm going to get a few shots while the band is busy."

He and Jessi watched her leave, then she turned to him. "We haven't really had much of a chance to talk. I've been wanting to thank you for the opportunity you gave Knight Rivers."

"Oh, well, that thanks should go to Aaron. Inviting Knight Rivers to do this tour was his idea."

"But you made it happen, and you've been a big help. Kyle has told me about several times when you stepped in to smooth things over or fix something that's gone wrong."

"That's what managers do."

She touched his arm. "Accept the compliment, Nick. I've managed a team before, so I know how hard it can be at times."

"Thank you, but Knight Rivers is easy to manage."

"You cut your teeth on the hard guy," she said with a laugh.

"He would have been much harder if I hadn't already traveled with him. I became pretty familiar with Aaron's quirks, idiosyncrasies, and demands during the last tour he took."

"I heard you and Kenzie went out a couple of nights ago."

"She told you?"

"No, Jeremy told us."

"Yeah, Jeremy wasn't too happy about our date."

She waved a hand. "Ignore him. It's not his life or his decision. He'll always feel protective of Kenz."

"I understand his concern. If I was in his position, I'd be doing the same thing."

"Onto another subject, how's your daughter?"

"She's good. I got to see her last week."

"She's adorable."

"Thank you. She is pretty adorable most of the time, but, like any child, she does have her moments."

Jessi stood and turned her back to the stage. "Do you see Knight Rivers going places?"

He looked up at the concern in her tone. "I do. Does that worry you?"

"I've been doing a lot of research about country stars with families. You know"—she waved her hand again—"like how they travel for tours and how many hours of their day they work."

"And?" he asked, wondering what she was getting out.

"And I'm pregnant. Please don't react," she quickly added when he started to stand. "I haven't told Kyle yet. In fact, I haven't told anyone." She made eye contact. "You're the first."

"That's amazing news, Jessi. And I'll keep your secret."

She sat down but turned toward him. "It's not really a secret. I just don't know if the timing is right."

He chuckled. "If we all waited for the perfect timing, the world would be mostly unpopulated."

"That's probably true." She hung her head. "I'm worried the news may hinder Kyle or the band from taking off."

"It won't. I can make sure of that. And Kyle's dad set him up before his death. With a few alterations, the practice studio can become a recording studio right there on the ranch."

"I hadn't thought of that."

"With the capable ranch manager Kyle hired, he can concentrate on his music and his family."

Jessi blew out a breath. "I'm glad I talked to you before telling Kyle. Thank you. You've eased a lot of my anxiety."

He leaned into her hug. "This should be a happy time for you. Go tell your husband the great news."

"Thanks, Nick." She stood up and headed toward the stage.

Kenzie made eye contact with him. He smiled, and she smiled back. He'd been scared of marriage before he started playing for Aaron. Not anymore. His marriage to Juliette had been brief and anything but happy, but imagining a life with Kenzie was completely different. He could see everything so clearly.

He wondered if she was thinking along those lines, or if it was way too early for her. She used to bring marriage up when they dated. Not often, but enough to make him nervous. There had been so much of the world he wanted to see, so much he wanted to do. Now all he wanted was to be home with his daughter, and hopefully Kenzie.

Jessi's announcement made him more anxious than ever for things to work out.

~

"*E*ek!" Kenzie grabbed Jessi in a tight hug, then turned to her brother for another hug. "I'm going to be an aunt!"

"I told you she'd be excited," Kyle said to Jessi while patting Kenzie's back.

"When do you find out if it's a boy or girl?" Kenzie asked, bouncing on the balls of her feet. She couldn't wait to start stocking up on cute toys, adorable little shoes, and soft blankets.

"It's still a little early," Jessi said with a laugh. "I haven't even been to the doctor yet."

"I'm so excited for you both. And for me. We're going to have a little Rivers running around the ranch! I wish—"

"—that Dad was around to see," Kyle finished when Kenzie stopped short.

Kenzie's eyes filled with tears. "I do. He would be so proud and excited."

Kyle tugged her into a hug. "Don't cry. This is a happy moment."

"I know. I'm sorry. I'm just so excited and happy for you both."

Kenzie wished she could take them out for a celebratory dinner, but they were due on stage in an hour. She'd moved her stuff out of the bedroom on the bus to give Jessi and Kyle some privacy, but didn't really have a place to get ready without her bathroom.

She was sitting up front putting on makeup when someone knocked. Opening the door, her heart jumped as soon as she saw Nick.

He only came up a couple of stairs and leaned his arms on the railing separating them. "Hi."

"Hi, yourself."

"Want to spend some time exploring Breckenridge tomorrow?"

"Yes. I've heard it's a really cute little town."

"Let's meet in the lobby at ten?"

She nodded. "I'll be there."

CHAPTER 18

*A*aron was getting moodier. He and Nick seemed to be at odds over something new almost every day. They used to keep most of their disagreements just between the two of them, but their yelling matches had started to involve everyone.

Kyle was determined to keep Knight Rivers neutral. Aaron had given them a rare opportunity, but by representing them for the price he charged, Nick had also contributed to their success and the offer of a recording deal once the tour concluded. Kyle tried to enforce impartiality. Everyone but Jeff agreed. He argued that, because of the opportunity, they should side with Aaron on all arguments.

Kenzie usually just left the venue. Aaron seemed to enjoy drama and conflict, and these days started an argument over every tiny little thing. She was sick of listening to the same disagreements.

Jessi and Cara's visit turned out to be fun for her in two ways. First, she was so glad to have female company, and second, Cara took Jeremy's attention off her and Nick. He still watched them like a hawk, but Cara was a nice diversion.

As they traveled through northwestern Wyoming and Montana, Kenzie fell in love with their surroundings. She was in awe of the mountains and rushing rivers. Writing was forgotten as she sat with her nose to the tour bus's window, wanting to memorize the beauty. Every time they stopped she found a place to buy postcards of the fabulous vistas they passed.

The crowds who were there for Knight Rivers had grown until they were bringing in almost as many people as Aaron at some of their stops. Of course, Kyle hoped that would encourage Kenzie to change her mind about leaving the band, and he told her every chance he got about how much the audience loved her. Her nervousness about performing had faded with every show, and she did love the life, but in large part, because she knew it was coming to an end.

Nick found her by the hotel's pool, where she'd escaped after another Aaron-against-his-ban-members blowout.

He sat on the side of her lounge chair. She scooted over to give him room, but not enough that her leg wasn't touching him.

"If you're trying to get some rays, you should be sitting in the sun."

"I came out here for peace."

"Yeah," he said resting his forearms on his thighs and lacing his fingers together. "Me too. After Spokane tomorrow, we only have two more weeks."

He glanced at her, his intense blue eyes sending her heart galloping. "Want to get some dinner after the concert tonight?"

"I'd love to."

They'd been to dinner twice since their lake picnic. There hadn't been time for anything else, although he'd hinted at something special for their night off in Tacoma two nights from now.

"Can I kiss you in public yet?" he asked a twinkle in his eye.

"You've already kissed me in public."

"Yeah, but some of the guys are over there. Are you okay with them seeing?"

His eyes scanned her face, landing on her mouth. Heat swirled around inside her in a luscious way she remembered so well. Time to let him—and everyone else—know how she felt, so she grabbed his shirt in her fist and pulled him to her. He showed a moment of surprise before their lips met. She noticed his breathing change along with her own, felt his heart pounding against her fist.

She sat back when she heard Tripp's obnoxious whistle and Ryder's shout to "get a room."

Nick grinned with raised brows, his eyes going back to her lips. "To be continued later."

She nodded, a little embarrassed that she'd been so aggressive.

He stood and pulled his phone out of his back pocket. "I have to make a call, so I'll leave you to your peace."

Like I can have any peace now. She nodded and took a deep breath to settle her heart rate and slow her breathing.

Jeremy blocked her rear view of Nick before he disappeared inside.

"Can't even sit by the pool without Nick searching you out," he said, stretching out on the lounger next to her.

"Or you."

"What does that mean?"

"It means you wouldn't have come out here if you thought Nick wasn't here."

"Excuse me for caring." His eyes were closed, his voice monotone.

"What will it take for you to let up on him?"

He glanced at her. "When he turns his attention to other women, then I'll let up on him."

When she didn't respond, Jeremy sat up and turned to face her. "I don't trust him, Kenz. I've tried, but there's something going on just under the surface with him and Aaron."

"It's obvious what's going on. Their personalities clash."

"No. This goes deeper." He leaned forward. "This involves more than just the two of them."

The night at the fair when she saw Nick with Jeff flashed through her mind. "What do you mean?"

Jeremy shook his head, a troubled expression clouding his face. "I just don't trust him."

"Kyle does," she countered.

"And I don't get it. I've tried to talk to him about Jeff and Nick. He just pushes my concerns away. I can't wait until this tour is over and we're rid of Aaron and his band. I already expect Kyle and I will go a round or two about finding a manager who isn't Nick."

She rolled her eyes. "Shouldn't I be the one who's mad?"

"I saw Nick buying drugs from Jeff the other night," Jeremy blurted out.

No. No, no, no. Kenzie sat up. "I thought the same thing when we were in Mississippi, but I was wrong. He wouldn't risk everything. He wouldn't risk losing his daughter. He just signed new clients—"

"I know what I saw, sweet pea."

"I asked him point-blank if he was doing drugs and he said no."

"Then he's dealing."

"No, Jer. You're wrong. I talked to Kyle about this, and he said everything is fine."

"Kyle's head is in the clouds because of this tour. All our heads are in the clouds, but reality is going to come back and bite us if we're not careful."

"That might be true, but Kyle wouldn't make stupid decisions because of the tour. He wouldn't put any of us in jeopardy. Ever. You know that."

"Kenz, you need to stay away from Nick."

She jumped off her lounge chair, grabbed her book, and headed for the door. The niggling in the back of her mind told her she should listen because of what she'd seen, but her heart told her Jeremy was wrong. She'd known Nick for so long, she just couldn't believe he was capable of doing what Jeremy said.

But she hadn't believed him capable of cheating either.

Thoughts and doubts were racing through her mind as she hurried toward the lobby. Nick crossed from the elevators, heading toward the front doors of the hotel. She started to call his name, but something—the look on his face, the determination in his step—stopped her. Once he exited, she hurried after. He headed across the parking lot to a shopping center next door. Instead of going to one of the stores, he made his way between parked cars, weaving in and out until he reached a dark sedan and opened the passenger door.

He started to climb in, but stopped and looked over the top of the car toward the hotel. Their eyes locked. She couldn't read the expression on his face. He watched her for several heartbeats, then slid into the seat and shut the door. She couldn't make out who was driving but watched the car turn out of the parking lot and disappear from view.

Hours later Kenzie searched the audience for Nick. He had certain places he usually stood, but she couldn't see him anywhere.

Their four o'clock concert ran smoothly and the crowd rocked right along with them. Knight Rivers meshed so easily. They knew each other's moves so intimately. She really might miss this, at least for a little while. She'd miss seeing these guys every day, and their gross jokes, and the great laughs they shared. She'd miss singing with them and goofing around on the bus and dancing with Ryder almost every night.

After the concert, they retired to the hotel karaoke bar for some more fun, and still, Nick didn't show up. She'd started to worry that maybe something was wrong with London and he had to fly home, but he hadn't been carrying any luggage. And who'd been driving the car?

When she came off the stage after singing "Different for Girls" with Bodhi—their names entered by Tripp—Aaron met her halfway to her table, holding out a glass.

"That was quite a performance. Thought you could use a drink."

She bent and sniffed. "What is it?"

"Ginger ale."

Taking the glass, she looked up at him. "Thank you."

"Can I talk to you about something?"

Ah, the reason for the drink became clear. Aaron usually expected something for his offerings. "Sure."

He took her elbow and led her to a small table by the door.

She took a sip of her ginger ale after they settled into the semi-circle booth. "What's up?"

"I've lost all ability to write. Lyrics and music used to come fairly easy to me and now, nothing."

Quit getting high or sloshed every night. She'd seen the dilated-pupil stare and agitation more and more often, and his mood swings were getting on everyone's nerves.

"What's your secret? Do you ever experience writer's block?"

"Sure. I think everyone has days when things don't come as easily."

"Days? I'm going on months now. I haven't been able to

write anything since you turned down the song I wrote for us. What didn't you like about it?"

"Aaron, you didn't write a bad song. It just wasn't for me, like a pop song wouldn't be for you."

He took a long pull of his beer, then stared at her for a moment. "This tour isn't going the way I expected."

"Why? You have a sold-out crowd at almost every venue. Your merchandise is selling like crazy. Your fanbase is grow—"

"It's not enough. I need a number one song that *I* write. And I need a girlfriend," he mumbled, voice low enough that she almost missed it while the karaoke singer was belting out Katy Perry's "Firework." The woman was actually quite good, and Knight Rivers showed their support with plenty of cheering.

She took another sip of her drink, set it on the table, and looked at him. "So why do you want to talk to me? I can't help you with either one."

"Actually, you can."

"Yeah?" She leaned her head back, feeling sleepy after their long day. "How? If I help you with a song, it won't be yours. And I'm not attracted—"

"Okay, okay." He held up his hand to stop her. "Just hear me out."

She half-turned to him, slouching in her seat. "I'm listening."

He leaned close. "If you help me write a song that reaches number one, I'll pay you for all the rights, but I want it published under my name."

As thanks for giving Knight Rivers this opportunity, she'd be willing to do that for him. But she'd want some kind of contract, even if they wrote it themselves. A notary could sign it rather than a lawyer or someone they knew. She nodded.

"I'll also pay you to be my girlfriend," he said in a low voice. "You help me clean up my reputation, and I'll pay you double."

"You're the only one who can clean up your reputation, Aaron. If you have a problem with alcohol or drugs, you need to get into rehab. I'm sure your uncle can help you keep things quiet."

"I need a girlfriend with a clean image."

She shook her head.

He glanced around. "Can we go somewhere quiet to discuss this? Please?"

"There isn't anything to discuss."

Sliding out of the booth, he held out his hand. "Please, just give me ten minutes. I promise to make it worth your while."

Blowing out a breath, she held out her hand and let him pull her to her feet. Her head spun and she closed her eyes. "I can't believe how sleepy I feel."

"You okay?"

"Sure." *The sooner we get this over with, the sooner I can fall into bed.* Only Ryder glanced her way when she turned toward Knight Rivers' table, so she gave him a wave. "You're not going to change my mind, Aaron."

"We'll see," he said, with a little too much confidence.

Aaron stuffed his hands in his pockets, which she was glad about while they made their way to the elevator.

"I want you to listen to what I have to say with an open mind."

"Okay." When the doors opened, she stepped inside and leaned against the wall. Though her head was spinning, she felt light—almost like she was floating—and extremely happy. She could help Aaron.

The elevator doors opened on the top floor, and as she followed him to the end of the hall, she could hear music before they reached his room.

"Sounds like a party."

"Yeah, I told the guys they could come over."

Wait. He said he wanted to talk in private. She wobbled on her feet.

"You need to sit down," he said taking her arm with one hand and opening the door with the other.

Loud music played around the noise of a room full of people. She didn't see anyone she recognized and wondered where all these people had come from. Her head spun with the noise and lights. She tried to pull away from Aaron's grasp, but his grip on her arm tightened. She looked at his out-of-focus face.

"I don't want to be here."

"We'll go into the bedroom."

"I don't want to."

Someone bumped into her, but Aaron's hand on her arm kept her on her feet. Aaron moved her to walk in front of him, and she spotted Nick and Jeff. Jeff pulled something out of a backpack, and Nick handed him money in a way that looked like they were shaking hands. She jerked away from Aaron's grasp and stumbled toward them. Nick turned and his eyes widened in surprise, but not before she grabbed his hand and saw the clear bag holding white powder in his palm.

"What's she doing here?" he shouted at Aaron. "Kenz, you need to get out of here, now!"

Her vision narrowed to a pinhole before everything went black.

CHAPTER 19

*N*ick pushed up on an elbow and checked Kenzie for the hundredth time. She was sleeping peacefully, her breathing steady. The effects of the roofie Aaron slipped into her drink would last for hours. When she woke up, she'd suffer a miserable hangover despite never drinking a drop of alcohol.

What scared him was how pliable she'd been. After she collapsed, he'd carried her to his room, set her on the bed, and handed her a glass of water. She held it until he told her to drink. She did as she was told with no emotion and a blank stare. He pulled a long T-shirt out of his suitcase and walked her to the bathroom. Like a robot, completely expressionless, she stared through him when he told her to change. He kept the door ajar, afraid she'd lock it and he wouldn't be able to get to her if she needed help.

When she came out wearing his shirt, he put her in his bed and pulled the covers up, all the while thinking that tomorrow he'd kill Aaron. No need, because flashing lights made him turn to the window. Handcuffed Aaron, Jeff, and many others were being led to waiting police cars. The party had been loud enough that he was surprised the cops hadn't been called earlier. If they'd arrived when he and Kenzie were in the room, they'd be joining Aaron and Jeff in the back of a police car right now. Kenzie would be released immediately, but he wouldn't.

He lay down on top of the covers and closed his eyes. He could probably get some sleep before Aaron called unless he decided his uncle would be more help. Marc Vance would have Nick on the phone if Aaron didn't.

Nick startled at the relentless pounding on his door. Checking Kenzie, he was relieved to find her breathing normally. He knew the police would come, but hoped not before morning. Swinging out of bed, he looked through the peephole to see Jeremy's mug.

Great just what I need right now.

When he opened the door, Jeremy's eyes went from him to his bed. Nick stepped back just as Jeremy's fist connected with his cheek, banging his head against the wall. Nick didn't have time to recover before Jeremy dove at him, knocking him to the floor and punching him in the face again. Nick squinted up preparing for another blow, but Jeremy's weight was lifted off him by Kyle and Bodhi.

"Jeremy, stop," Kyle said. "You don't know what's going on."

"Kenzie's in Nick's bed. That's all I need to know."

"It's not what it looks like, Jer," Nick struggled to say while trying to push up from the floor. "Aaron roofied her drink and I brought her here to sleep it off."

"More like *you* roofied her drink!"

"Nothing happened between us, Jer. She's out of it and will be for hours. I brought her here before anything *did* happen."

"Ryder said Kenzie left with Aaron. Let's be glad Nick was there," Kyle said, pushing Jeremy back against a wall.

Just as Bodhi held out a hand to help Nick up, two police officers walked in. "Nick Marshall?"

He dropped his head back and looked at the ceiling. This would all be over soon. "Yeah, I'm Nick."

"You're under arrest for possession of a controlled substance,"—While one officer was handcuffing him, the other patted him down and extracted the baggie of cocaine he'd bought from Jeff just hours earlier—"and intent to sell or deliver a controlled substance. You have the right to remain silent. Anything you say can and will be used against you in a court of law. *Blah, blah, blah . . .*"

"Wait. You have the wrong man," Jeremy said, suddenly coming to his defense. "Someone must have planted that. Tell them, Nick."

He glanced at the guys. Jeremy stood against the wall, still held in place by Kyle. Bodhi's mouth hung open, his eyes wide. Nick was glad Kenzie was still out, facing away from this moment in time.

"Kyle, tell them they have the wrong man," Jeremy said, pushing away from Kyle's hold and approaching them.

One of the officers held up a hand. "Stay back."

The other officer took Nick's arm and turned him toward the door. He glanced at Kyle. "Don't leave Kenzie alone."

"I'll take care of everything."

"Take care of what?" Nick heard Jeremy say as he was escorted out of the door. "Tell them someone planted those drugs on Nick."

The ride to the police station didn't take long. He was taken to a cell and flinched when the door clanged shut. He hated being put in this position, hated being behind bars, hoped he was out before the media got wind of the story. They'd have Aaron's mug shot in print before noon.

His thoughts turned to Kenzie as he touched his swollen

eye and tender cheekbone. *Thanks, Jeremy.* If the guy had given him five seconds to explain . . .

He wished he could be there when Kenzie woke up, so he could tell her the truth before she heard the news. The look on her face when she walked up to him and grabbed his hand last night—

It was a moment she might not remember, but one he'd never forget.

He dropped onto the mattress-covered cement slab, hoping he wouldn't be here long. They hadn't taken a mug shot or fingerprinted him yet. They'd have to take him out of his cell for that.

~

*K*enzie opened an eye at the sound of raised voices. Jeremy was yelling at someone, which was surprising since Jeremy seldom got angry.

She turned and winced as pain shot through her head and her stomach churned. What happened? How did she get into her room on the bus? She couldn't remember getting up this morning or even going to bed last night. In fact, she couldn't remember anything after . . .

"You're awake."

The bed dipped when Kyle sat down, and she put a hand to her head and groaned. "What happened? How did I get on the bus?"

"I carried you. Aaron roofied your drink last night."

She opened an eye and tried to focus on her brother. "No, he gave me a ginger ale."

"It doesn't matter what you were drinking, Kenz. Ryder said he saw Aaron hand you a drink and a while later you left with him."

Right. Aaron wanted her help with a song and a girlfriend. She remembered feeling dizzy and extremely tired. "After I got off stage, Aaron handed me a ginger ale, but it tasted fine."

"Well, you went to Aaron's room, where a party was in full swing. It was a good thing Nick saw you and got you out of there before anything happened."

"I don't remember any of that."

"What's the last thing you do remember?" Jeremy asked from the door.

She tried to blink him into focus, pretty certain she was going to die from the pain behind her eyes. "I remember Aaron asking for my help. He said he needed a number one song and a girlfriend."

"How were you supposed to help?" Kyle asked.

"He wanted me to write the song, but let him take full credit, and he wanted to pay me to be his stand-in girlfriend."

Jeremy snorted. "That guy's ego surpasses his talent and intelligence. Just the fact that he has to pay a woman to be his girlfriend explains a lot. We need to leak that to the media. Heck, call your buddy Travis. He can add that to his *Rolling Stones* article."

"Aaron wanted me to go to his room so we could talk in private. He didn't want anyone to hear our conversation."

"But you don't remember being in his room?"

"No." It scared her that her memory felt like it had been wiped clean. She was glad Nick had been there, but *why* was he there? "I don't remember anything after sitting in a booth with Aaron. I can't wait to have a little talk with that scumbag."

"There she is," Ryder said, elbowing past Jeremy and dropping onto the bed with her.

She grabbed her head and moaned.

"Careful, Ryder. She's hungover big time," Kyle said.

"Aw, sorry." He scooted close and cuddled her back

against his chest. "Too bad Aaron got arrested. I'd love to beat the crap out of him for what he did to you."

"He was arrested?" she asked, still holding her head.

"He and Jeff," Jeremy said.

"And Nick," Ryder added.

Nick was arrested? She closed her eyes and took several deep breaths, exhaling slowly. "Why were they arrested?"

"Drugs," Jeremy said.

"Wait. If Aaron and Nick were arrested, how are we finishing the tour?"

"Everything's been canceled. We're headed home."

Home.

That sounded so good to her. But Nick was in jail. How could he be so stupid? How could he have done that to his family? His daughter? She couldn't think straight, her thoughts jumbling into knots of pain.

"How is she?" Tripp asked.

"Awake and in pain," Jeremy said.

Bodhi appeared behind Tripp. "Hey, sweet pea, you scared us."

Kyle put a hand on her shoulder and Ryder's arm wrapped around her waist. She felt safe.

"Want some aspirin, baby girl?" Kyle asked.

"I would love you forever," she mumbled, her emotions in turmoil. She wished she remembered what had happened last night. How could she have been so stupid?

"I'll get it," Jeremy said.

A moment later, Kyle touched her shoulder. She got up on an elbow and took two aspirin with a gulp from a water bottle he held out. "Thank you."

"We took you to the hospital this morning and had you tested for drugs. The hospital called the police."

Thankfully, her memory was blank.

"You get some more sleep," her brother said. "We'll talk when you feel better."

Ryder started to move, but she clutched his hand to keep him close. She wanted to slip into oblivion, but she didn't want to be alone. He snuggled in again, and she drifted away.

*W*aking up to the sound of rain pounding on the window, Kenzie rolled over. Someone—possibly Ryder—had pulled the curtain, but she could tell it was dark out. Which meant she'd slept all day. At least her head felt better.

She needed a restroom and something in her stomach, but first, she changed out of the clothes she'd been wearing the night before. In the tiny kitchen, she made herself a sandwich and went up front to sit in the passenger seat, pulling the divider curtain so she wouldn't disturb the band members or Raymond.

They were parked at what looked like a campground. The rain ran in rivulets down the windshield. They'd been lucky on this tour, only running into a few storms, and nothing too terrible. At one of the county fairs, a rainstorm had blown through, quickly soaking them for the rest of their show.

Home.

Nick wouldn't be there, because he was in jail. She closed her eyes and tried to dredge up what happened last night from a black hole of nothingness. She remembered sitting in the booth, listening to Aaron and thinking okay on the song, but no way on the girlfriend part. The edges of her mind conjured the images of getting in the elevator with him, but not how she got there. If she couldn't remember, how had she been able to walk to the elevator?

Unease wrapped around her when snippets of entering his hotel suite came to mind. He'd propelled her through the people, tugging her toward a door. Where did Nick come in? Why was he there, and how did he know she needed help?

The thought of a plastic bag holding white powder played in the shadows. The image was so fuzzy, had it been real or imaginings from the drug Aaron had slipped into her drink? At least the hospital had a record of what Aaron had done. Would they call the police or was that something she needed to do? Hopefully there would be plenty of punishment for Aaron. She had every intention of telling his uncle. More than likely, with the tour being cancelled, Marc Vance already knew.

What would have happened to her if Nick hadn't been there? Would she have signed some kind of contract? Would it have been admissible in court? She knew Aaron was desperate to be number one, but how could he have thought drugging her was a good idea?

She couldn't imagine why Nick would have been there unless that was a life she didn't know about. Obviously, if he was arrested for drugs, he was living in a manner she didn't know or understand.

The thought made her angry and so sad for London. And Nick's parents, who would now become the little girl's primary guardians. And drugs? How could Nick have been so selfish? How many lives would he upend?

Including hers. Yes, her selfishness reared its ugly head. Going on that stupidly romantic date had opened her heart to possibilities. She started asking herself what-if questions, imagining a future she'd given up three years ago.

And in an instant, Nick had dashed her hopes and dreams a second time.

Suddenly the memory of Nick's eyes, wide in surprise, followed by anger flooded her mind. She was holding his hand, looking down at the plastic bag holding white powder. Nick had been at the party in Aaron's room to buy drugs.

CHAPTER 20

*K*enzie parked in the church's side parking lot, got out, and took a deep breath of home. They'd been back in Dove Hill for four days, and a peace had settled in her heart. She'd missed the rolling hills of the ranch and waking to the song of birds rather than traffic and an unfamiliar bed.

So much had happened in those four days. She'd called the police and filed charges against Aaron Vance for what he'd done, and they had her hospital record to back up her claim. Aaron had appeared in a Washington State court, pleaded guilty to the charge of putting something in her drink, and not guilty to the other drug charges brought against him.

Through the media, they discovered that Jeff was transporting drugs in a hidden compartment under Aaron's tour bus. Aaron was the one who had the compartment installed when he bought the new bus but insisted he didn't know anything about it.

"Aaron was giving Jeff the opportunity, not us," Bodhi said, as they searched for updates on their phones.

"Did he know Jeff before he asked us to go on tour?" Kenzie had asked.

Bodhi passed his phone to her. "Apparently, they've known each other for years."

Yes, Kenzie was glad to be home, living in her naïve little bubble. If that made her ignorant, so be it. She could live with ignorant.

Marc Vance had driven down from Nashville yesterday to check on her health and apologize for his nephew. He told her he spent the days since Aaron's arrest on damage control for his company while trying to hang onto his other clients.

After he talked to her, he stopped to offer Kyle a recording deal that was impossible to pass up. Knight Rivers had been auditioning singers since they got back and had narrowed down their choice to three. Now Kyle wanted her opinion.

She told her brother repeatedly that it didn't matter what she thought. They should make the decision without her. But Kyle and Jeremy argued that she had a good ear, and they wanted her input. She finally agreed, so all three women were sent home with new music and would be in Dove Hill the next week for final auditions.

She walked into the church foyer, but headed straight to the chapel, only waving to a couple of people she knew. The town was still abuzz with what had happened, and the church goers would keep her talking through the whole service if she paused.

"Hi, Mama!"

Kenzie hadn't even thought about London this morning. Not once. Unusual, since she'd been thinking of the little girl pretty regularly since Nick's arrest. Also unusual, she hadn't been able to find out any news about Nick. She figured his name would be mentioned along with Aaron and Jeff, but his name never came up.

She glanced across the chapel as everyone else turned in the seats to look at her. London was standing on the pew between her grandma and Nick—who was watching her with a wary expression.

Released on bail? She was surprised he'd been allowed to leave Washington State.

Waving at London, she dropped into the seat Kyle and Jessi saved for her. Kyle wrapped an arm around her shoulder, and she settled in for the hour-long service. The pew they sat in was on the other side of the chapel and two rows in front of Nick and his family, which kept her from looking across the aisle. She zeroed in on the podium and kept her attention on the preacher.

At the end of the service, before she could ask Kyle about Nick being out of jail, London ran toward her with her arms outstretched. "Hi, Mama!"

Because everyone around them was watching, and a few even "Awwwed," Kenzie sank down onto the bench and picked up London.

"Hi, pretty girl. How are you?"

"I fine."

Kenzie was glad London hadn't outgrown that adorable answer over the past three months. "You fine?"

London nodded, her dark curls bobbing. "I miss you."

A huge lump ached in Kenzie's throat. How could this darling girl's mother have left her? She just couldn't understand.

People passed them on the way to the doors, including Kyle and Jessi.

"You better go find your daddy," she said, right before a pair of male shoes stopped in front of them.

"Daddy." London pointed with a grin.

Kenzie glanced up and met his eyes. His smile was slow and sad. She hoped he recognized her look for the glare she meant it to be. He'd compounded London's not having a mother by being arrested. She wanted to punch him again—right in the nose this time. And might have if London hadn't been in her lap.

"Can I talk to you?"

"There's nothing to talk about. Whatever Aaron put in my drink didn't take away my memory of what you accepted from Jeff that night. I saw you, and I remember."

"Will you walk next door to the park with London and me so I can explain?"

"You can't explain this away, Nick." She covered London's ears with her hands. "Did you for one minute stop to think about your daughter and what will happen to her? I'm surprised your mother trusts you with her care."

"If you'll come to the park, I'll explain everything."

London slid off her lap and held out her hand. "Yet's go."

"You go with your daddy, sweetie." She glanced up at him. "Unless you're incapacitated."

"I'm not incapacitated." Nick took her hand and pulled her to her feet. "I've never done drugs in my life."

She gasped softly and jerked her hand out of his grasp. "We're in church."

He bent, picked London up, then put his arm around Kenzie's waist, guiding her out of the church and into the sunshine.

"Just because I bought them doesn't mean I take them," he said as they walked across the church's lawn.

"Then why buy? That makes zero sense."

"It makes perfect sense if I was helping the DEA."

"What?"

He put London in the bucket swing, and she grinned.

"High."

Kenzie stood back and watched him push London, whose giggles were bubbling over.

"I was helping the DEA. They knew Jeff was dealing and asked me to watch him. He would have been suspicious of me hanging around so much if I hadn't bought some. I also had to be *fake* arrested," he said using air quotes.

"Mama, push!"

Kenzie leaned forward and pushed the swing. "That is the craziest story I've ever heard. The DEA doesn't go around hiring just anybody to help them. You have to take law enforcement classes and go through training to be a police officer first." *Right?*

"You'll have to tell that to the DEA." Nick took a turn pushing. "Remember seeing me get in a car before your last concert?"

"Yes. You got into a dark car and drove away."

"Washington State DEA."

"So you're not out on bail?"

"Nope."

"How long did you have to stay in jail?"

"About four hours." He took a step closer. "In a gray, cold cell with only a thin mattress. And it started raining."

"Why didn't you call me? Why let me think you were involved?"

"I couldn't say anything to anyone until last night."

She stepped closer. "How did you get home?"

"Flew. All alone."

Biting her lip to keep from smiling, she raised a brow. "All by yourself?"

He reached out and took her hand. "Alone. While it was raining."

"Mama, down."

Kenzie stopped the swing and lifted London down.

"Swide," she said pointing toward the jungle gym.

Kenzie helped her climb the slide's stairs, and Nick stood at the bottom to catch her. As soon as she slid down, she ran back around and held out her hand for Kenzie's help with the stairs again.

As they played at the park, Kenzie felt the top of her brick wall crumbling. Not completely, but enough that she let herself relax, let herself enjoy the feel of a man's hand at her waist and the sound of a little girl's laugh.

She wasn't sure why, but she believed Nick's story. As far-fetched as it all sounded, she truly knew Nick would never leave London after what her mom had done.

London giggled. Nick smiled. And Kenzie felt joy spread through her from head to toe, larger than herself, larger than life, filling her to the brim.

~

*N*ick couldn't help but get his hopes up. He could tell Kenzie believed his crazy story, but one afternoon at the park didn't mean their situation was resolved. At the same time, he dared to feel encouraged. Kenzie was so patient with London, and his daughter adored Kenz. The sweetness of watching them together expanded his heart until it felt too big for his chest.

"Looks like I'll have to pass my baby girl crown to this cutie," Kenzie said when he called London by the nickname her dad had called Kenzie.

"I hungy," London said to Kenzie.

"Sounds like it's time for lunch," Kenzie said, glancing at Nick.

He took London's hand, and she held out her other hand for Kenzie. Like a family, they walked back to the church parking lot.

He picked London up when they reached his truck. "Can you say goodbye?"

"Bye-bye, Mama." London leaned forward with puckered lips.

Kenzie smiled before kissing London. "Bye, sweetie."

Nick wanted to lean forward and wait with puckered lips too but knew Kenzie wouldn't meet him halfway. Not yet. Instead, he watched her get in her car and drive away.

His mom had fixed a full-blown lunch of fried chicken, mashed potatoes, and black-eyed peas.

"You were gone a while," his dad said.

"London and I went to the park,"

"Mama," London said with a nod, waving a chicken leg.

"Kenzie went with you?" his mom asked, going for nonchalant but failing.

"She walked over with us, didn't she, baby girl?"

London's curls bounced, she nodded so hard, with a grin to match.

"We went on the slide and the swing. I held London up so she could swing on the monkey bars."

His dad raised his eyebrows. "Wow, such a big girl."

"Did Kenzie have a nice time?"

"Mom, don't start."

"What? I asked a simple question."

"I found a house to rent until I get something built," he said, attempting to redirect the conversation. He bought six acres just outside of Dove Hill during his last visit home, but he hadn't looked at house plans yet, still hoping, yearning, praying Kenzie would be involved in that process.

"You can stay here," his mom said. "Why waste money on rent when we have plenty of room?"

"We need a place of our own."

"All men need a little privacy when dating, Vicki," his dad said with a grin.

His dad knew exactly what he was thinking. He was surprised his mom hadn't already picked up on the same thing. He needed a place to take Kenzie without his mom and dad watching his every move.

"You can bring Kenzie here," his mom said.

Nick stood. "Time for a nap, London."

"I'll put her down," his mom said, waving him away. "You go . . . see someone."

He didn't have to be told twice. He kissed London on the cheek. "Love you, baby girl. See you soon."

When he pulled down the Rivers' driveway, he spotted Kenzie on her horse cantering around one of the fenced pastures. She'd changed into jeans and a T-shirt and braided her hair.

Parking near the big house, he walked out to the fence and rested his arms on the top rail, enjoying the smell of freshly mown grass and the call of several barn swallows in a nearby tree.

If she noticed him, she didn't show it, cantering around again. Then she slowed Poco to a trot. Instead of walking past him, like he expected, Kenzie stopped at the fence right in front of him. He reached out and rubbed Poco's nose. "Hi, boy."

Kenzie swung off the horse's back, and Nick opened the gate. Feeling a little nervous, he took his time following her into the stable. By the time he reached her, she already had Poco tied off and was removing the saddle.

"I thought we could talk some more about what happened," he said, cringing at how hesitant he sounded. He wanted her to think he was more confident than he felt.

"Why?" She picked up a currycomb, and he followed with a hard brush.

Poco whinnied in happiness at double attention as they combed and brushed his coat.

"I just want to make sure you believe me."

She patted her horse's neck. "I believe you."

Her admitting it so quickly surprised him. "You do?"

"Sure. You buying drugs didn't make any sense to me. Especially with your daughter to consider," she said as they continued to work their way around Poco. "You mentioned acquiring new clients and wanting to build a house, so I kind of pushed what I saw the night of the fair to the back of my mind."

"You mean the night you went with Travis to make me jealous?"

"Pfft! I wasn't trying to make you jealous," she said making eye contact, then quickly looking away with a shrug. "Travis asked me to go, and I said yes. It had nothing to do with you."

"Pfft," he repeated the sound she'd made. "Yes, it did. You didn't want to fall madly in love with me again, so you started looking for an out."

She rolled her eyes. "Whatever makes you feel better."

He took the comb out of her hand and backed her up against Poco's stall door. "You know it's the truth. You just don't want to admit it. At least to me."

She put a hand on his chest. He could feel the heat radiating through the fabric of his T-shirt and warming his heart, which was pounding wildly. He was sure she could feel the rhythm of love beating just for her.

"I want to show you something."

He loved the sound of her breathy, "What?"

While he unclipped Poco and led him into his stall, she put the brushes away. Then he took her hand and led her into the sunshine, to his car. She slid into the passenger seat and he jogged around to the driver's side.

"Where are we going?" she asked after he got behind the wheel.

"Not far."

They didn't talk much while he drove through quaint Dove Hill, took a left, and drove west for a couple of miles.

"You have me curious."

"Patience. We're almost there." Taking another left onto a dirt road, he drove until he topped a hill, then stopped, got out, and walked around to open her door, nerves skittering through him.

He had decided to be bold. Tell her what he wanted, then take it like a man if she turned him down.

She slid out and let him take her hand. He led her away from the car, stopping after about a hundred feet. "What do you think?"

Looking around, she smiled. "It's beautiful."

He pointed. "You can see the edge of Rivers Ranch from here."

She turned to him, her eyes shining.

"This is mine. I bought it the last time I was home."

"What're you going to do with it?" she asked with a barely-there smile.

"I thought we could build our house here at the top of the hill. We'll put the stable over there. I want to build London a playhouse in that tree by the creek."

She lifted a brow. "We? You're being awfully presumptuous."

"Am I?"

Turning her back to him, she took a couple of steps away. "We've only been on a couple of dates. And I don't know if I even like you enough to go on another."

He walked up behind her and put his hands on her waist. "I haven't asked you on another."

"Well, if you did, I'd probably say no."

"That's too bad. I thought I'd add a nice writing studio with plenty of room for a piano and guitars, maybe even a drum set, but I can take that out of the house plans." He wrapped his arms around her and pulled her close so that her back rested against his chest.

"You already have house plans?"

"No, I thought we could work those out together, but if you're not interested . . ."

She turned to face him. "I need time, Nick. I need to know for certain that I can be a mom to another woman's child. I need to feel safe that you won't—"

"I won't."

She looked down.

He lifted her chin. "I won't, Kenz. Never. Ever. I'll spend my life making up for what I did to you. I understand you need to make sure about London, and I'll give you all the time you need."

"What if it takes me a year?"

"I'll wait."

"Or two?"

"They'll be the two longest years of my life." He ran the fingers of both hands down her cheeks to her shoulders. "But I'll be right here waiting."

EPILOGUE

*K*enzie adjusted the darling wreath of flowers Vicki had placed on London's head. In all the history of flower girls, there would never be one more adorable than the now three-year-old. She was beaming under her halo of white and yellow.

"You look so pretty."

"You pretty, Mama."

Yes, she was still being called Mama, and after today that title would become official. After the ceremony, she, Nick, and London would become a real family.

"You really do look beautiful, Kenzie," Vicki said.

"Thanks, Mom."

Yes, she was calling her soon-to-be mother-in-law Mom, which only seemed fitting. Vicki had been a surrogate Mom ever since her own mother left so many years ago.

Vicki held out her hand. "London, let's go show Daddy how pretty you look and visit the bathroom one more time."

Yes, after months of fighting it, London had decided to potty-train days before the wedding. She'd taken to shouting, loudly, "I have to pee," so all of Dove Hill could hear.

Becky breezed in looking pretty adorable too. Kenzie had let her pick her own bridesmaid dress, and Becky chose a very fitted-to-her-pregnant-belly lavender sundress. She loved London's flower halo so much Kenzie had ordered one for her too.

"Is the bride ready?"

"Nervous."

"Why? You look lovely. Everything is set up perfectly. The cake is beautiful. The band is ready for the rocking reception, the flower girl hasn't spilled punch on her dress yet, and the groom is drop-dead handsome."

She couldn't wait to see him for herself.

"He wants you to meet him on the other side of the front door in ten minutes."

"What?"

"I'll orchestrate everything so he doesn't see you. Ten minutes," she said, pointing a finger at Kenzie's nose.

"Okay."

After Becky left, she walked over to her bedroom window and gazed toward the main house. A flower-covered arbor was in place near the sparkling pool, and chairs were lined up under the spring shade of several poplars. The dogwoods scattered around the ranch were in full bloom, giving the setting a soft yet vibrant fairyland effect.

Yes, she'd taken Nick at his word and made him wait. From September until spring. She'd taken the time to fall completely in love with him all over again. And London. Everyone loved London. She was so funny and so darling and so loving. She wished her dad were here to meet her. She'd be more spoiled with attention than she was already.

Kyle walked in and whistled. "Wow, baby girl, you look gorgeous."

She smoothed both hands down the skirt of her white dress. "Do you think?"

He took her by the shoulders. "Yes. I wish Dad was here to see."

"I was just thinking that. Well, not about seeing me, but to meet London."

"He'd love her," Kyle said. "Remember when Dad was in the hospital, I said I'd put a picture of him in my pocket?" He reached into his tuxedo pocket, pulled out a picture, and held it out for her. A passing stranger had taken a picture of the three of them the one time they went to the Gulf Coast. They were all smiles as they tucked in close.

"Thanks for remembering."

"I promised him I'd walk you down the aisle. Are you okay with Doug taking over that job?"

"Yes. I want you up front with me."

He hugged her close. "I see you're all packed."

"Yep. I moved the last of my stuff to the new house yesterday."

"I'm glad Nick is keeping you close. I was afraid he'd whisk you off to Nashville."

Nick had picked a plot of land that was situated in a way that she could see River's Ranch. "I can stand on my back patio and wave to you," she said, feeling tears sting the back of her eyes.

"Don't cry," Kyle said, holding up his hands in a helpless gesture. "Becky will kill me if I make you cry."

She ran the tip of her finger under her eye. "This will be the first time in my life that I'll live somewhere besides the ranch."

"Okay, okay, we'll talk about this when you get home from your honeymoon. In the meantime, no crying." He backed toward the door.

Jessi and Cara walked in and both turned to Kyle with glares.

"What did you do?" Jessi demanded.

"Nothing. I didn't do a thing." He escaped quickly.

"Don't go far," Cara yelled. "It's almost time to start."

Becky leaned into the room. "Come on, bride. Nick's here."

"No," Jessi and Cara chorused together.

"Relax. He won't see her." She took Kenzie's hand. "And she won't see him."

She led Kenzie into the living room, past the photographer, opened the front door, and positioned Kenzie behind it. "No peeking." She leaned through the crack. "For either of you. Now, give me your hand."

Kenzie held out her hand, and Becky placed it in Nick's. He rubbed his thumb over her knuckles, sending tingles down her spine. She felt his lips on her skin and covered her mouth when tears burned her eyes again.

The photographer moved around the living room taking pictures from one side of the door, then the other, until Becky pulled her and her clicking camera into the kitchen.

"I'm so sorry for hurting you, sweet pea. I'm sorry I stole three years from us. I promise you my deepest love, my greatest devotion, and my tenderest care through the pressures and uncertainties of life. I promise my support and faithfulness. I pledge to support you through all your endeavors, to respect your unique talents, and to lend strength to all your dreams. I'm so grateful for this second chance, Kenzie. I'm grateful for your love for me and for my daughter—soon to be *our* daughter. I will be eternally grateful that you accepted my proposal. I promise to care, protect, and love you forever."

Kenzie wiped at the tears streaming down her face. Becky was going to be so angry.

"Don't cry, Kenz. This is the happiest day of my life, and I want it to be the same for you. I'll be the one waiting under the arbor." With that, he kissed her hand again and left.

Becky walked in and stomped her foot. "No!" She grabbed Kenzie's arm and hustled her into the bedroom. "We have to get your face cleaned up before they start the wedding without you. I told him not to make you cry," she muttered under her breath.

Kenzie grabbed a tissue and blew her red nose.

~

*N*ick was a bundle of nerves and couldn't seem to get enough air into his lungs. Fainting up here in front of friends and family would certainly make for a memorable wedding. He glanced at the guests, and Jeremy gave him a thumbs-up. Yep, Jeremy had finally accepted him back into the group and into Kenzie's life.

The priest clapped him on the shoulder. "Remember to breathe, Nick. Thirty minutes and it will all be over."

But he didn't want it to be over. He wanted to remember every second of this day.

Kenzie's piano had been moved out by the pool, and sweet Mrs. Bowen changed the tune as the bridal party approached. First down the aisle was his darling daughter, who couldn't bashfully walk while sprinkling rose petals. Instead, she danced and twirled while throwing the petals at the guests with gusto. She got plenty of laughs, and people had their cameras out taking pictures. Her performance would probably go viral by tomorrow.

His sister, hanging onto Kyle's arm, followed her pregnant belly down the aisle. She looked radiant, and he couldn't wait to meet his niece, who was due in three weeks. London would have a little cousin to play with.

Mrs. Bowen changed the song again, and everyone stood and turned for a peek at the bride. Nick's heart stopped when she appeared on the path, holding his father's arm. He couldn't stop the tears that filled his eyes. The priest pulled a handkerchief out of his pocket and passed it to Nick. "My gift to every groom. You men very rarely come prepared for that first glimpse."

"Thank you." Nick wiped his eyes enough that he could see beautiful Kenzie moving down the aisle toward him. Her dress was lace from neckline to waist. The lace continued over her hips and down each side. She wore her hair up with soft tendrils curling around her beautiful face.

His heart expanded, filling his chest while emotions swept over him. He loved Kenzie with every fiber of his being, and he would spend his life proving himself to her.

Once they reached the front of the aisle, his dad kissed her cheek and handed her over to Nick. He could feel her trembling and hoped his smile calmed some of her fears.

"Hi, Mama. Hi, Daddy."

They both laughed along with their guests and waved at London, who sat on the front row between his mom and dad.

He listened to all the words spoken but didn't take it in as much as he did Kenzie's expressions. She seemed to be watching him just as closely. They exchanged their vows and the rings they'd chosen for each other. He watched Kenzie slip the perfect ring on his finger. She knew him and his tastes so well.

When he held her hand and slipped Kenzie's ring in place, her eyes filled with tears. He raised her hand and kissed her knuckles for the third time that afternoon.

"I now pronounce you husband and wife. You may kiss your bride."

Nick took Kenzie's face between his palms and kissed her as tenderly as possible. He wanted her to feel every bit of his love with the press of his lips. She wrapped her arms around his neck, and he pulled her close, deepening the kiss to the cheers and applause of the guests. They weren't able to linger long before London was pushing between them.

"I have to pee!"

~

If you enjoyed *Rhythm of Love*, grab *Finding Eden*, the first book in the Eden Falls Series.

To keep up to date on new releases join my newsletter at TinaNewcomb.com.

Following is an excerpt from *Finding Eden*.

EXCERPT FROM: FINDING EDEN

CHAPTER ONE

Colton McCreed peered down at the approaching ground as a shimmer of fear worked its way up his spine. The Cessna jolted and his stomach dropped. He'd landed at a lot of small airports, but never on such a tiny strip of asphalt. Would the pilot be able to stop before the plane plunged into the very cold looking lake on the far side?

He glanced at the burly bear of a man sitting in the pilot's seat who sported biceps the size of hams. The guy looked more like a wild mountain man than pilot.

"Your name is Beam?" Colton had asked at their introduction.

"Because I like my Jim."

"But…not before you fly. Right?"

A crazy gleam flashed in the man's eyes before he covered them with reflective lenses. Not the response Colton had hoped for.

"Are you sure you have enough room to land?"

"Pretty sure." Beam raised his sunglasses and squinted at the runway as if seeing it for the first time. "There's a life-jacket under your seat, just in case we slide into the drink.

You'll want to put it on quick before the temperature of the water sends you into hypothermia."

Great. "Shouldn't you be reassuring your—?" Colton lost his train of thought when the plane jolted, again.

Beam grinned and turned his ball cap backwards.

Colton's business manager suggested he fly, rather than drive into this small town. "You've never lived in rural U.S.A. If you want your story to be believable, you've got to integrate yourself into the community, live as the natives do. Attend town meetings and celebrations."

"Why can't I drive my own car?"

"You won't mix with the population driving around town in a Maserati."

"How rural is this place?"

"Eden Falls, Washington, has all the amenities you'll need. The crime rate is non-existent, so the residents will have an inherent sense of unity and trust, which is exactly the setting you wanted to portray in your next murder mystery." Jorge had held up his hands as if framing a movie screen. "Just imagine a serial killer moving unseen through a town idyllically named Eden Falls. Not a fictional place, but a real town. Mingle with the folks, visit the local tavern..."

For your sake, Jorge, there better be a tavern.

Colton held his breath as he zeroed in on the advancing patch of tarmac. One quick flash of a fire-blazing death shot through his mind, but he pushed the image aside—*too dramatic.* He used slow, calculated methods of demise in his novels.

Every muscle in his body tightened when the wheels of the single engine Cessna touched down. The pressure of the seatbelt strained across his chest as the pilot applied the brakes. Still braced, Colton's hand fumbled under the seat for the lifejacket and came up empty. He opened his mouth to yell at the pilot when the plane suddenly veered to the right. He exhaled a groan as his tight muscles dissolved.

Beam maneuvered close to the only building around, a white aluminum shed just big enough to hold the small plane. They jerked to an abrupt halt. "Didn't need that life-jacket after all, huh, city boy?"

He waved his enormous hand. "There's your welcome party."

Colton had been too preoccupied with his impending polar swim to notice a girl standing beside a rusted Jeep.

Beam popped his door open and climbed out before Colton could unbuckle his seatbelt. By the time he swung his own door wide, the bear of a man had engulfed the girl in a hug that took her feet off the ground. He frowned in their direction as he stumbled from the plane. Jorge told him Eden Falls was thrilled at the prospect of becoming the setting for Colton McCreed's next novel. He also said Mayor Alex Blackwood would be here to greet him. Instead, this pea-sized town had sent a girl.

As Beam unloaded Colton's bags and guitar case from the plane, she came forward and held out her hand. "Welcome to Eden Falls, Mr. McCreed. I'm—"

"Not Mayor Alex Blackwood."

A look of confusion passed over the girl's face and she retracted her hand.

"I was told he would be here to meet me."

The girl glanced at Beam who grinned as he swung Colton's bags into the back of the Jeep. Her eyebrows lifted over a pair of eerie green eyes. "Mayor Blackwood extends *his* apology. An unavoidable emergency came up."

Beam chuckled.

Colton glanced from the pilot to the girl. "He was supposed to show me around Eden Falls."

She flashed a smile that didn't quite make it to her eyes.

"I'll be happy to show you around town and answer any questions."

They were in the middle of nowhere with mountain peaks surrounding them. There was no way out unless he wanted to fly with the maniac, again. He should have known Jorge would distort the truth, lead him to believe there would be a welcome party awaiting a recognized author's arrival. He hadn't expected a parade, but at least the mayor could have shown up. He blew out a resigned huff. Jorge had accomplished his goal. He'd gotten Colton to this remote setting to write the story that had been tripping through his brain for several months—the story that wasn't coming together. For the first time in his career, he was experiencing writers block. That fact alone set him on edge.

Hands on hips, Colton turned to the girl. "I guess you'll have to do."

"I guess you'll have to do." Who does this guy think he is?

Jorge Reis—*just call me Jorgie*—had been hounding Alex Blackwood for weeks to shower *New York Times* bestselling author Colton McCreed with all the warm fuzzies she could muster. Well, she didn't have time to coddle some guy who thought he deserved royal treatment. Sure, it would be good for tourism to have Eden Falls mentioned in one of his books. Look what *Twilight* had done for Forks. As mayor, she was open to the possibilities this opportunity might hold for their beautiful little town, but if she had to put up with Mr. McCreed's attitude, it would be a very long summer for both of them.

She dialed her patience to "Pamper" and smiled. "Climb in and we'll get started."

The author tugged on the Jeep's rusted door twice before

it opened with a protest. Alex ignored his mutter of disgust and turned to Beam. "Thanks for making a special trip inland today."

He tipped his head toward her passenger who was scowling at them through the dirty windshield. "I might have scared the city boy a little."

Alex winked.

"How long's he staying?"

"All summer."

Beam took off his baseball cap and ruffled his hair, standing it on end. "Good luck."

"Thanks. I think I'm going to need it. Are you in town overnight?"

He plopped his cap back on his head. "Yep. Staying with Rowdy."

She thumbed over her shoulder. "Do you need a ride?"

"No, thanks. Someone's picking me up."

Curiosity nudged Alex like a prodding finger. "Someone?"

"Don't be nosy, cuz'." He pulled her screeching door open. "Tell Charlie I said hi. I'll see him on Memorial Day."

"He'll love that."

She slid behind the wheel and cranked the engine, which coughed and sputtered before grumbling to life. She really needed to break down and get a new mode of trans-portation. This rusty old bucket wouldn't last much longer, but it had been Peyton's and she wasn't willing to give it up. From the corner of her eye, she caught the author shaking his head. His self-imposed importance had her fighting a smile, but perhaps provoking him further wasn't a good idea. He'd learn his attitude wouldn't fly around here soon enough.

"How do you know him?"

His demanding tone filled the small confines of the Jeep, crowding her and she didn't like to be crowded. She did like his cologne though. A subtle, masculine, scent surrounded her pleasantly. "Beam is my cousin. Our dads are brothers."

"His parents named him Beam on purpose?"

"His real name is Everett, but he acquired the nickname when he started playing linebacker in pee-wee football. The coach said he was like an I-beam, plowing down the opposition. The name Beam stuck."

"And he makes his living flying in and out of this place?"

This place didn't appear to be meeting Colton McCreed's expectations. Lucky for him, patience was one of her virtues. She smiled as she shifted into reverse and backed up with a jerk, hitting a nice-sized pothole in the process. "No. He lives in Seattle and makes his living flying tourists around in seaplanes, but he also flies into smaller Washington towns when someone needs a ride."

With a quick wave to Beam, she turned the Jeep around and headed down the rutted dirt road that led to the highway. Yes, *this place* really did have a highway. The bumpy ride would give Mr. McCreed a taste of Eden Falls right from the start. No sense in sugarcoating the town's shortcomings.

Colton braced a hand against the dashboard. "How long have you lived here?"

"All my life." She was born and raised here, and couldn't imagine living anywhere else. "Eden Falls has some of the prettiest views in the state. The drive in is gorgeous. Just about any outdoor activity you could wish for is available. We're situated between the two largest cities in Washington. Everything you need, if not within our own town limits, is close at hand. I think of *this place* as heaven on earth."

He turned a cynical eye her way. "You sound like a travel agent."

Her passenger grew quiet and Alex glanced at his profile. He had a nice face, not movie star handsome, but appealing. He had that in-fashion, messed-up style going on with his sandy hair. His eyes were a blustery gray with heavy brows that hung low like threatening storm clouds to match what seemed to be a permanent frown. The feature that drew her attention was his nose. Alex had long ago dubbed herself a connoisseur of noses. If there were ever a contest, she'd be the first to volunteer as a judge. His was long and slender, but widened out right before the nostrils, with a definitive bump at the bridge. Yes, he had a very nice nose.

If he wasn't married, and if Misty Douglas didn't get to him first, he'd be a nice diversion for the single women of Eden Falls, as long as they didn't mind the perpetual scowl. She wondered if his frown was an L.A. thing, a brooding author thing, or just an unhappy with life thing.

When Beam pointed out Eden Falls from the sky, Colton had estimated about thirty streets with a river running along the north side. Nestled neatly within the surrounding mountain peaks, it was tiny compared to his hometown of Los Angeles.

Would there be a decent cup of coffee or pizza delivery available? Could he live in this place for three months without everything closing in on him? Was he renting month-to-month or had he paid for the summer in full? Jorge knew he didn't like to be tied down. Claustrophobia had a way of wrapping its tentacles around his roaming nature.

He pulled a notebook and pencil from his backpack as their surroundings turned more civilized. Even with smartphones, laptops, and tablets available, he preferred a pencil and paper for taking notes.

The girl pointed to the left. "That's Eden Falls High School. The middle school is across the street."

He didn't care how many schools were in town. He didn't

like kids, didn't want them, and had no plans to include them in his novels—or his life. "I assume, by the cars in the parking lot, school isn't out for the summer."

"Two more weeks."

"Are there enough kids to hold graduation?"

"We'd hold graduation for one senior or twenty, Mr. McCreed."

He smiled at the girl's snarky tone. He'd ruffled her feathers, but wasn't sure how. His questions seemed plausible. "I might be interested to see how a small town graduation differs from one in L.A. Would it be possible to attend?"

"I'm sure the student body and faculty would be thrilled to have you. The post office is on the right. My dad has been the postmaster since he graduated college."

He glanced up from his notepad. Jorge would be sending his mail there.

"Douglas Hardware and Lumber is on the left. The fire station is across the street."

Two firemen were in front of the red brick building washing a truck. The girl honked, and one of the men waved. The other flexed his bare chest muscles in a bodybuilding pose, and the girl broke into a smile. He cupped his hands and yelled something Colton didn't catch.

He studied her long enough to realize she wasn't as young as he'd first thought—college age rather than high school. Still, in her business suit and heels, she looked like she was playing dress-up—undoubtedly to impress him. "Friends of yours?"

"Friends of my brother. There's a gas station on either end of town and another one on Cascade Boulevard along with the IGA grocery store and a gym. If you like barbecue—"

"Is it members only?"

She turned a puzzled glance his way.

"The gym, is it members only?"

"Oh, yes, but you can get a month-to-month membership. My Aunt Glenda and Uncle Dawson—Beam's mom and dad —own it. I can talk to them for you, if you'd like."

Colton nodded. "Any good pizza around?"

"Renaldo's Italian Kitchen is on the square. They have great pizza and pasta dishes, and they deliver. We have Chinese and Mexican restaurants. Noelle's Café is great for home cooked meals. The café is also a popular breakfast destination. If you have a sweet tooth, Patsy's Pastries is a must."

He had an enormous sweet tooth, hence his interest in the gym.

They arrived in downtown Eden Falls. Town Square was a two-block park in the center with a one-way street that circled it. Shops around the perimeter wore welcoming exteriors. The streets and sidewalks were clean, and the park's grass was a vivid green. Purple and yellow flowers bordered the trees and huge pots of flowers hung from lampposts. A raised stage sat at one end with a banner advertising a Memorial Day concert.

He noted the Roasted Bean Coffee Shop, Renaldo's Italian Kitchen, One Scoop or Two ice cream shop, Eden Falls Emporium, Dahlia's Salon, and Pages Bookstore as just a few of the businesses they passed. The girl took a left, doing a three-sixty all the way around, pointing out places like Town Hall and the police station along the way.

"Do you fish?"

"As in sitting in a boat holding a pole?"

She flashed a you-are-a-moron glance. "Yes."

"Not so far, and if I can help it, I never will. Why?"

"I was going to point out The Fly Shop, but it doesn't sound like you'll need to visit. There's a drug store and two banks here on the square. The movie theatre is small, only one screen, but they play new releases."

As she took another left, he continued to take notes of the businesses along the way, impressed that there were only a couple of empty storefronts.

"Any bars in town?"

"The Cascade Club is across the street from the gym. Rowdy's Bar and Grill is down Main Street a block further."

The girl made a right turn into a residential area, left onto Cedar Drive, and pulled into a driveway halfway down the street. When she turned the key in the ignition, the Jeep's engine shuddered so violently, it rattled his brain. "Here you are. Home sweet home for the next three months."

Colton stared open mouthed. *No. No, no, no. This can't be right.* The whole house would fit inside his living room. He could already feel claustrophobia clawing at his throat. *I can't live here for three months.*

He shoved the passenger door open with a screeching protest and stared at the little green house with its white trim and black shutters. A concrete path from the sidewalk to the wooden porch steps cut the pristine lawn in half. Waist high bushes bordered with little red flowers flanked the front. He looked around at all the tiny houses of the neighborhood. Perfect, if he were a hobbit.

He pulled out his cell phone, ready to blast Jorge into the next century. The least his business manager could have done was ask for pictures of the place. He would have seen it was too small for Colton. He scrolled to Jorge's number and hit call. Of course, he got Jorge's voicemail. *Big surprise.*

The girl circled to the back of the Jeep to unload his bags, but he stopped her. "I want to see inside first."

"Sure."

She pulled a set of keys from a pocket as Colton followed her up the front steps. A metal glider and a couple of chairs with decent cushions made the porch look inviting, and afforded a spectacular view of the mountains. He followed her inside, cringing at the twang of the screen door spring. Prepared to hate the place, he was, instead, pleasantly surprised. It was small, but the high ceilings created a roomy feel. The living room had an overstuffed sofa and two easy chairs. A nice sized flat-screen hung on the wall.

She must have noticed his glance at the fireplace because she walked over to it and flipped a switch. "It's gas. You might like to use it since the nights are still cool."

He nodded without comment, still not ready to commit.

She led him into a small kitchen with a dinette set, but what grabbed his attention was the screened patio just beyond. The room was bright and spacious, and he knew it would become his writing area. He'd pull the kitchen table out there. This place just might work.

Beyond the window was an excess of green grass. "I don't do lawns."

A smile danced in her eyes, which were a spooky black-cat green. "I'll be here on Saturday mornings to mow, usually around eight or nine. I have to be at the baseball fields early, so I hope that won't be an inconvenience."

He was an early riser, so he shook his head, but curiosity got the better of him. "Why do you have to be at the baseball fields? Do you mow lawns there, too?"

She laughed for the first time since they'd met. She had a sexy, rusty laugh that didn't match her young face or petite form.

"No, I just watch the games."

His eyes wandered the room. The place was small, but not as bad as he'd first imagined. Maybe he could make do after all, although making do wasn't his habit. "How many bedrooms?"

"Two."

He followed her down the hall, his gaze dropped from the top of her head, where her blonde hair was tied into a crazy knot, to her waist, then dipped further south. She stopped abruptly at the first door, and turned. When she noticed him looking at her assets, she rolled her eyes.

"There's a full bath here and a half bath off the kitchen." Her words dripped with annoyance. "The washer and dryer are just inside the garage door."

He glanced in the bathroom. No Jacuzzi bathtub or multiple shower jets like his had, but he could make do. The next door opened to a bedroom, which held a bed, dresser, nightstand, and no room for anything else.

"The beds have clean sheets on them. There are extra sheets, blankets, and towels in this hall closet." She opened the door as if she needed to prove her words. "The kitchen is fully stocked with pots, pans, and dishes. Everything—"

"I don't cook. Or do laundry."

She lifted a shoulder, shrugging him off. "Well...everything is there if you change your mind."

He swiped a thumb across his lips. "I was told there would be a housekeeper."

"Felicia Kerns lives next door and cleans several houses in town. She said she could come in once a week."

Once a week? His housekeeper was at his L.A. home all day, everyday except Sundays and Mondays. She did the cooking, cleaning, and laundry. "Once a week won't be enough."

The girl's mouth twitched, but she kept her smile in check. "Felicia is pretty flexible. If you ask *nicely*, I'm sure she would be willing to work something out with you."

Colton frowned at her obvious dig. He thought he'd been more than nice, considering. He looked over the second bedroom, which wasn't much larger than the first, but he wouldn't be spending much time in here anyway. The place was small enough that he should be able to handle some of the mundane domestic duties himself.

After she helped him with his luggage, they ended up back in the kitchen. "Is the owner okay with me renting for three months with the option for longer if I need it?"

"She is."

"I was told I'd have the use of a car."

"There's a small Ford in the garage. It's an older model, but it will get you from point A to point B. The gas tank is full and the tires are new. The oil was just changed and all the fluids topped off." She pulled a set of keys from a kitchen drawer and handed them to him.

"Whom do I call if I have any problems?"

"Me. My home phone and cell numbers are here on the counter, along with some others that might be helpful. I printed out a map of Eden Falls and the surrounding—"

"I mean, *whom* do I call if the water heater goes out or the furnace blows up? Shouldn't I call the owner?"

She tipped her head, her green eyes locked on his. "I am the owner."

Colton couldn't have stopped his laugh if he'd tried. "You? Own this house?"

Any hint of the smile she'd shown earlier disappeared. His gaze dropped to her full lips and stayed longer than it should have. Too bad she wasn't a few years older.

"Do you need anything else?"

He raised his eyes to meet hers. "No. I think I'm set."

"Welcome to Eden Falls and happy writing," was said in an eat-dirt-and-die tone.

She walked out and climbed behind the wheel of the rusted jalopy. After she cranked the engine to life and drove away, he realized he hadn't asked her name.

ACKNOWLEDGMENTS

As always, I want to thank my Beta Readers, Jeanine Hopping, Chris Almodovar, Holly Hertzke, and Marnie Giggey. Love to each one of you beautiful women.

Thank you to my editor, Faith Freewoman at Demon for Details. She polishes my work without removing my voice.

Thank you to proofreader Sara Olds for catching my missing or extra commas and rewriting a sentence or two so they'd make more sense.

Thank you to my cover artist, Dar Albert, at Wicked Smart Designs. She usually knows what I want before I do.

Thank you, Stefan Newcomb, for keeping my web page current.

Thank you to Chris, Marnie, Carly, Sara, Kristen, Andrew, Richard, and Stefan for your love and support!

A huge thank you to Rick, just for being you. Love you!

Last but certainly not least, thank you, dear readers. I feel so honored that you take the time to read, review, and share my books.

xox

Tina

ALSO BY TINA NEWCOMB

The Eden Falls Series

Finding Eden

Beyond Eden

A Taste of Eden

The Angel of Eden Falls

Touches of Eden

Stars Over Eden Falls

Fortunes for Eden

Snow and Mistletoe in Eden Falls

Rumors in Eden Falls

Second Chance Romance Collection

When You Love Someone

Endless Love

Rhythm of Love

Second Chance Romance Collection

ABOUT THE AUTHOR

Tina Newcomb writes clean, contemporary romance. Her heartwarming stories take place in quaint small towns, with quirky townsfolk, and friendships that last a lifetime.

She acquired her love of reading from her librarian mother, who always had a stack of books close at hand, and her father who visited a local bookstore every weekend.

Tina Newcomb lives in colorful Colorado. When not lost in her writing, she can be found in the garden, traveling with her (amateur) chef husband, or spending time with family and friends.

Follow Tina on:

- facebook.com/TinaNewcombAuthor
- instagram.com/tinanewcombauthor
- bookbub.com/authors/tina-newcomb
- goodreads.com/tinanewcomb
- pinterest.com/tinanewcomb

Manufactured by Amazon.ca
Bolton, ON

29473048R00157